Frogs & French Kisses

sarah
mlynowski

delacorte press

Published by Delacorte Press
an imprint of Random House Children's Books
a division of Random House, Inc.
New York

This is a work of fiction. Names, characters, places, and incidents either are the product of the author's imagination or are used fictitiously. Any resemblance to actual persons, living or dead, events, or locales is entirely coincidental.

www.randomhouse.com/teens

Educators and librarians, for a variety of teaching tools, visit us at
www.randomhouse.com/teachers

Library of Congress Cataloging-in-Publication Data
Mlynowski, Sarah.
    Frogs & French kisses / Sarah Mlynowski.
        p.   cm.
    Summary: Love spells run amok in New York City when high school freshman Rachel asks her younger sister, who is a witch, for magical help in winning the affection of heartthrob Raf Kosravi.

    ISBN-13: 978-0-385-73182-9 (hardcover)—ISBN-13: 978-0-385-90219-9 (gibraltar library binding)
    ISBN-10: 0-385-73182-5 (hardcover)—ISBN-10: 0-385-90219-0 (gibraltar library binding) [1. Witches—Fiction. 2. Magic—Fiction. 3. High schools—Fiction. 4. Schools—Fiction. 5. New York (N.Y.)—Fiction. 6. Humorous stories.] I. Title: Frogs and French kisses. II. Title.
    PZ7.M7135Fr 2006
    [Fic]—dc22

                                                                                  2005016141
The text of this book is set in 12-point Goudy.

Printed in the United States of America

June 2006

10 9 8 7 6 5 4 3 2 1

First Edition

For Laura Dail, my awesome agent.
Because she loves Rachel as much as I do.

Acknowledgments

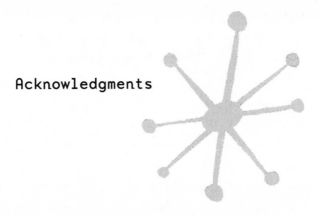

Thanks to the power of a trillion to:

Wendy Loggia, my extraordinary editor, as well as the rest of the Delacorte Press Random House Children's Books team: Beverly Horowitz, Chip Gibson, Isabel Warren-Lynch, Tamar Schwartz, Gayley Carillo, Kenny Holcomb, Adrienne Waintraub, and Jennifer Black. Special thanks to Christine Labov for her tireless (and always cheerful) publicity skills. The superb group on the other side of the pond: Ruth Alltimes, Sarah Davies, Lisa Grindon, Laura Burr, and everyone else at Macmillan. Artist extraordinaire Robin Zingone for creating the gorgeous cover art. The people working like mad to make the movie: Lisa Callamaro, Claire Lockhart, Helen Wan, and everyone at Fox 2000 and Storefront Pictures. Shannon Browne for her fabulous assistance. Gail Brussel, my superb publicist.

My trio of longtime readers, whom I would be helpless without: my mom, Elissa Ambrose (who always knows just what I'm *trying* to say); Lynda Curnyn (my partner in crime); Jess Braun (who's never afraid to tell me when some-

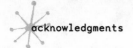

thing sucks). And my newest and youngest reader and test audience, Avery Carmichael. You guys rock.

Dad, Louisa, Robert, Vickie, John, Jen, Bonnie, Robin, Ronit, and Jess D., for their love and support. Aviva, my sister and inspiration for Miri. (No, Squirt, I promise you weren't, um, that geeky.) Gary and Darren, the Swidler brothers, who were kind enough to teach me how to give a mooshie. Special thanks to Todd(ie), the littlest brother, my own personal superhero (and husband), who not only knows *everything* but is kind enough to let me steal his best lines.

frogs
&
french kisses

My Love Life Is Up in the Air (and So Am I) 1

I'm perched on a floating broom, my arms squeezing the life out of my little sister's waist.

"You girls all right?" my mom calls down. She's watching us from behind the second-story cottage window. "You're not airsick? Maybe I shouldn't have let you talk me into this."

"I'm fine," Miri chirps.

"Me too," I lie as the two of us wobble up and down like we're on a haunted seesaw. We're straddling a plastic broom four feet above the dewy ground. In what deranged world would I be fine? My eyes are cemented closed, I'm biting my lip, and every one of my muscles is clenched in fear.

"I don't want you girls gone for more than an hour," my mom warns. "So be back here at eleven p.m. sharp. I'll leave the window open so you can fly straight back in. If you think anyone has spotted you, return here immediately. And, Rachel, don't you dare take off that helmet!"

How does she know my secret plan? "But it's itchy!"

"She won't." Miri pats my knee. "You ready? Here we go!"

Nausea and dizziness wash over me. Maybe this isn't such a brilliant idea. My legs are dangling like a rag doll's, and the broom is starting to chafe.

"Don't go too fast," I plead in a super-high-pitched voice, like I just inhaled a balloon full of helium. "And don't go too high. We don't want to smash into an airplane. And don't—"

The broom jerks forward, I swallow a scream, and suddenly we're flying through upstate New York.

"Be careful!" my mom hollers in the background.

I'm flying. I'm flying! I'm flying!!!!!!!!!!!!!!!!

I may be dreading going back to school, but at least I'm flying high during spring break. Literally.

I gingerly open my right eye as we shoot past the gate to our rented cottage and zoom over the dirt road. The wind caresses my cheeks, my arms, my hair. . . . I think the wind just blew a leaf up my nose. But who cares? How cool is this?

Don't look down, don't look down!

I look down.

My shoelaces are hanging over the sides of my new pink sneakers like floppy dog ears. I really should have double knotted. These are the new pink sneakers that my mom bought to cheer me up. To make a long, heartbreaking story short, I spent the first few days of vacation moping because Raf Kosravi, the love of my life, hates me because I (unintentionally) stood him up for Spring Fling to go to my father's wedding.

Buying the shoes was really thoughtful of my mom. She's definitely trying to be more understanding. On the same night she surprised me with the cheer-up present, she dropped her slice of pepperofu (vile, flavorless, pepperoni-

2

shaped slabs of tofu) pizza and announced, "Miri, banning you from using witchcraft isn't working. If you're going to do it anyway, as you've been doing for the last two months, I want to teach you to use magic responsibly. The three of us are going on a trip. Start packing."

My jaw fell open in midchew. Mom was finally seeing the light! See, I've only just recently discovered that my mom's a witch. My sister, too. Everyone's a witch except me. Well, not my dad or any of my friends. But everyone I live with. And my mom had a very strict rule: absolutely no magic until Miri finishes her training. My mom is antimagic herself, preferring to be a nonpracticing witch. So this change of heart was a major coup.

"Yes!" I cheered while debating what to pack. Going-out clothes or won't-be-seeing-anyone-worth-impressing sweats? I didn't mind leaving the city, mostly because my best and now only friend (since I embarrassed myself phenomenally at the school fashion show), Tammy, is spending spring break in the Gulf of Mexico with her mom and stepmom (yes, her mom is married to a woman). "Magic for everyone! Can we put a love spell on Raf?"

"Don't push your luck" was my mom's response. "Love spells are *not* what I consider responsible."

What is the point of having a witch for a mom if she won't perform one measly love spell on the boy of my dreams? If only she were more like a friend and less like a mother.

Anyway, the next morning we left extra food for Tigger, our cat, and Goldie, our goldfish, rented a car, and drove from our cozy downtown Manhattan apartment to a rented

3

cottage in the middle of nowhere, where Mom claimed we'd have no nosy neighbors to witness our shenanigans.

We arrived on Wednesday night, two entire days ago. Forty-eight hours in a two-bedroom cottage that smells like a mixture of mothballs and apples. Forty-eight hours of no cable. No DVDs. No Internet. I've had nothing to do except watch while my mom trains Miri, which surprisingly isn't that much fun. Fine, it's semifun. At least my mom is finally letting Miri perform practical magic instead of just making her recite the history of witchcraft. But watching Miri attempt to levitate inanimate objects gets old *fast*.

The peach-colored coffee mug's hovering three inches above the kitchen table is unbelievable. Four inches is awesome. Five is funky. Six . . . yawn. After two days, rising kitchen dishware gets a wee bit repetitive. Actually, downright sleep inducing. It wasn't until this afternoon, while my mom was showing Miri how to float a paper towel, that it occurred to me that if Miri could make a towel fly, why couldn't she make *us* fly?

I found the broom in the hallway closet. It was old and scraggly, and some of the bristles were bent at odd ninety-degree angles, but it would do the trick. "Is there any truth to the witches-flying-on-brooms legend?" I asked, yanking it out, causing a dustbin to fall on my head.

"Well . . ." My mom hesitated. "No."

I didn't buy it. If a paper towel could levitate, why couldn't a broom? I walked over to her and looked deep into her green eyes. "Do you swear?"

Instead of answering, she ran her bitten fingernails through her shoulder-length bottle-blond hair and shrugged.

4

"What?" Miri cried, jumping out of her chair and causing the paper towel to float back down to the table. Good thing she'd raised glasses the day before. "You told me flying brooms were a myth!"

"I know." My mom took a moment to bite her thumbnail. She and my sister share this disgusting habit. "But I was worried about you. I didn't want you flying around Manhattan, bumping into the Empire State Building."

I clapped with gleeful excitement. From now on I'd travel in style. Sweaty overcrowded subways? Never again. Running late to school? I don't think so. The only road I'm taking is Highway Broom. "Teach me how!" I shrieked.

"You mean teach *me*," Miri said snidely.

"If I'd known I was going to teach you to fly, I would have brought cigarettes," my mom said.

"You promised to quit!" I muttered.

"I know, I know. I quit, all right? It's just that letting you fly is going to be stressful." She bit her thumbnail again. "I'll teach you, but you have to promise—"

Be careful, go slow, stay low, whatever, yes, yes, yes!

"—to wear your bike helmets."

Groan. Only my mom could make something as cool as flying look geeky.

The ferocious wind blows a lock of my shoulder-length brown hair into my mouth. But it's worth it. I'm flying! Yes, the loser helmets are fastened and itching, but I'm still feeling pretty lucky. Come on, how many fourteen-year-olds get to fly outside the pressurized cabin of an airplane? No peanuts, no exit doors, no flight attendants. No crying babies. No stranger hogging the armrest. No fidgety traveler climbing over you every two seconds to go to the bathroom. This is far more civilized.

Plus my mom showed Miri how to add a cool night-vision visor to the front of each helmet, so Miri and I can see in the dark.

Whoosh! Whee! Cool! Cold.

Even though it's already April, it feels like we're smack in the middle of winter. Despite the tights I'm wearing under my jeans, as well as the sweater under my jacket, my body is covered in goose bumps. I'm convinced that if I let go of Miri with even one hand, I'll be sent plummeting to an early death. Yet I really want to scratch under my helmet.

6

"Where do we want to go?" Miri shouts from the front.

"Who cares? Just fly!"

I'm a bird soaring through the night. A kite coasting along the beach. We pass over the tops of budding trees, and in spite of my head problems, I can't stop smiling. "Higher!" I shout.

She lifts the nose of the broom, and though I have to cling tightly to her so I don't slip off the rear as we sail upward, I want more. "Do a three-sixty!"

"I can barely go straight!" she says. "And quit talking; I'm trying to concentrate!" Even though she and Mom enchanted the broom, flying still requires Miri to manually (and magically) steer it.

We pass another dark road. The town is completely

empty, which is why Mom is letting us fly. We won't be spotted. It's a bird, it's a plane, it's two girls on a broom!

"Look!" I squeal, pointing with the toe of my new shoe to a farm below. At least fifty cows are grazing and watching us as we pass overhead. I get a whiff of manure and wish I didn't need my hands to cling to Miri, so that I could hold my nose. Ew. "What's over there?" I shoe-point to a gleam of colored lights in the distance.

She redirects the broom and we head toward the flashing blues, reds, and yellows, which as we get closer start to look like a giant woman's face.

"It's a drive-in!" I cheer. Only one car is there, which can't be good for business. But it does mean fewer potential spotters. Miri hovers behind a tall tree so that the driver and his date won't see us. I have always wanted to go to a drive-in movie. I didn't think they existed anymore. What a blast from the past. The ground is paved with cobblestones instead of concrete. Leading up to the massive screen are two rows of lanterns casting a tender glow through the night. How romantic. Sigh.

If I were a witch, my one wish would be for Raf to like me again. I don't even care that I have just one friend left. Nope, my only request would be Raf.

Okay, and maybe that my head would stop itching. But it's a far second on the list.

I close my eyes and swallow the lump in my throat. Mustn't think about Raf. Mustn't think about what could have been. Must keep moving. "Can we get out of here?" I ask. Miri kick-starts the broom and we reverse back onto the

7

neighboring road. "Be careful," I warn her. "There's a car driving toward us."

She jerks the front of the broom up so the small white Toyota Tercel won't see us. "I think it's parked," she says.

Fantabulous. Probably two people making out, just to rub my face in it. Everyone has a boyfriend except for me. I've never even had a first kiss. Not a real one. And I probably never will. Unless Raf forgives me. . . . Three days till R-day. Raf day. Rekindled Romance day. At the moment, he's in New Orleans for spring break. If I knew which hotel he was staying at, Miri and I could fly the broom down there and serenade him with songs of sorrow.

No way. Too stalkerish. (As if walking by his locker forty times a day wasn't.)

Wait a sec. That's not a couple in the car. It's a woman. By herself. Banging her head against the steering wheel. And now she's opening the car door. She's walking around to the back and opening her trunk.

Omigod. Maybe there's a dead body in there! Maybe we're about to witness the tail end of a murder. But we won't be able to tell the police how we know, so we'll have to make an anonymous phone call from a random pay phone and use one of those voice modifiers that will make us sound like men—

She pulls out flares. Oh well.

Itch. Itch, itch. It's not like my mom would know if I took it off for half a second.

Miri's about to make a U-ie out of there when I tell her to hold on.

"What?" she asks, annoyed. "We can't let her see us.

What if she has a cell camera and e-mails a picture of us to the tabloids? And then we're institutionalized in a top-secret government facility like Area Fifty-one?"

"Just stop!" I order. Besides, I'm not the one who'll be put in the rubber room with electrical wires rammed into her head. I'd definitely visit her, though.

She grinds the broom to a halt, and we resume hovering, bobbing up and down over the road. "She can't start her car," I say.

"So?" Miri asks, turning her head to face me. "What are you, a mechanic?"

So dense, this little one. "Don't you think we could help her with some of our other skills?" Hint, hint. Her forehead wrinkles in confusion. "You're a witch!" I remind her. How are her powers not on the top of her mind? They're *always* on the top of mine.

Still wrinkled. "You think I should start her engine?"

"No, I think you should make her car fly. We can drag race." I kick the toe of my shoe into her calf. "Of course, start her engine!"

She elbows me in the arm and I almost go sailing off the broom. "Are you trying to kill me?" I yell.

She turns back toward the lone woman and rubs the spots on her helmet where her temples would be. "Shush. Let me concentrate."

We drop two feet toward the ground. "Careful!" I scream through clenched teeth.

"Oops. Sorry." The broom wobbles. "I'm trying to help her, but it's not so easy to concentrate on two things at once."

9

"Just do it quickly."

Miri's entire body tenses, and then with a burst of cold and a whoosh the Tercel roars to life, and the woman jumps at least a foot in the air, not knowing what just happened.

"Yes!" I say, and pat Miri's back with the forehead of my helmet.

"I did it!" she squeals, lifting her arms in a V. And that's when the broom starts making circles.

"What are you doing?" I ask nervously.

"I-I d-don't know," she stammers.

"Just stop it, please!" Getting dizzy again. Super dizzy. Flashbacks to the hora dance at my dad's wedding. "Slow down!" I scream—not that she listens. My jaw is clenched, my teeth are grinding into each other, my feet are dangling, and I may have just lost one of my new cheer-me-up sneakers. Hair spilling in all directions. Think I just swallowed a bird. Now would be a superb time for my own powers to kick in.

Or now.

We're making wide circles. Ten feet in radius, twenty feet. Thirty feet. We're both clasping the broom and screaming, and I don't know which way is up and which way is down and why am I smelling manure again?

Blur of speckled white and black. Oh my. Oh, no. I think we're circling the farm. We're *descending* onto the farm. We're about to *plunge* into the farm.

"Hold on tight!" Miri yells as we—

Oh, no. Please no. It's too gross! It's—

—crash.

Got Milk?

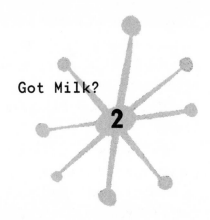

2

Moooooooooooooooooooooooooooooo.

You've got to be kidding me.

"I think I broke my head," Miri says.

I'm lying on my stomach, my legs splayed froglike, my eyes clamped shut. "If you broke your head, you wouldn't be talking," I tell her, secretly thankful for the wisdom of moms and their helmet nagging. Despite my sister's being a brown belt in Tae Kwon Do, she's only twelve years old, four and a half feet tall, weighs only seventy-five pounds, and is quite fragile.

I feel warm breath on my face. I really hope that's Miri. I open my eyes. A cow's mouth is inches away.

I shut my eyes again. "A cow is about to eat me. Mir? Seriously, are you in one piece?" The breathing stops, and I look up again to see the cow already bored and moving on. Ouch. My leg is burning. I sit up to find my left knee bleeding right through a rip in my jeans *and* tights. Ow, ow, ow. And my chin hurts too. I think I broke my face. It chlorine-in-my-eyes stings.

"Yes," she grumbles.

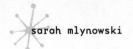

At least fifty black-and-white speckled cows of all sizes are surrounding us. I roll to my feet gently, careful not to disturb the livestock. I'm pretty sure cows don't eat humans, but I don't want to provoke them. Are they attracted to blood? I eye my scraped knee nervously. I *think* that's sharks. I hope.

Once on my feet, I help Miri up. "Ouch," she says. "You cut your chin. Does it hurt?"

"Not too much. But I'm sure it's gorgeous. My leg hurts more. Are you okay?"

"Fine. But the broom has seen better days." She points to what's left of it. It's cracked down the middle and now lies in shreds on the muddy (I hope it's mud) ground.

I hoist off my helmet and scratch my head like crazy. Ah. I point at one of the animals. "Any chance we can fly one of these things home?"

Moooooooooooooooooooooooo.

I leap back. "Maybe not."

Miri sneaks toward the cow and gingerly pats him (her? I'm not checking) on a black patch on his/her side. "Come see," she says. "He's not scary up close. He's kind of cute." (She's obviously decided on its gender.) She pats him, like he's a dog.

Moooooooooooooooooooooooo.

Only my sister would think a nine-hundred-pound cow is cute. "He's useless unless he's sprouting wings and taking us home," I say. "We have to get out of here. Ideas?" Happily, I didn't lose a shoe after all. But they're definitely not looking their pinkest. I step up on tiptoe and scan the area for an exit. Ow, ow, ow. Knee hurts. About twenty feet away there's a fence.

Moooooooooooooooooooooooo.

"What do you think Moo means?" Miri wonders out loud.

"No idea." And at the moment I don't really care. "Any clue how far we are from home?"

"I bet it means he's happy. Like when Tigger purrs."

"Miri! Focus! Home—how far are we?" Our cat hardly ever purrs. Not when I'm around, anyway. He prefers my mom and Miri. Must be the witch thing.

She stops caressing the cow and glares at me. "We only flew for ten minutes, we can't be too far away. Let's go if you want. Good-bye, sweet cow! Moo!"

We hurry toward the fence—Miri skips, I limp—and try to find a gate. Even with the night-vision visor, I'm having problems seeing.

"And you're sure you can't cast a spell on the cow?" I ask. "So we can fly it home?"

She shakes her head. "What if someone sees us?"

"Come on, what's the difference? Someone could have seen us on the broom."

"Maybe another witch. And then we could hang out," my sister says, pining for a witch peer. Apparently I am not enough for her.

"As if there's another witch in upstate New York. Bet they all live somewhere cool like Transylvania, or Salem. Now come on, Miri. Make the cow fly!" My leg is really starting to burn.

13

"I'm not making an animal fly. A broom is one thing, but I won't treat a cow like an object!"

"We're not doing circus acts," I say, exasperated. "We just want to ride him. People ride horses, don't they?" I can see I'm not getting anywhere. "So how are we going to get home?"

She points to my shoes. Now she's talking! "Perfect," I say. "I'll click them together three times and we'll be zapped back to the cottage?"

She rolls her eyes. "Nooooo."

"Hot-air balloon?" I ask hopefully.

"Your shoes are made for walking."

Groan. "Here's the gate," I say, spotting the hinge.

"What do you think this place is, anyway?" Miri asks.

An instant milk bar? "A dairy farm, dummy."

Once we're back on the road, we notice a sign on the door. "It's called Sammy's," I say, rubbing my still-burning knee.

"Good-bye, cute cows!" Miri sings, waving.

And then we walk all the way home, the broom sadly dragging behind us.

Forty-five minutes later, we're back at the cottage. My mom is sprawled on the mossy green couch in the living room, reading a romance novel. "Why didn't you use the window?" she inquires. Her gaze falls on my ripped jeans. When Miri tells her about the broken broom, she has a full-blown panic attack. "That's it," she asserts as she examines my chin. "No more flying. And why, oh, why did I quit smoking?"

The next day is full of disasters. First, I wake up to see that my small facial scrape has ballooned into a massive red blob on my chin. The second happens when we're at the grocery store that afternoon, picking up dinner. My mom is considering brands of veggie burgers, Miri is squeezing tomatoes, and I've just thrown a box of matzo into the cart because I feel I should have some since it's Passover this week—not that anyone would know that from all the bread we've been eating. My mom is so not religious. My dad isn't religious either, but he usually keeps Passover, which means no pasta, no pizza, no bread of any kind in the house. And he always has a Seder on the first night. No Seder this year, though; he and my new stepmom are on their honeymoon in Hawaii. I kind of miss the Seder. Last year my stepsister, Prissy, asked the traditional four questions, we sang that song about the goat ("Then came a cat and ate the goat, that my father bought for two *zuzim*. One little goat, one little goat." I have no idea what a *zuzim* is or why a cat is eating the poor goat, but we all sang along at the top of our lungs), and we hid the matzo. My dad eventually gave us twenty bucks each to give back the matzo, as is the custom. I wonder what I spent my money on? I could really use that twenty bucks now.

15

Anyway, after taking the box of matzo, I look longingly at the beef filets, knowing that there's a better chance of Mom getting us all makeovers than making us steaks. Zilch for both. And that's when I see it. The sign over the luscious, juicy meat reads SAMMY'S GRADE-A BEEF.

Sammy's? Oh, no. Step away from the aisle. *Step away from the aisle.* Sammy's is no dairy farm. It's a slaughterhouse! I take a quick step back and almost trip over a spice rack. Then I step on a small sneaker. Miri. Maybe she didn't see?

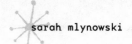

She shakes out her foot. "Be careful, clumsy. What's wrong with you?"

"N-nothing," I stutter. I oh-so-casually turn so that my back is to the meat section and stretch out my shoulders so that I'm blocking the sign.

"What are you doing?" she asks, and tries to peer over my left shoulder. I lean farther to the left. She tries to look over my right. I shift. Left, right, left, right.

I need a distraction. "Did you see the tomatoes? Yum."

"Are you hiding something?"

"The inner workings of my soul?"

She takes a bite of her thumbnail and the accompanying skin. "I know they sell meat here, Rachel. I'm not an idiot."

You'd think a vegetarian wouldn't bite her own body parts, but no. I wrap my arm around her thin shoulder and usher her toward the cereal aisle. She wiggles out of my grasp and turns back toward the meat fridge, her eyes filled with disgust as she inspects the beef chunks. Maybe she won't notice. Maybe someone will scream *fire*. Maybe—

Her face pales. Her jaw drops. Her eyes tear. I think she noticed.

"Oh, no," she moans.

"Miri, don't get upset."

"But all those cute cows are going to die!" Her lip is quivering and her shoulders start shaking and she looks a bit like she's trying to do a body wave. "They're going to be someone's dinner!"

I nod. "Unfortunately not mine."

Which doesn't help, because it causes Miri to fully cry right in the middle of the grocery store.

Where is our mother? I peer through the aisles and spot her tangled in those impossibly frustrating plastic vegetable bags. No need to bother her. I can handle this.

I hate watching my sister cry. I know she's being psycho-dramatic here, as well as taking this cow thing too personally, but only a soulless person can watch her sister be this upset and not feel pain. It's like having a clump of hair ripped from my head. Or a lung from my chest. Or a kidney from my . . . Hmm, I don't know where kidneys are. I should definitely pay more attention in bio. I got a B on my last assignment. But this month I'm going to focus and study and do my homework when it's assigned, just like Miri, and maybe I'll be able to save my final grade. . . .

What I really need to save is my love life.

What Miri really needs, I gather from her expression, is a tranquilizer. But back to saving . . . Eureka! "Miri," I say, tapping my temple. "If it makes you so upset, why don't you save them?"

She stops crying, and I see, beyond her ridiculously long, glistening lashes, the hope in her eyes. "How?" she asks.

Must I think of everything? "Use your powers, silly. You can't save all the cows in the world, but you can probably come up with a plan to save the ones at Sammy's."

She fingers a package of beef and then wipes her hand on her jeans. "You think I can?"

"Of course. We'll look through A²." Otherwise known as *The Authorized and Absolute Reference Handbook to Astonishing Spells, Astounding Potions, and History of Witchcraft Since the Beginning of Time.* My sister prefers using spells to cast her magic, rather than just zapping something with her raw will, since mixing the ingredients and chanting gives the witch more control. After last night's impromptu car-starter spell and subsequent nosedive into the cow field, I whole-heartedly agree with the strategy. "And we'll need to buy a new broom," I add.

"You think Mom will let us fly again?" she asks dubiously.

"Of course. When I fell off my bike, didn't she insist I get right back on?"

"I guess." Miri doesn't look convinced.

"Leave the permission stuff to me. You focus on finding the right spell." Maybe we can make the cows indestructible. Maybe Miri can put a spell like that on us, too.

"I flipped past a safety spell a while back," Miri says. "That might work."

"Or you can find an immortality spell." Nothing could hurt us! We'd look a little worse for wear when our hair started to fall out in a few centuries but we'd be as indestructible as vampires, without having to drink blood, but getting to wear the sexy red leather outfits and high-heeled shoes.

The safety spell wins. It seems Miri believes she has more of a say in this magic stuff than I do. I can't imagine *why*. On the plus side, I manage to convince Mom that Miri will be scarred for life if she doesn't get back on the broom immediately. So Mom takes her on a test run around the neighborhood before letting us go out alone again. We opt not to tell her about the Protect the Cows plan. She's in bed, reading, and there doesn't seem to be a point in worrying her over nothing. After all, she said Miri was allowed to use magic, right? And saving cows shows a social conscience (for the cows), so that makes it definitely responsible.

"Can you stop bumping into me?" Miri whines as my knees once again (unintentionally) smack the backs of her calves.

Okay fine, that last one was intentional. "If you stop zigzagging, I'll stop bumping into you," I say, negotiating.

She jerks the front of the broom up and I slide backward, nearly falling off the back end. Excellent. Maybe being in a body cast will help my social status. Not. My redesigned chin sure won't do me any favors.

My stomach is somersaulting and I don't think it's because we're suspended twenty feet in the air. Although I'm sure that's not helping. Now that school is less than forty-eight hours away, I can no longer be in denial about the trauma I'll be forced to endure.

19

See, a few months ago I convinced Miri to cast a dancing spell on me so I could be in the JFK High fashion show and finally be on the A-list. But when my mom freaked out and reversed the spell, my dancing ability sank to zero and I made a complete fool of myself. And I don't mean that in the annoying I-look-so-fat-says-the-ninety-pound-model sort of way. I knocked over castmates like they were bowling pins. I smashed up the sets. And then I (sob) stood up Raf, because I thought he'd never want to be seen with me. I'm officially socially ruined.

Maybe Miri will sprinkle some of the safety spell on me. I need to be protected from London Zeal, the senior who headed the show, whose leg I broke when I accidentally knocked her off the stage.

Although I might need the spell more to protect myself from Melissa Davis, I realize as we pass over Sammy's fence. I know it's wrong to hate, but she's evil. She's a mini London Zeal, a fellow freshman who tortures anyone not A-list, flirts with my quasi-used-to-be-almost-boyfriend, Raf, and stole my ex–best friend, Jewel. Although Jewel might be slightly evil these days too, since the fashion show corrupted her. Like it did me, temporarily. But at least I'm reformed. I realize that there are more important aspects to life than the A-list. I'm practically a do-gooder. I'm saving cows!

"Ready?" I ask as Miri steadies the new broom. I tried to convince her to buy the one with the hot pink bristles, but she thought we should get traditional straw to blend in. And so potential witnesses don't think they're seeing a fuchsia comet.

"Yup."

We spent the day finding a spell, finding the ingredients, and mixing, and now all we have to do is sprinkle the concoction over the cows. I keep one arm around Miri and use the other to open the fanny pack around my waist and pull out the Ziploc bag. The pack is my mom's, obviously. I would never own anything this obscenely orange and tacky. Or anything referred to by the word *fanny*. In the bag is a potpourri of garlic, mint, salt, and rice. It looks more like laundry detergent than magic ingredients if you ask me, but what do I know?

Miri takes a deep breath and recites:

"From a danger direct,
I vow this day forward,
To cherish and protect."

Who writes this stuff? I cringe at the bad poem. The spell sucks up the energy and warmth around us, causing the air to become instantly freezing. All right, I admit I can't really tell the difference between the magic and the cool April wind.

Meanwhile, Miri sprinkles the substance onto the livestock, reminding me of throwing rice at a wedding. Congratulations! Mazel tov! The concoction lands on the cows, sticking to them like snowflakes on a playground, or dandruff on a black sweater. It's all very scenic.

And then the cows disappear. Yes, vanish. Evaporate. Like a stain being washed out of a shirt. Or like Raf's feelings for me.

I can feel the (super-small, practically nonexistent) hairs on the back of my neck standing at attention. "Um, Miri?"

"They must be moving somewhere safe," she says, speculating as she continues sprinkling.

Eventually, all that's left is an empty field. The spots where the animals were grazing are bare. The night is suddenly quiet. Not a moo anywhere. Kind of creepy. "They're not . . . dead, are they?"

"No way. That would kind of defeat the purpose of a safety spell," she says, handing back the Ziploc. "We saved the cows."

"At least they've escaped their cheeseburger destiny, right?" I say, trying not to slip off the broom as I zip up the fanny pack. Why would my mom even own something so ugly? She's a witch! She could zap up the hippest purse in the world! Louis Vuittons on Monday mornings; Izzy Simpson bags for the afternoon. She doesn't even have to carry a purse at all. She could just zap up money, credit cards, keys, lipstick (not that she wears lipstick) whenever she needed them. She doesn't even need credit cards. She could zap up whatever she needed into the living room, direct from the Home Shopping Network or the Internet.

"Let's get out of here before the butcher spots us," Miri says. "I was thinking we'd fly back to the drive-in and see if anything good is playing. We deserve to reward ourselves. We'll tell Mom we had a really long practice session."

"You're the best, Miri." I'd give her a hug, but I don't want to mess up our balance. My sister snaps her sneakers together, and we jet off toward the drive-in. As we approach, I see the latest Spider-Man movie blasting on the screen. Fun! Some entertainment, finally.

Miri hovers over a tree.

"Why don't we get off and sit on the branches?" I suggest. "That way we'll have a good view."

I gingerly climb down first and find a makeshift ledge in a fat V-branch. Miri parks the broom and then squeezes in beside me. I'm watching a drive-in movie! There are no branches directly above me, and I can see straight up to the twinkling stars. I am the luckiest girl in the world.

Fine, if I were the luckiest girl in the world, I'd be here with Raf in a Mercedes and not with my little sister up in a tree, but whatever. And the branch is hurting my bum. I try to make myself comfy as Spider-Man swings from telephone line to building. "You know," I whisper over a budding leaf, "in a way, you're kind of like Spider-Man."

22

Miri turns to face me and her eyes glow in the moonlight. "How so?"

"You have powers, and you can use them to help the
world. Like you did tonight by saving the cows."

She bites her pinky nail and asks, "But what else can I
do?"

"You can do anything you want," I answer, suddenly excited by the idea of being a superhero's mentor. "Stop wars,
find homes for orphans—"

"Save the whales!" she squeals.

"Exactly. And you could wear a silver cape, a pink leo-
tard, and some kind of sexy eye mask. With sparkles! Of
course, I'd wear something similar as your sidekick." We're
like Batman and Robin!

She reaches for the thin branches above her and pulls
herself up. "Let's go home and make a list," she says excitedly.

I was wrong. My mom is clearly not the only person who
can make magic geeky.

The Wheels on the Bus Go . . . Kazam!

3

"Girls," my mom says as she swerves into the right lane, totally cutting off an unsuspecting driver, "I have a confession to make."

I've ridden with my mother three times in my entire life, which is three times too many. She. Is. The Worst. Driver. Ever. She's caused at least six almost-accidents in the last twenty minutes. I cling to my seat belt for safety. "Let me guess," I say. "You don't have a driver's license?"

My mom giggles. "Hilarious. Actually, smarty-pants, I'd like to discuss something important. Something serious . . ."

Maybe she'll finally tell us why she gave up witchcraft! About what caused the rift between her and Aunt Sasha, the aunt we never see.

"I want to talk about dating."

Oh, no. A sex talk from Mom. Can anything be more embarrassing? To add vinegar to the wound, I'm trapped in a car driving back to the city, so I can't even feign doing homework. My only option is to fake sleep. I roll my head so that it leans against the passenger's side window, close my eyes, and exhale a thunderous fake snore.

"Rachel," she says, "relax. Not about you dating. About me dating."

I pop my eyes open. That I can handle. "You dating?" This should be fun. My mom dated a bit after the divorce, only on weekends when we were at my dad's (she didn't want to be the type who brought home lots of "uncles"), but then she gave up. She hasn't so much as grabbed a cup of mocha joe with a man since then. "Anyone special? Someone at work? Do you have a crush?" Cuteness! Mom with a crush! Mom with a secret boyfriend? Has she snuck out of the apartment to see him at night?

"There's no one in mind. But I'd like to start again. Seeing your father remarry has made me think that it's time for me to move on. And I wanted to know how you two felt about it."

A new boyfriend! Fun! Someone who will explain the inner workings of the male mind to me. Or—someone who has a hot son. Now we're talking. They'll get married and I'll have a sizzling stepbrother. Too bad Raf's parents are still together. What a horrible thing to think. Wishing him years of divorce anxiety just so my mom can marry his dad. And anyway, then he'd be my brother, which would make it *mucho* creepy if we got married. Or worse: what if my mom and his dad then got divorced? Raf and I would be forbidden to see each other. Just like Romeo and Juliet. How romantic.

"You should definitely start dating again," I say. "It's time." At the very least, we would have a man around to change lightbulbs. My mom is so lazy about that. The one in my bedroom ceiling lamp blew out just the other day. And what was my mom's response to my claim that she should change it? That I should do it myself. Come on. What if I got hurt? That's such a stepdad's job. So is taking out the garbage. And setting the table. And taking my mom on trips so I can have wild parties.

"Miri?" my mom asks. "What do you think?"

"I . . . I don't know," Miri mumbles.

"Come on, Sis, be supportive!" I twist my body sideways to glare at her. Doesn't that girl ever watch Oprah? A "Go, Mom, go!" or at the very least a "Go, girl!" seems situation appropriate.

My mom sighs. "I asked for *her* opinion."

Miri wraps a frizzy strand of her brown hair around her thumb, making the tip turn red. "It's just that I'm not ready to wear another pukey pink bridesmaid dress so soon."

My mom laughs. "I said dating, honey, not marriage."

I roll my eyes. "Yeah, Mir. Way to get ahead of yourself."

"Whatever makes you happy, Mom," Miri says.

Anyway, there's no chance we'd wear pukey pink dresses to Mom's nuptials. I'm thinking long, sexy black. Maybe we should get out of the country and do a location wedding. Like in the Caribbean. Fun, no? Then we can get married on the beach—I mean, she can get married on the beach—and we can tan at the same time.

"So do you have anyone lined up?" I ask, excited. She should ask out Fireman Dave from the second floor. He's *hot*.

"No," she says. "Truth is I don't even know how to go about meeting quality men these days. The last time I had a real boyfriend was seventeen years ago!"

Ping! "I've got it!"

"No, you are not signing me up for one of those dating Web sites again, Rachel. They're so humiliating."

"That's not what I was going to suggest, big shot," I say haughtily. I was actually thinking she could apply to the re- ality show *Who Wants to Marry My Mom?* Even though I hate watching reality TV, at least I'd get to star on it. But if potential for humiliation is her litmus test, I'd better think of something else. "It's best you realize now that it won't be so easy to meet good men in Manhattan. Don't you watch TV? Aren't the chances of remarrying in your forties like one in a hundred? Aren't most men in your age group mar- ried, dead, gay, or jerks?"

"First of all, I'm thirty-nine." She veers into the path of an oncoming car but just before impact swerves back to her lane. "Maybe you're right. My single friends haven't found it so easy. Where am I going to meet men?"

I wish that my mom has more luck than I have. If I haven't been able to find a guy in my age group and none of them are married, dead, or out of the closet yet, the odds are not in my mom's favor.

She raises her hands as if in question and veers to the left, cutting off a bus diagonally behind us. She really is the worst driver. As the bus passes us, I peer into the windows and almost faint in shock.

One hot man. Two hot men. Three . . . omigod. It's a bus *full* of hot men.

I don't believe it. My heart pounds against my rib cage. Did I . . . did I just make that happen? Maybe I'm

27

finally a witch! I attempt telekinetically to roll down the car window.

Nada.

A coincidence. But still. How lucky is that? "Chase that bus!" I scream, pointing.

My mom gapes at me like I left my brain at the cottage. "Excuse me?"

"It's a bus full of men! Talk about a dating pool. Go get it!" I'm bobbing up and down in my seat like a yo-yo.

"I am *not* chasing a bus," she says, shaking her head. "I don't want a speeding ticket."

"Do you see a cop?" I do an exaggerated look out the window. "I don't see a cop. Go get 'em!"

"You're crazy."

"Use magic!" I cry.

"I don't use magic! I'm a nonpracticing witch!"

"Mom! It's a new chapter in your life. Make some changes!"

The gulf between us and the bus is widening. "I don't know," she says. "That's not what I meant. . . ."

"Now is the time. Give the bus a flat tire! Empty its gas tank!" The bus is now almost a football field away. Two football fields! Three! They're getting away! "Follow that cab!" I scream.

"It's not a cab," Miri snarls from the backseat.

Why must she be so literal? Anyway, I know, but I've always wanted to say that. It sounds glam.

"Rachel, give it a rest," my mom says, but as her mouth forms the words, her eyes tell a different story, lusting longingly for the Hunks-on-Wheels. And that's when a gust of cold air bursts through the car.

I'm wondering why the air conditioner just kicked on when *boom!*

The bus is tilted to its right. Oh my. Oh yes! My mom just gave the bus a flat tire! It grinds to a halt and pulls to the side of the road.

I'm bursting with pride, like I just watched my child take her first steps. "You did it!"

"I—I—I," my mom stammers.

"Quick, pull over beside it," I instruct.

She listens and parks the car on the shoulder of the road, right behind the bus.

"Well, what do we do now?" Miri asks, kicking the back of my seat. Big baby.

"We offer our assistance," I say. "I know I'm not the best wingman at the moment because of the scrape on my face, but it's better than it was yesterday and Miri looks pretty cute in her overalls—"

"What if they're dangerous?" my scaredy-cat sister complains. "They could be serial killers."

"Yes, a bus full of serial killers, that's realistic." Come on, Miri, get with the program. "Let's go!" I sing, and unlock my door.

I glance over at my mom. She looks completely shell-shocked, blinking repeatedly as if specks of dirt just flew into her eyes.

"Come on! Now or never!"

She ogles the bus, looks at me, and then, just when I

think she's going to reverse right out of there, flips open the overhead mirror and gives herself the once-over. "All right, let's do it."

Wahoo! I wish she wasn't wearing her nerd-o jeans pulled up right to her waist. Although they do make her butt look all J-Lo.

I flip open my mirror for a quick peek. Besides the chin absurdity, everything looks normal. Complexion = clear, nose = small, eyes = brown, teeth = straight.

"This is so stupid," Miri says, sulking. "What are you going to do? Help change the tire?"

"We're not going over to help them. We're going so Mom can meet men. Now, put on a pretty please-date-my-mother smile and let's go."

"Forget it. I'd rather stay here and edit my Save the World list. And leave me the cell phone in case you two get accosted, so I can call the police for backup."

Such a drama queen.

"Keep the doors locked," my mom says insistently, and then jumps out of the car. She cautiously checks for oncoming traffic, hesitates, and then, holding my hand, leads me toward the bus.

Before we can get to the front, the door swings open and a tall, skinny man wearing a brown suede hat (in an obvious attempt to cover his thinning gray hair) steps outside. He's wearing a thick green Patagonia sweatshirt, and a badge that says *Baseball Hall of Fame, Tour Leader* dangles from his wrinkled neck. A baseball tour! Excellent. The tour guide stretches his arms over his head and then scratches his burly gray eyebrows, looking startled to see us approaching. His

30

gaze sways from Mom to me, then back to Mom, and then he smiles. "Hello."

My mom stands up straighter. Go, girl! "Hi," she says, sounding almost . . . coy?

"Hi," he says. Excellent to the power of two! We've made contact.

I elbow my mom in the side.

"Anything we can help you with?" she asks, feeling my not-so-subtle cue. "Give you a ride?"

Old Man Tour Guide shakes his head. "Nah. Thanks, though. Much appreciated. Very sweet of you to offer." He (oh yes) tips the front of his hat as if he's some sort of cow-boy. Maybe he was a cowboy. In the 1940s. "The driver just called Triple A, but it will take them at least thirty minutes to get here."

"Great," my mom says, eyes still on him. Old Man Tour Guide doesn't look away.

Yikes. Old Man Tour Guide is flirting with my mother! He's a hundred years old! Fine, he's at least fifty.

OMTG sticks out his pale hairy hand. "My name is—"

"How's it going, Lex?" says a booming voice. As the owner of the voice steps off the bus, my heart literally swoons. Like if I were a cartoon, it would pop out of my shirt and jiggle. He's *gorgeous*. About half OMTG's age, at least six feet tall, thick light brown hair, and topped off with deli-ciously chiseled cheekbones. He's wearing faded jeans and a Yankees jersey. I wonder if he's a ballplayer.

"I think the boys are getting restless," he says, and cracks his knuckles. "Hello, ladies," he adds as he notices us.

Ten more men follow him off the bus. Ten more *hot* men.

31

As each man steps off, he smiles at my mom. This is the dating pool jackpot.

"So what kind of tour is this?" my mom asks Lex, who hasn't yet realized he should get out of the way. I mean, come on. My mom should not be spending precious time with him when there are more appropriately aged stepfathers available. Lex could be my stepgrandfather. I could fix him up with my *bubbe*.

"I lead a day-trip tour to the National Baseball Hall of Fame in Cooperstown every Sunday from April to October. Have you been?"

"Nope," she says. And bats her eyelashes. Oh, no, what's she doing? She's wasting her flirting! I raise my eyebrow as a suggestive cue to move on.

"I'd be happy to take you one day, Mrs. . . ."

My mom blushes a deep fuchsia. "Ms., actually. But please call me Carol."

"I'm Lex," he says, and sticks out his pale hairy hand again. Mom takes it, apparently oblivious to my eyebrow signals. Abort plan!

"And this is my daughter Rachel."

I shake his hand reluctantly. And then I turn to the crowd of younger, hotter men and extend my hand to the specimen closest to me. "And what's your name?" I ask.

"Jimmy," the guy says. He's cute. Red hair, jean jacket, nice teeth.

I tug my mom away from Lex. No need to date the frog when we're surrounded by princes. "Mom, meet Jimmy."

She giggles. "Hi, Jimmy. I'm Carol."

32

"Nice to meet you," he says, sounding gruff yet sexy. "You live in New York?"

"Yes, I do," she answers in a chirpy Mouseketeer's voice I didn't know she had. Impressive. Somewhat nauseating. The old broad has some tricks up her sleeve. "You?"

Go, girl!

"Nah," he says, shaking his head. "Florida. I came up to visit my wife's brother and . . ."

I should have looked at his ring finger before getting excited. Oh, no. What if these men are all married? Or if they all live in Florida?

I can handle Florida. I'm not opposed. New school, perma-tan, Disney World . . . But my mom's being a high-priced mistress? Not so much. Too much drama. I'd see the other woman's kids at school and would have to pretend I didn't know where their father was spending his nights. What if I fell in love with his seventeen-year-old son? Would it be my ethical duty to tell him, even if it would tear his soul apart?

I snap back to attention just as my mom is being introduced to Adam, the hot guy in the Yankees jersey, Florida Man's single brother-in-law (no ring). Much better. "I live in Jersey City," he's saying. Oh well, no tan for me, but being nearby will make their courtship easier. Fewer flights.

"I'm a travel agent," she's saying.

"One of the best in the city!" I pitch.

The apples of her cheeks redden.

"Isn't she cute when she blushes?" I add, and she inserts

her thumbnail into her mouth and is about to take a nibble when I gently yank her hand away. Must she gross them out?

"Very cute," Lex says, startling me. Enough, old man! Stop stalking my mom!

"I was thinking of planning a trip down to visit Jimmy, my sister, and the kids," Adam says, sidling up closer to her. "Do you think you could give me advice?"

"Actually," she says as she picks at her fingers behind her back, thinking I won't notice, "I specialize in honeymoons. . . ."

I quickly step on her foot. Is she that clueless? "Mo-ther, I'm sure you could help him out. Why don't you give him your *business* card. And then he could *call* you." I try to use my nonexistent telepathy to help her get it. Card . . . phone call . . . date . . .

34

She nods and then stops picking long enough to reach into her purse and pull out a card.

Adam smiles as he reads it. "Thanks."

"I need to book some trips too," pipes up Lex. "Is there one for me?"

Sigh. How transparent can you get, old man? I thought cowboys were supposed to be suave.

Smiling, my mom starts handing cards out like candy canes at a mall in December.

"Where do you recommend this time of year?" Lex asks, once again hogging the conversation.

"France is beautiful in the spring. . . ."

Where you should go, Lex, so you can leave my mother alone! Just as I'm about to interrupt, a new hottie, a blond hottie with big green eyes, butts in for me. "Are you a travel agent? I could use some help with my miles. . . ."

Wink, wink. Sure he can.

Twenty minutes later, we're back in the car and Operation HM³ (Help Mom Meet Men) was a smashing success. What can I say? I'm brilliant.

"I can't believe that worked," Mom says giddily. "I gave out eleven business cards!"

"You took forever," Miri moans. "It's freezing in here. Can you start the car already and turn on the heat? I'm going to catch a cold."

I turn on the heat and then the radio and do a little seat groove to the beat. Maybe I'll become a matchmaker. I'm like a puppeteer, commandeering the emotions of unsuspecting innocents. Who needs magic? All I need are clever strategies. Fine, we needed the magic to stop the bus, but otherwise it was all me. I can do anything I set my mind to, just like my mother always told me! Well, not anything. There's nothing I can do about school tomorrow. If only I could conjure up a cancel-school spell. Or at least a freak snowstorm.

I *cannot* face going to school tomorrow. Is it possible the JFK kids have forgotten about the fashion show fiasco? It's been an entire week.

Yeah, right.

Even if the masses have forgotten, there's no way the fashion show horribles have. London has probably spent the entire week preparing ways to torture me. After all, I did knock her off the stage and thus break her leg. Oh God. I

35

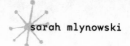

need to go into hiding. Maybe my bruised chin will act as a disguise? No, I'm pretty sure it will be gone by tomorrow. The red has already started to fade.

But Miri had the right idea. If I catch a cold, I can stay in bed the entire day.

I turn off the heat.

"Are you crazy?" Miri asks. "It's freezing in here. Do you want to get sick?"

"Yup." I roll down the window and inhale.

Not Quite Gone,
Not Quite Forgotten **4**

Beep! Beep! Beep! Beep!

Nonononononononoooooo. It's seven a.m. Monday morning and my throat doesn't hurt at all. How is that possible? I inhaled bitterly cold air. I showered last night and walked around the block—without blow-drying! I purposely didn't take a vitamin before bed! (Don't tell my dad; he's obsessed with vitamins.) Also I didn't have my evening glass of fresh orange juice. And I love my evening glass of juice. The rush of vitamin C gives me sweet dreams.

Maybe I have a fever. I *am* feeling pretty headachy. I could have at least 101, maybe 102. My throat isn't sore but I'm burning up. Might have to be hospitalized. Maybe the kids at school will feel guilty about bad-mouthing someone who's sick and send me flowers and one of those life-size cards that everyone signs in different colors. In fact, they'll probably realize that my horrendous fashion show performance was a result of this sickness, and I'll be forgiven, because you can't be mad at someone who's sick. A-list, here I come! Plus I'll have a superhot doctor nursing me to health. Yes!

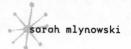

I hurry to the bathroom, park myself on the edge of the bathtub, and shove the thermometer under my tongue.

"Oh, give it up. You're perfectly healthy," Miri says, barging in and flipping on the faucet.

" 'et ot!" I mumble, which translates to "get out" in non-thermometer-speak. "I'm thick. Pwobably contaios."

She applies toothpaste to her brush. "Suck it up and go to school. You'll be fine."

I will not be fine. I catch a glimpse of myself in the mirror and gasp. My chin has completely crusted over and seems worse than ever. It looks like a beard. Isn't this all Miri's fault to begin with? Losing my dancing skills, bruising my chin . . . I'm about to tell her where to get off but decide to try to calm myself down instead. I shouldn't be getting so emotional when I'm deathly ill.

The thermometer beeps and reads . . . 98.2?

What? That's impossible. How could I not have a fever? I'm perfectly healthy. How can this be? Hmm, isn't normal body temperature 98.6? Perhaps there's a dangerous medical condition that causes your temperature to drop. Maybe by noon it'll be down to ninety, by this afternoon eighty, and by this evening I'll be a frozen Popsicle, unable to move without my fingers snapping off like ice-capped branches.

Miri grabs the traitorous thermometer from my hands. "You're fine. Go get dressed."

Speaking of ice, maybe it's snowing outside. Then the school will call a snow day and I'll get to stay home. I sprint back to my room and hurl open the window blinds.

Sunny. A beautiful sunny day. Shouldn't the weather know that it's supposed to reflect my mood?

"Mom!" I holler. "Can I stay home today? Pleeeeeease?"

"No!" she yells back through the walls.

I flop onto my unmade bed and pull the covers over my head. "But I'm going to be a social outcast! And I have a beard!"

"I told you, if you're mature enough to use magic, you should be mature enough to face the consequences. Besides, you can't hide away forever."

Not forever. Just until my classmates graduate. So I'll be a few years older than the others when I finally go back. At least my body will have caught up to them. Hopefully. Even my own little sister has me beat in that department, with her B-cup breasts. How unfair is that? "But I look like a man!"

I can hear her laughing. Ha-ha. "It's not that bad, Rachel. Get ready for school."

Get ready for social mortification is more like it.

If I make my steps really small, I'll be late. Because I don't have a note, I'll get expelled. And then I'll never have to go to school again! Although then I won't get into college. I'll never get a good job and the only place that will hire me will be McDonald's and all I'll eat will be Big Macs and fries and one day my neighbor will find a five-hundred-pound me unable to squeeze through the front door of my cat-infested apartment.

I make my steps *slightly* bigger. And tighten my puffy black coat. The bright sun deceptively makes the weather look warm when it's actually even colder than yesterday.

As I approach the last few blocks before school,

39

something seems off. Like a silent Times Square. A crowd of students have gathered outside the building. Jeez. Are they *all* waiting for me so they can mock me? Am I so famous?

"This rules, man," a passing senior says. "I'm going back to bed."

I'd like to go back to bed. I'd like to go back to middle school. I sprint toward the mob and try to eavesdrop on a cluster of sophomores to hear what's going on.

". . . cows in there. How funny is that? It was so the senior prank," one of them says.

Cows?

"Best prank ever," someone else comments. "How did they do it? Get fifty cows into the school gym without anyone seeing?"

Fifty cows?

The words and noise around me swirl, like I'm on a merry-go-round.

". . . doubt any of the seniors were smart enough to pull this off . . ."

". . . probably those jerks at Brentwood High . . ."

". . . classes are going to be canceled . . ."

". . . major property damage . . ."

". . . health officials have to decontaminate . . ."

I feel instantly light-headed, like I just gave blood. They couldn't be Miri's cows. The Sammy's cows? No. Maybe. Did Miri wish them into the school gym? Why would she wish them into *my* gym? She doesn't even go to this school. She's still in middle school.

Am I partly responsible for the destruction of school

property? I feel sick. On the other hand—no school! How sweet and sour. And then I spot Raf.

My cheeks heat up despite the cold.

Even though he's not facing me, I can tell it's him by his camel leather jacket. It's his fall/spring jacket, the one he wore when I first spotted him back in September and thought he was cute. For the rest of my life I will think of Raf whenever I see a boy in a camel jacket. Or anything camel colored. Like caramel sauce. Which is just as delicious.

Raf is not wearing his gloves. He dropped one of them at my apartment the night he came to pick me up (unsuccessfully) for Spring Fling. Since a piece of clothing is the key ingredient in a love spell, of course I asked Miri to whip one up for me. Unfortunately, she's still scarred from the mess caused by the love spell we put on Dad and isn't quite eager to get back in the fake-affection saddle just yet. (Small disaster involving us trying to break up my dad and his fiancée's wedding. Obviously we sorted it out, since they're currently honeymooning in Hawaii. Long story, but let's just say our stepmother turned out to be not as bad as we first feared.)

I hope his hands aren't cold. I guess, since it's April, there isn't much point in buying a new pair. Although he could probably find a fantastic sale.

Did he see me? Does he hate me? Should I duck or apologize again? You've got to make things happen, I remind myself. If I can fly on a broomstick with no seat belt, I can talk to a guy who used to like me.

First I need to hide my chin. I unroll my turtleneck so that

41

it covers the lower half of my face. Much better. Okay, now I'm going over. In ten. I tap my feet against the ground and count.

Nine, ten.

Ten more seconds.

He's leaving. My knight-in-camel is disappearing into the horizon like a setting sun. I know I should run after him, but my new shoes are stuck to the ground like lumps of pink clay. I wallow in my own pool of sadness until I'm snapped out of it by the sound of snickering.

I look to my right and see Jewel Sanchez, Melissa Davis, and Stephy Collins standing in a semicircle, all smirking at me. With their brown, red, and blond hair, they remind me of evil Charlie's Angels. They are all wearing brand-new trendy back-to-school outfits: tight jeans, designer spring coats, sunglasses perched on freshly highlighted hair. Even though I know that Melissa is the same height as Jewel, five foot six, she seems to tower over Jewel. The ego must add inches the way the camera adds pounds. Jewel's mahogany curls are clipped to her head in a style that tries to look like she just threw it back, even though from our years of Bee-Bee (Best Buds) status I know it took her at least an hour. Stephy's long blond pigtails are gone, and her short Tinker Bell do, along with her petite frame, makes her look like she's seven years old. A malicious seven-year-old, the kind who steals your candy. The three of them and Doree Matson were lucky enough to be London's chosen freshman four in the fashion show. They are therefore super A-list. Unfortunately, if their three pairs of eyes were laser beams, I would have disintegrated by now. I instantly look down at my shoes. I'll just walk away before they can attack me. Slowly, controlled. One step, two, three. Run, run, run!

Flump.

Controlled means not tripping over a bike rack and falling on my elbows, doesn't it?

I see a flash of light and I hope I've fallen unconscious. I'll wake up in the hospital, finally living the pitiable loads-of-flowers/life-size-card/hot-doctor scenario. But no such luck. I can hear the trinity of freshman evil cackling. I can't believe that Jewel, my ex–best friend, is actually laughing at me. Ignoring me is one thing, but laughing? From my spot on the ground, I see my surroundings blurring, mostly because of the prickling at the backs of my eyes.

Until a familiar hand reaches to help me up.

"Hi!" says Tammy. "There you are!"

I've never been happier to see my new best friend's face. "Thank God," I say, scrambling to my feet and brushing dirt from my coat. "I missed you! When did you get back?"

"Last night at eleven." She wrinkles her nose and gently touches my chin. "That looks like it hurts."

"It's fine, and you look amazing," I cry, and give her a bear hug. Unlike me, she's tanned and relaxed looking. "How was it?"

She drops her backpack to the pavement. "Fantastic. I went shark diving!"

"Excuse me?"

"I was in a cage underwater surrounded by great hammerheads! It was so cool."

"Is that safe? Why would you want to do that?"

"The cage totally protects you. And what do you mean, 'why'? Where else could I see sharks?"

I motion to Jewel, Melissa, and Stephy with my chin and then roll the turtleneck back up. Those girls are sharks in the sea of high school. "Maybe I should bring a cage to class."

Tammy laughs and then steps on tiptoe and scans the yard. "Have you seen Aaron?"

"No. Have you spoken to him since you've been back?"

"No. And he hasn't e-mailed me since I left on Sunday. Why? Do you think something is wrong? I know he was going to Mick Lloyd's party on the night I left for the Gulf of Mexico. I'll die if he hooked up with someone. You haven't heard anything, have you?" She immediately rubs the tip of her nose, like she always does when she's feeling insecure. It's a little on the large side, and she's convinced that its size is the reason she never had a boyfriend before Aaron.

"From who? You're the only person still speaking to me." Not getting an e-mail from your boyfriend for eight days doesn't sound promising. Not that I'd tell her that. There are certain things a best friend must never say. One is "I don't think he likes you." Two is "Yes, your nose is big." But the truth is her nose isn't why she's never had a boyfriend. She's never had a boyfriend because boys are morons. I mean, I've never had a real boyfriend, and nothing's wrong with me, right? Well, except for my extreme slobbiness and weirdo family. And my beard, but that's new. But in any case, I think it's bad news he hasn't been in touch over the break. Especially since after my dad's wedding they kissed for three hours on her couch, and that was barely eight days ago. "I'm sure he's just busy," I say.

She scowls disbelievingly and then yawns, covering her mouth. "I'm tired."

"Probably because of the time zone difference."

"It's only an hour," she says, and laughs.

"Students! Hello? Students?" Mrs. Konch, the principal, is shouting into a loudspeaker. She's short and plump and reminds me of a dinner roll. "Everyone, please vacate the premises! Check your school e-mail tonight for an update!"

"Insane," Tammy murmurs. "Do you think the cow rumor is true? Seems unbelievable." She shrugs and yawns simultaneously.

"Um . . . yeah. Unbelievable." I know I should be more worried about the cows, but at the moment I'm more concerned by the laser beam of a glare coming at me from London Zeal. She's a few feet away, surrounded by her über-glam and shiny fashion show friends. The girls are all made up with their heavy lipstick, short denim skirts, and black knee-high boots, and the guys are wearing their coolio black leather jackets and crumpled jeans. London is all white: white jacket, white leather skirt, and a white two-inch heel on her unbroken foot to match the all-white full-leg cast. She wouldn't want to break her one-color-per-outfit rule.

I shouldn't make fun; the cast on her leg is all my fault, and I feel awful. I timidly approach the crowd. "London, I am so sorry," I say sincerely. Even though she's evil, she does not deserve to have a broken leg.

The group snickers. London shuffles toward me. "Sorry?" she hisses. "You'll be sorry. Very sorry when I'm done with

45

you." She jabs her french-manicured nail into my chest and then hobbles back to her friends.

Having the freshman A-list hating me is one thing. But the senior A-list too?

I'm doomed.

"Let's get out of here," Tammy says.

"Let's. Wanna come over?"

Tammy does a final scan around the yard, seemingly searching for Aaron. Then she gives me an okay sign with her right hand. In scuba diving, this can mean anything from are-you-OK to do-your-ears-hurt to yes-I'm-OK to I'm-terrific. So sometimes I'm not entirely sure what she means, but at the moment I think she's saying "Sounds like a plan."

"Please vacate the premises!" Principal Konch says again, sounding frantic and angry, as though it's our fault the cows have invaded our gym.

As though.

46

*

"The cows are in the gym?" Miri shrieks at six that night, stamping her foot on my carpet.

"Keep your voice down," I say. "Mom is watching the news in her room."

"How is that possible? Are you sure we did it?"

"No, but it makes sense. You zap them to safety, they disappear, and this morning there are fifty cows in the school gym. A coincidence? I don't think so." She kicks her chair and it teeters on its side. "Careful," I warn her. Miri's kicks are like mini weapons. "The spell was more of a moving spell than a safety spell," I add, nodding. "Although maybe your raw will stupidly thought that the cows were safer in the gym. Who knows?"

She waves her hands, clearly exasperated. "But . . . but . . . what's going to happen to them now?"

"How should I know? You tell me; you're the one who moved them!"

She tries to bite her fingers, but I hit her hand away. "They must be our cows," she says. "But how did they end up at your school? Do you think I was subconsciously trying to get you out of going to class?"

Aw. "Miri, that's so sweet! But listen, as much as I appreciate the thought, I think you should just do a spell reversal."

"No way," she says, shaking her head. "First of all, the spell reversal is a five-broomer, and I don't want to screw this up any more." Next to every spell in the book are broom icons. One broom means the spell is light and easy; five mean extremely intricate and difficult to cast. "And second, I'm not sending the cows back there. There must be another way. We'll have to move them somewhere else."

"And how are we going to do that?"

"We'll go over and zap them." She nibbles on her finger, then swallows.

"Did you just eat your skin? That is so vile." I shake my head in disgust. "And no, we can't just hop over to the school. I heard police sirens when I was leaving. It's hardcore there now. Someone will see us."

She looks panicked. "Do they know it was us?"

47

"Yes, Miri, when they spotted cows in the gym they assumed one of their student's little sisters had cast a magic spell."

She throws her hands over her eyes. "Oh, no!"

"I was being sarcastic. Of course they don't know! They think it was a senior prank."

She takes a deep breath. "Well, what's going to happen?"

"I just got an e-mail. School is closed tomorrow and Wednesday but reopening on Thursday. So the good news is I get two more days off. Thanks for your help!"

The phone rings and I grab it.

"He has mono!" Tammy says happily. "That's why he didn't e-mail! He was too tired to even make it to the computer. Isn't that great?"

"Hold on," I say, and lead Miri out of my room.

"Can you call her back, please?" Miri cries. "Hello? Important?"

"Give me two secs. This is a private conversation," I say, and push my door closed. "Tam, I'm happy that he wasn't breaking up with you, but aren't you worried you're going to get sick?" And then she'll have to miss school. Some people have all the luck.

Pause. "I feel fine."

I whisper into the phone since Miri's a little young to hear this. "But it's the kissing disease. You know? Passed from saliva? And you guys . . . made out."

"I'm healthy. And anyway"—now her voice drops to a whisper—"my mom would kill me." You'd think that having two moms would make Tammy's household super-liberal, but Tammy doesn't tell them a thing. "But isn't that great news?"

"You fell asleep on my couch today. Watching *Casablanca*. You love that movie," I say, more to myself than to her. Sleepiness is one of the signs of mononucleosis.

"I was tired, Rachel. Diving is exhausting. Especially with sharks."

Miri is banging on the door. And Tammy so has mono and is going to desert me at school. "Terrific. I gotta go. Wanna come over again tomorrow and watch *Titanic*?" She likes anything that won an Oscar. And maybe we can share toothbrushes and I'll catch mono from her. Awesome.

We hang up and I let my sister back in. "What are we going to do about the cows? Should we tell Mom?" she asks helplessly.

"Rachel!" my mom, apparently psychic, screams from her room. "Your school is on TV!"

Miri and I run to my mom's bedroom and there, on TV, are the cows.

A reporter is standing in front of them. "Today, at JFK High School, a school prank has been taken to a new level. Someone has mooooooooooved"—I groan—"fifty cows into a high school gym. In related news, this explains the mysterious Saturday disappearance of the cattle at Sammy's, a slaughterhouse in upstate New York."

The scenery changes to Sammy's. "Hey!" my mom says from under her purple duvet. "Isn't that near . . ."

La, la, la. Miri starts biting her nails. I twirl my hair. An elderly man is on TV. "It was the strangest thing," he says,

49

looking utterly mystified. "The animals were here grazing at seven p.m. but gone by four a.m. We didn't hear a thing. It's almost supernatural. If we didn't know better, we'd think it was the work of aliens. . . ."

"Girls," my mom says, her eyes bearing into us, "something you want to tell me?"

Squirm.

"Rachel," she begins. "This is your plan to get school canceled?"

She thinks I did this? Hello? I'm the kid who was left behind. The child to whom nature forgot to hand down the witch gene. "Mom, I swear, I did *not* know this was going to happen."

She thumps the still-tucked-in spot beside her. "Why don't you two sit down and explain."

Miri's face squishes up like a raisin. Here come the waterworks. "It's my fault!" she wails, tears spilling. "I was trying to save the cows!" Sob. "I didn't mean to put them in the school gym, I swear, and now someone innocent is going to get blamed. And it can't be me because then people will know, but I don't want it to be someone else because that would be so unfair." Miri then climbs into the spot next to our mom, and I plop down on the corner of the bed.

My mom pats Miri's hair. "So you were trying to save the cows," she says.

We nod frantically. "Yes!"

"I see."

Okay, now that she knows, everything will be fine. Mom will tell us how to fix the situation, and all will be taken care of. Problem solved!

"So how are you going to fix it?" Mom asks.

What? "Um, us?" I say.

"I said you're allowed to use magic. But I also said that you have to face the consequences. And that means not expecting me to clean up your messes." She shakes her index finger at us. "You two are on your own."

Miri sinks into the mattress. "Do you have any advice?" she squeaks.

"Yes. Next time you cast a spell, think about what you're doing. Where did you think the cows were going to go?"

"Somewhere safe?" my sister answers.

"Yes, but where?"

"I don't know."

"Now you do," Mom says sternly. "So you'd better be more careful next time." And then she . . . smiles?

Where did that come from? "Are you okay, Mom?"

"Sorry," she says, still smiling. "Just thinking about something else."

Something else? What could possibly be distracting her from our moving cows across the state? "What's up with you?"

She aims the remote at the TV and clicks it off. "Lex called today."

"Lex?" Miri looks confused. "Luthor?"

"Yes, Superman's nemesis called Mom," I say, and lie across Miri's legs. "What planet were you hatched on? Lex is the old guy from the bus." I can't believe he called already. It's only been a day since we got back. He's obviously desperate. "What did he want?"

"To take me out to dinner," she says, her smile widening.

Miri pulls the covers over her head. "I don't want you to date again! You're going to forget all about us!"

"Never ever," Mom says reassuringly.

"Well, I'm not worried," I say. "I want you to date again. Just not him. You're not going to go, are you?"

"Of course I am," she says. "Why wouldn't I? Didn't you think he seemed nice?"

"Nice and old," I say. "He probably eats dinner at five o'clock and orders the early bird special." Miri giggles from under the covers and I add, "You should be dating younger guys." I join Miri under the covers and then sit up so it feels like we're in a tent.

My mom sighs. "Don't be mean, Rachel. And it's not like any other guys are knocking down my door."

"When are you going out with him? Saturday night?" At least someone in this place has a date. I lift the comforter and pull my mom underneath with me.

"No," she says, sitting up beside me. "I told him I'd be happy to go out with him on the weekend of the eighth."

Apparently Mom plays hard to get. No last-minute plans for her. Someone's been reading her dating books. "That's in three and a half weeks!"

"It's not that long," she says. "And it's the next time you girls are at your dad's."

"We're not babies, Mom," I huff. "You're allowed to have a life when we're here. Dad has a life. You should too." I can make out her shrugging shoulders in the dark. "So what did you agree to?" I ask. "A Saturday-night dinner?"

"I didn't. I told him to call back closer to the date."

"That's good," Miri says casually. "Since he's so old, by then he might have kicked the bucket."

My mom snorts, and then the three of us laugh, and our tent feels warm and cozy like a cocoon. "I should start dinner," Mom says, and reaches to dismantle our hideaway.

"Don't," I beg. I don't want her breaking this bubble. I don't want to return to reality just yet. I don't want to worry about cows or going back to school or Raf or London or any of that.

"It'll be fine," she says, patting my knee.

Maybe she's right. The cow problem will eventually go away. And how bad can London's revenge be?

www.ineedtobehomeschooled.com

5

Kick. Kick.

Thank goodness for Tammy. If she weren't sitting next to me, I would definitely have to transfer.

The last two days went by too quickly. Why do good things disappear so fast? Vacation. Money. Ice cream.

The two of us are sitting on the right side of the auditorium, in the fifth row. I warned Tammy that her proximity to me would contaminate her social status, but she was convinced that, after a week and a half, the fashion show clique would have forgotten all about me. Teen years are like dog years. Thirteen days translates into thirteen months.

As always, there's good news and bad news. The bad news is they have not forgotten. London Zeal is kicking my chair. Yes, London and her posse of slick A-list seniors followed me to my seat so they could sit behind me and harass my back with their pointy-toed boots. Very mature, no? I'm pretending to ignore them. The other bad news is that the entire school has a lingering smell of cow excrement.

The good news is that my beard is gone. Since I

very cleverly hid it under my turtleneck on Monday, no one ever knew it was there, and now it's as if it never happened.

Kick. Kick. If the auditorium didn't have built-in seats, my chair would have been jolted across the room by now.

Kick, kick. She's making me wish I had broken both her legs.

Tammy yawns.

"You sound tired," I say. "You're not, right?"

"Nope."

"And your throat doesn't hurt?" Swollen glands are another sign of mono.

"Nope. Poor Aaron has mono. Not me."

We're both in denial. Tammy fell asleep on my couch again yesterday. But I cannot bear to be at school without her.

Kick. Kick, kick.

Enough! I spin to face my nemesis. "Yes, London?"

Her good leg is raised in midkick. "If it isn't Rochelle Weiner," she says.

"It's Rachel Weinstein," I say. "Can I help you?" What does she want from me? One of my good legs? I already told her I was sorry.

"I'm surprised to see you."

"I *do* go to school here."

"Yes, but it won't be a pleasant few months for you, I can promise you that. You may want to transfer. Unless you're enjoying all the coverage." The fashion show lackeys beside her giggle.

What is she talking about? What does she mean by

coverage? I look at Tammy for an explanation but she's sound asleep. I have no retort, so I spin back to the front. How did I manage to get the most popular girl in the school to hate me?

Onstage, Mrs. Konch, Vice-Principal Earls, and Will Kosravi, Raf's brother and the student council president, are huddled together. Then Mr. Earls clears his throat into the microphone. London kicks my chair again.

I nudge Tammy with my elbow. "You okay?"

Her eyes pop open. "I'm not tired."

Mrs. Konch takes the microphone. "I wish we could welcome you back under happier circumstances, but unfortunately, the school was a victim of a terrible prank." She glowers at the rows and rows of students. "We are currently investigating who is to blame. If anyone has any information, there will be a reward. And for those of you responsible, punishment will be less stringent if you turn yourselves in."

I slither in my seat. Kick.

"The animals," she says, frowning as snickers wave through the rows, "have caused severe damage to the gym floor—"

They have?

"—as well as damage to the ten classrooms neighboring the gym, the changing rooms—"

Those, too?

"—and the cafeteria."

Stupid, hyperactive cows.

"We will have to undergo a few changes," she continues. "First, all gym classes will now be held outside, so please dress appropriately. Second, until the classrooms are repaired, some freshman classes will be doubled up. Check the revised class schedules on the activities board. Finally, the library will be open for lunch."

Would you like some fries with that Shakespeare? Maybe Raf will be in some of my classes.

Kick.

Snore.

Groan.

Just my luck. Instead of getting doubled up with Raf's homeroom, I get Melissa and Jewel's.

I pull a groggy Tammy into the back row. As I'm about to sit down, Melissa slides into my seat. I lunge for the desk in front of her.

57

"Saved for Doree," Melissa says.

I point to the empty desk beside her. "And that?"

Jewel slides into the chair with a shrug. My stomach sinks. Not that I expect her to help me out.

At this late stage in the game, only one empty seat remains. It's by the window, so I sit Tammy in it—perhaps the fresh air will keep her awake—and crouch down beside her on the cold, hard linoleum. By the time I look up, Tammy's cheek is already flat on her desk. Which leaves me with no one to talk to.

Doree Matson, by far the most annoying of all the A-list freshman girls, mostly because she thinks she's smart and never stops talking in class, sashays into the room. "Hello, darling!" she sings to Melissa as she sits in the saved chair.

Janice Cooper, a friend of Tammy's, sits on the floor beside me. "I am so sorry," she says in a very serious voice. "How are you dealing?"

"Sorry about what?" I ask cluelessly.

She stares at me. "That you were added."

What is she talking about? "To what?"

Instead of looking at me, she fidgets with the gold barrette in her long brown hair. "You haven't seen?"

"Seen what?" Panic is taking hold like a straitjacket.

"Oh, you know. Never mind." She flushes and looks down at her book.

This is bad news. Cockroach-in-the-bathroom bad. I stretch upward and shake Tammy's arm and try to keep my voice down. "What's going on?"

Tammy opens her eyes. "Not tired."

"What have I not seen?" I whisper.

She reddens and snaps to attention. "Oh, Rachel, I'm trying to find someone to take it down. . . ."

Has something been written about me on the bathroom walls? My bra been hung up on the flagpole? "Take what down?"

"Your picture on the freaks Web site."

"What?" I shriek. I didn't even know there was a freaks Web site.

Tammy leans down toward me and whispers, "Rachel, I'm so sorry. I didn't see any point in telling you since I knew it would just freak you—I mean, upset you. It's a stupid thing started by some of the senior girls. Aaron told me about it, and I've already spoken to Mrs. Konch, demanding that the site be taken down, but I guess the administration is too busy with the cow stuff to do anything right now."

I think I might hyperventilate. "What does this Web site say?" I whisper.

"You don't want to know. But don't worry. We'll get it deleted."

I'd like to get myself deleted.

The day goes from very bad to very worse. Our math class isn't doubled because we're advanced, but Hayward gives us a pop quiz, which I completely fail because I can't concentrate. And I've never failed a math test in my life. Math is my thing. I swear I'm not being conceited, but some people have even called me a math genius. During the quiz, though, I can barely remember what a polynomial is because all I can think about is getting online.

And then Jewel, Melissa, and Doree are also in my bio class, something I would have loved a month ago, but now I just want to knock them over the head with my beaker.

I spot Raf as he's about to leave for lunch. His dark hair is curling over his eye. He slips his arm into his leather jacket. I need an icebreaker, something that can lead to real conversation. So how about those Mets? Sunny out, isn't it? Come here often? I could tell him that he dropped a glove at my apartment. But then I'd have to give it back. And then what would I sniff when I miss him?

I'll just apologize. I take a deep breath, as if I'm about to dive underwater, and then I walk straight over to him and say, "Hi."

59

He zips up his jacket without making eye contact. "Hey."

"How was New Orleans?"

"Fine."

"Did you have shrimp? I heard the seafood there is supposed to be . . . um . . . amazing. Was it? Is it Mardi Gras this time of year? No wait, it's in February. Or March. I just read something about it in *Cosmo*. Did you read it? Probably not. . . ." My babbling trails off. "Raf, I am so, so sorry that I stood you up for the Spring Fling."

He closes his locker. "Whatever."

He smells so good. Why was I so stupid? I should have told him that I had my dad's wedding that night. I should have known that he wouldn't care that I screwed up the show. I should have trusted him. I lean against the neighboring locker. "No, really. I thought that you would never want to be seen in public with me after what happened at the fashion show."

"Why would I care about what happened at the show?"

"Because I made a fool of myself." I keep my eyes on the floor.

"So?"

I was kind of hoping for a no-you-didn't. I look up and realize he's looking right at me. I meet his dark brown eyes. "So, I thought you'd cancel."

There is green in his eyes too, emerald speckles I never noticed before. "Listen," he says. "I couldn't care less about a stupid show. But it's too bad you think I'm so superficial that I care about what other people say. Plus," he continues, "the whole wedding thing was weird. Why did you say yes to being my date? You must have known your dad's wedding was on the same night."

"Well, I . . . I didn't think the wedding . . ." My voice trails off. Explaining that I was trying to cancel my dad's wedding will make me look even more psycho. "I'm sorry" is all I can manage.

"Whatever," he says again. "See ya." And with a shrug he takes off down the hallway.

Ouch. It's so unfair. Doesn't he know that I would have given my molars as well as my eyeteeth to go to Spring Fling with him? I've missed three of JFK's dances: Fall Ball, Winter Mixer, and now Spring Fling. Since prom is exclusively for seniors and their dates, I will officially be the only person in the entire school not to go to one single dance in a given year. Not that I know how to dance, but that doesn't mean I don't really, really want to go.

61

Tammy slides up beside me and puts her arm around my shoulders. "Wanna go out for lunch?"

I nod without saying a word.

I finally get online during seventh period, when we have computers. Since we pick our own stations, I arrive extra early to get the window seat way in the back. At least this class isn't doubled up.

Tammy sits next to me. "I don't think you should look," she says, resting her head on her hand. "I don't want to see it again."

"Well, you don't have to sit next to me if you don't want to. In fact, you shouldn't get this close to anyone, since you

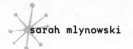

have mono. And I have social leprosy. Now, what's the name of the Web site?"

She types it in for me.

Maybe it isn't about me. Maybe it's about a girl who looks just like me . . . my doppelganger. In Russia.

And that's when a close-up image of me and my beard fills the screen.

Okay, it's not just me. There are other people on the screen too, about ten or so additional students unfortunate enough to have made it onto this site. There is also the heading: The Freaks of JFK High. But I can't breathe. My beard is on the Web, and here I thought I concealed it so well. There's also a picture of my tripping over the bike rack. I guess that light I saw was a flash.

"Don't look up," Tammy says. So of course I do. London is standing at the door. All in white. Smirking.

I thought, It can't get worse than Thursday! How could it ever get worse than Thursday?

It gets worse on Friday.

"I'm sick," Tammy says via the traitorous telephone receiver.

"I'm going to pretend you didn't say that."

"I have a doctor's appointment this morning. My throat is burning."

"No. No. No! You're not sick! Mind over matter!"

"I'm so sorry."

I can't believe she's making me go to school by myself. When I'm the star of the freak Web site.

And it gets worse. I sit on the floor in almost all my classes. Even though I didn't fail my math quiz, like I thought I did, Ms. Hayward is very concerned by my A- and makes me stay after class. When I'm done, there is a picture of me and my beard glued to my locker.

It starts to rain. I have gym outside. JFK's obnoxious gym teacher makes you participate no matter what. Rain? Cramps? Broken leg? Doesn't matter—yesterday I even saw London in her gym clothes. We play softball, since April is softball month. I drop the ball repeatedly and get very wet.

Since I have no one to go out to lunch with, I eat alone in the library.

I don't see Raf all day.

I spend Friday night alone, definitely not at one of Mick Lloyd's legendary A-list-only parties. (I'm so far off the A-list I'm practically Z-list.) On Saturday, I wake up with a miserable cold with no fever, which means, unfortunately, I don't even get to have mono. Since I have no friends, I do nothing but work on assignments and stare at my picture on the freak Web site. I change the screen whenever my mom or Miri is around. Letting them see what a loser I am is just too humiliating. And Miri is in too good a mood for me to upset her. Because of some chemical in our gym floor, the cows cannot be used for beef production. So Miri called SALA, the Saving Animals' Lives Association, and they raised money to have the cows moved to a refuge in Alabama. Guess they were safer in the gym after all. They will now be able to live long and happy lives. Yay, them. I wish I were a cow.

On Monday, the lock on my locker doesn't work.

63

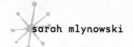

Someone had my lock clipped and put on a new one. I have to get the janitor to snap it open.

No matter how hard I look, I don't see Raf all day.

On Tuesday, I find a caricature of me and my beard in the first-, second-, and third-floor bathrooms, drawn right onto the backs of the stall doors, alongside the graffiti. And I'm not saying this because I'm oversensitive, but it so looks more like a caricature of a caveman than one of me. If it weren't accompanied by the slogan "Rachel Weinstein is a man," I wouldn't even have known it was supposed to be me. I attempt to wipe one off with the cheapo school soap, but it won't budge. The janitor, my new best friend, promises to take care of them over the weekend.

I see Raf only once, in the distance, but he doesn't see me.

On Wednesday, my clothes are stolen. Since we no longer have access to the gym lockers, I leave my jeans, sweater, and shoes in a bag by the bleachers while I'm playing third base. Unfortunately, by the end of the period, the bag, along with my clothes and my (sob) new shoes, is gone. So I have to wear my smelly gym shoes, a long green T-shirt, and my green gym sweatpants for the rest of the day. And the pants are giving me a wedgie, which I constantly have to stealthily adjust. Okay, fine, pick. Of course, once I'm in my gym clothes, I see Raf every four seconds. In the hall, on the stairs, at the water fountain. I can feel him watching me too, staring. Once, he opens his mouth as if to say something, but I quickly duck out of view. I don't need him making fun of me too.

On Thursday, as I walk through the senior hallway on

my way to second period, I hear hysterical laughter. And I see a large crowd of students circling London, who is dressed in another all-white outfit. Her arms are shuddering above her head. Her hips are bumping from side to side. Her one good leg is quaking. What's wrong with her?

"You look just like her," one of her lackeys shrieks. "You're nailing it!"

London's nasal voice pierces my eardrums. "I call it the Electric Rachel."

Oh, no. Ah, jeez. I knew it looked like I was being electrocuted when I danced. I knew it! Miri always told me I wasn't *that* bad, but this proves it. Keep your head down, and speed up, I tell myself.

"There she is!" one of the other lackeys cries as I pass them.

Don't look up, don't look—

"Rochelle! Why don't you show us how it's done?" London cackles.

Ignore them. Just ignore them. Pretend they don't exist.

"Rochelle!" I hear her hollering as I turn the corner, away from them.

By the end of the day, patches of kids all over school are doing the "Electric Rachel." In the hallways. In the classrooms. In the library. It's become more popular than the Macarena was.

By last period, I can't take it anymore, and I hide in the bathroom. Tears spill over my cheeks as I stare at my bearded self. Okay, I know I deserve some karmic punishment for all the awful things I did last month . . . but come on. I have no friends except an absentee best friend (mono

65

now confirmed), the love of my life hates me, and now the entire school is mimicking me? This is too much.

And if London can name a dance after me, how come she can never remember my name? Huh? Huh?

When I get home, I am beyond depressed. Mom is working late, so I am free to wallow. I lie facedown across my floor, letting the pink carpet absorb my frustrated tears. Tigger chooses this moment to sit on my back.

The phone rings and rings and rings, and I know it's Tammy calling to check on me, but I can't bear to get up.

When Miri gets home from Tae Kwon Do, she picks up Tigger and sits beside me.

"Howdy," she says. "Why are you lying on the floor?"

"I . . . they . . ." Though I promised myself I wouldn't, I break down and tell her the whole story, except for the freak Web site. That was *too* humiliating. "And I wouldn't even care so much, but the fact that Raf doesn't like me anymore is the worst part."

My sister looks horrified. Like Tigger just got run over. "What a you-know-what. I hate her. What can I do to make you feel better?"

I turn over and face the ceiling. "Zap them into cats." Although they'd probably circle me and scratch me to death. "Don't bother. What's the point? There's no point to anything."

"I know what will cheer you up!" Miri says, eyes brightening. "Let's do something from the Save the World list we made on vacation."

"Why not?" At least I'll have something to do. And I knew she would ask me to help her with the list eventually. Too bad I kind of fell asleep while she was making it.

She runs into her room and then returns, waving an article from the *New York Times*. "I've done some research on number one, helping the homeless. This article is all about the malnutrition of the people living on the streets in Manhattan. I was thinking we could zap up some food to hand out."

"All right," I say lifelessly. They can have my dinner. I'm not even hungry. I didn't have lunch today. The library was packed, so I hid in the bathroom and talked to my caricature.

Miri peers at me strangely. "Why don't you relax? Take a bath. Watch TV. You look stressed. We'll work on this over the weekend." She skips back to her room.

67

Instead of watching TV, I pull myself off the floor and turn on my computer. And it's just as I feared. There's a new picture of me right beside the beard one. I'm in my gym clothes, picking the wedgie in my butt. It's so pathetic looking that I start to laugh. I've officially hit rock bottom. And on the bottom I have a wedgie.

"What's so funny?" Miri asks, and before I can switch the screen, she sees it. A younger sister just shouldn't see her big sister looking so humiliated. It's like seeing your dad cry or your favorite actress without makeup. I expect her to start sobbing, but instead her face turns red, and her clenched fists pound against my desk. "London did that?"

"Don't worry. It's a joke."

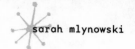

"Don't say that! You're making me really mad!"

"I'm a loser, all right? Your big sister is a social failure!"

I cry through dinner. I cry while I take a bath. By the time I climb into bed, my eyes are swollen and I look like a raccoon. Hope London brings a camera tomorrow. The shot should be a real winner.

I fall into a dreamless sleep. At about three in the morning, I wake to a shadow looming over me.

"What are you doing, Mir?"

"I'm not Miri; I'm the tooth fairy," the shadow says. "You're dreaming."

Weird dream, I think as I fall back asleep. When the alarm beeps me awake, I rub the crusted tears from my eyes. I'm not going back to school. I'll just hide. I pull the pillow out from under my head and cover my face with it. I lie on something scratchy. Something that smells . . . like a boy? Raf's gray wool glove? Why is his glove under my head? I don't remember taking it out of my T-shirt drawer to cuddle with. I squeeze it. And then I look up . . . and see Miri in the doorway.

"I came up with a few plans to make you feel better," she says sheepishly.

Sweet scratchy glove. I look back at Miri. Then back at the glove. Does this . . . does this mean what I think it means? "Tooth fairy my butt! Did you do the love spell?"

She gives me a shy smile. "I did."

Yes! Raf is going to *like* me again! And once he *likes* me again, he'll always like me—even when the spell wears off. At least, I hope so. "But I thought you were afraid of doing love spells."

"I was. But I couldn't stand seeing you so sad. So I got over it. Got to get back on the broom, right?"

How sweet is she? The cloud over my head dances away. Boogies away. Electric Rachels away. "I love you!" I say, and rub the glove against my cheek. Okay, it's itchy, but who cares? Raf is going to love me again! We could be frenching by lunchtime!

"Now, remember, emotion spells are temporary. And a love spell only lasts like three to four weeks. And it takes a day or two to kick in."

Drat. "Another lunch in the bathroom for me."

She smiles again and holds up what looks like a home-made tennis ball, except it's made of rubber bands, glue, and aluminum foil. "Not necessarily. But you have to bounce this against London Zeal."

"What?"

"Throw it at her, let it bounce, and I promise your day will get better."

I feel a flush of excitement. "What did you do?"

She tosses me the ball and winks. "You'll see."

69

Bounce, Baby, Bounce

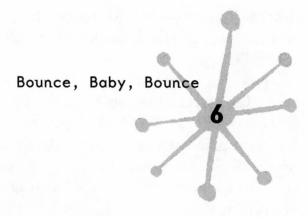

6

I don't see Raf or London all morning. Unfortunately, I do see the drawings of me still on the stall doors.

I finally cross paths with Raf when I'm on my way outside for softball, in full gym attire. He hesitates but then gives me a half smile and walks away. *A half smile!* Wahoo! Does that mean the spell is working?

After gym, I spot London hobbling down the hall alone, looking like an icicle. White baggy pants, white hoodie, white fedora. She must have invested in an entirely new leg-cast-appropriate colorless wardrobe. "Nice outfit," she snarls at me. "It really suits you."

Now's my chance. I've been carrying the gluey ball around with me all day, gripping it in my hand, which didn't improve my note-taking or softball skills one bit. I throw it at her leg.

"What are you doing, you freak?" she demands as it hits her in the good ankle, bounces twice, and then rolls down the hall.

I lunge. Got it!

"You are such a weirdo," she says. Nothing happens. Too bad. I was kind of hoping she'd turn into a frog.

"Have a good day," I say, and run toward the stairs. It's not like she's going to run after me. She's not very mobile these days. I sprint to my locker (where I left my clothes for safekeeping) and try to remember my new combination. Doesn't work. Oh, no. Did she change my lock again?

The thing is . . . this lock looks a lot like my old lock. My original lock. I try the combination: 27, 12, 33 . . . It works! My old lock is back! How did that happen?

I open my locker and find my clothes. And not only the clothes I was wearing today but the clothes I was wearing on Wednesday. As well as my—gasp!—pink shoes. Abracatastic!

Miri's spell must have something to do with all this. I grab an outfit and run to a bathroom stall to change. And on the door where the beard drawing was? There's a picture of a girl inserting a wad of Kleenex into her bra. It's a rough drawing in black marker, but I know it's of London. How do I know this? Because on the picture are the words "London Zeal stuffs."

71

"You have to tell me what that fantastic spell was," I say, throwing myself onto Miri's bed. I haven't stopped smiling all day.

She swivels in her chair. "With this rubber and glue, your actions will bounce right back to you. It's temporary but still a goody."

I laugh. "It was awesome. You have no idea. When I got to computer class, everyone was on the freaks site, and it was filled with weird pictures of London. London bleaching her mustache. London before her nose job. London drooling on her pillow. All of my photos were replaced with shots of her! She was furious and yelling at her entire posse, because apparently they're the only ones who know the password to get on the site. And then, when I walked down the hall, everyone was doing this weird dance-shuffle thing. And you know what they were calling it? The Hobbling London Limp! Ha! By the end of the day, she was practically Z-list!" Okay, fine, maybe just B-list, but still, she had undergone a definite demotion. Her own posse was avoiding her! "But do you want to know the best part of the day? Her clothes went missing! She had to wear her gym clothes all day." At least they're all green, so she didn't have to break her one-color rule.

Miri giggles. "And what happened with Raf?"

Sigh. "Not much."

"I thought so. I warned you it might take a while."

"I know, I know. I'm just so excited! It was the best day ever!"

"You know," she says coyly. "Being happy is really the best revenge. And one way to be happy is to help others. So will you help me with the feeding-the-homeless spell tomorrow?"

"Absolutely," I promise. "Your wish is my command. And I owe you big time."

I'm still hopping about at dinner.

"Girls," my mom says, dishing us mashed-potato-and-broccoli stew. Ew. "Remember Adam from the tour?"

"Um, yeah," I say. "The Yankees hottie."

My mom laughs, her arm jiggles, and the gravy she's holding splashes on her shirt. "Oops. Yeah, him. He left a message asking me out."

"Go, Mom, go!" I shriek. Score! "I knew my plan would work. See? I told you. Now do you promise to listen to me whenever I have suggestions?"

"Yes, Rachel, you were right. I promise to take your dating advice."

I pass her a napkin. "So when are you going?"

She scrapes the spill and shakes her head. "Going? I'm not. I already have a date with Lex."

I don't believe this. "Hello? Don't be crazy, Mom. You can date more than one man."

"Rachel, that's not fair to them," she says.

Snort. "Mom, until there's a ring on your finger, you can date a hundred men. A thousand." Although I don't know how she'd remember all their names. Sometimes she has difficulty remembering mine. I guess it comes with the territory when you're over thirty. Anyway, she'd definitely need some sort of dating filing system.

"I don't know, honey. I don't have that much free time."

"Mom, what are your plans for tonight? Read a romance novel? Tomorrow a murder mystery? You'll find the time."

She chews a piece of broccoli, looking thoughtful. "Maybe I'll see how it goes with Lex first and then set up a date with Adam."

I throw my spoon down in disgust. "Mom, Adam called today. You're not seeing Lex for two weeks. Adam is a hot

73

commodity. In two weeks he could be engaged." She obviously doesn't read *Cosmo*. "This is what you're going to do," I say authoritatively. "You are going to call Adam back. You are going to tell him that you *will* go out with him *this* weekend."

"But—"

"But nothing. I know Miri and I are in town. Big deal. We're practically grown-up. We don't need to be babysat."

She looks doubtful. "Are you sure?"

"Yes!" I scream, and kick Miri under the table. Backup?

"Yes," she adds reluctantly.

My mom takes a sip of her zucchini juice, sets down her glass, and then says, "Okay, I'll call him back."

"When?" I ask.

"Tomorrow?"

Zap! Wrong answer. "Call him now before you chicken out." I reach over and pick up the phone. "What's the number?"

She shakes her head. "I can't talk to him with you two watching."

"We'll go to the other room." I drag Miri out by her arm.

Once we're safely on the other side of the closed kitchen door, Miri smacks my hand away. "She's not ready."

"She's ready. And she's dialing, so let her do her thing."

"What do you know?" Miri grumbles. "You've been on, like, one date."

I shush her with a wave of my hand. "How did you know how to make a broom fly? Some things are innate."

"You're innate," she counters.

74

"That didn't even make sense. Can you shut up now?" I press my ear against the door.

"Hi, Adam? . . . Yes, it's Carol. . . . Good, thanks, how are you? . . . Saturday night? That's tomorrow. Well . . . I . . ."

Normally I would never recommend that a woman accept a date *the day before*. But this is a special case. I push my way back into the kitchen and nod vigorously.

She shrugs at me and says, "Okay, sure. Why not?"

Wahoo to the power of two! My mom has a date!

"Does he have any sons?" I mouth to her, but she doesn't get it. Oh well. I need her to hurry up the call anyway, to keep the line free for Raf's declaration of love.

"I can't go," my mom cries, blond hair dripping down her shoulders, fluffy pink towel wrapped around her skinny body. "I have nothing to wear."

That's true. And trust me, I've attempted to raid her closet on many occasions. "Try on what I put on your bed," I say.

Luckily for her, while she was in the shower (for an entire hour, I might add; I hope she took the time to shave her legs for the special occasion), I set out the outfit I felt was her most date appropriate. Her sexy (sexiest, anyway; she seriously needs to do some shopping) black pants, a lime green low-cut sweater, her highest black heels, and her heart-shaped silver necklace that she bought years ago and never wears. I asked Miri if she agreed with my choices, but she

75

wasn't the least bit interested. Not that she'd be any fashion help. She thinks polka dots and stripes match. Anyway, she's too busy finishing up her homework. Yes, English essays on a Saturday night. Real winner, huh? Not that I have anything wild and crazy on deck. No A-list parties to go to. No plans except helping Miri with her Save the World spells.

"How do I look?" my fully-dressed mom asks, pirouetting.

"Awesome." She looks feminine and classy. Her boobs are sagging a bit, but there's nothing she can do about *that*. I promise you, I'm never breast-feeding. What I should do is encourage her to buy a push-up bra. I might have to become her full-time stylist. Maybe that's what I'll do when I grow up. Seriously. I could work exclusively for stars. Designers will send me all their latest, desperate to dress my clients. Of course they'll send extra pieces for little old *moi*.

Although I'm not sure I really want a career in which I have to deal with people's fragile egos all day. I need to find a job that I can do on my own. Maybe I'll be a painter. Or a novelist. After all the pain I've been through lately, I'm sure I could come up with something really dark and terrifying, something that will really sell.

"What's your makeup strategy?" I ask my mom. Not that she isn't cute on her own, but adding color to her cheeks won't hurt. If we had some extra time, I would encourage a visit to the hair salon (i.e., make the appointment) so that she could get rid of her absurdly dark roots.

"I want to look natural," she says. "Some blusher?"

"All right, that'll work." I lead her to the bathroom mirror as though she's on a leash. "With a little mascara and lip gloss."

She sucks in her cheeks and applies the color. I didn't even know she had blush! I flip the compact over. Plum Fairy. I'm impressed. She seems to know what she's doing. Why doesn't she put on makeup more often?

When she's finished, she starts fidgeting with her outfit and biting her nails.

"What time is he coming?" I ask.

"Not till seven-thirty."

"It's only seven! You'd better relax or you're going to be too eager and he'll sense your desperation."

"I'm not desperate. I'm nervous. Why am I nervous?"

I take her quivering hand and pull her toward the kitchen. "Why don't you pour yourself a glass of wine, sit down, and read one of your books? Get in the mood for romance."

77

Nodding, she uncorks a bottle of Merlot. "Now just chill," I say, and hand her a book. For the next twenty minutes I don't hear a peep from her. Until . . .

"Oops."

A large blob of red wine has somehow landed on the left breast of my mom's pretty sweater. "What did you do?" I ask incredulously.

"Spilled."

The clock on the wall says she has five minutes. What am I going to do now? I've searched her wardrobe and there are no other choices. And that's when I notice her teeth.

Why do they look so . . . dirty? "Mom, have you brushed your teeth lately? They look brown."

She rests the wineglass on her book and runs to the mirror. "I think it's because of the red wine. They're stained."

"Well, brush them again! You can't go on a first date with stained teeth!" The clock now says four minutes.

"But what am I going to wear?" She's eating her fingers in distress.

"I don't know! I'll find something while you scrub your teeth." Who knew red wine did that? It should be illegal.

Three minutes.

I frantically grope through the clothes in her closet. Too frumpy, too ugly, too worky. Maybe something of mine? The cute V-neck . . . No, too young.

Two minutes.

"Is it coming off?" I scream.

"Almost," she says, and then I hear gurgling. Spit. "Did you find anything?"

"Yes. I found the lime sweater, but you ruined it." If only there was some way to get rid of the stain. Yeah, right. Even I know red wine doesn't come out so easily. If only we had some superstrength stain remover. If only . . .

If only my mom was a witch and could zap the stain away.

She's standing in front of me, clad only in her pants and beige bra. "So? What should I wear?"

I put my arms on her shoulders, look her straight in the eye, and say, "What you had on before."

"But it's stained," she says, bewildered.

78

"Zap it clean."

Her nostrils flare. "Rachel, you know I'm a nonpracticing witch."

"No, Mom, you used to be a nonpracticing witch. But it's time to evolve. There will be no consequences to cleaning your shirt. Seriously, what can happen? All the dry cleaners in the country will unexplainably burn down? I know you didn't use magic when we were kids because you wanted us to have normal childhoods, and that totally worked. We experienced lots of lows, not to worry. But you promised to take my advice. And I'm telling you to zap it. Trust me. Just do it." She zapped the wheels of the bus, so what's the big deal about zapping a stain? She should really just zap herself a new wardrobe, but let's take this magic stuff one baby step at a time.

She pushes past me into the closet. "Rachel, there must be something else for me to wear." She holds up a boring white button-down.

"Will your date be at the office?"

Then a black long-sleeved sweater.

"A funeral home?"

A striped turtleneck.

"Ski hill?"

The buzzer rings, interrupting our fascinating exchange. Panic drains the Plum Fairy right off her cheeks. I hold up her lime sweater and wave it like a flag. "Just zap it!"

"I . . . but . . ." She gnaws on her thumbnail. The downstairs buzzer rings again.

"Mom?" Miri calls out. "Do you want me to get that?"

"Zap it!" I holler.

"Fine!" Her lips purse, the temperature in the room drops, and the stain is . . . gone.

Whoa. That was cool. And freaky. How did she direct her energy right at the shirt? What if it's like radiation? Should I have worn one of those X-ray blankets like at the dentist? "Well done. Not so bad, was it?"

The buzzer goes off one more time.

"Miri, can you get it?" I scream, and toss the sweater to my bra-clad Mom. She slides it over her head and models in front of the mirror. "Perfect," I say. "Go get 'em! Oh, and Mom? Now that you're comfy using magic . . ."

"I won't need to use more magic," she says, tight-lipped.

"Yeah, yeah, I know, but if the date is boring, like if he starts droning on about sports or his job or something, zap your cell phone to ring, and pretend it's one of us with an emergency."

She rolls her eyes, which isn't her most appealing look. "Don't do that on your date," I advise.

By the time Adam gets to the front door, my mom and I are ready to greet him with smiles. I try gently to move Tigger out of the way with my foot, but he isn't budging. Miri is there too, and she's scowling.

Actually, I'd like to be the one Adam is taking out. He's hot. In his copper sweater (upgrade from the Yankees jersey, definitely) and with his modelesque cheekbones, he looks like a Greek god. I wonder if there's really such a thing as a Greek god? If witches are real, then maybe Adonis is too! Maybe he's Adam!

Would a Greek god live in Jersey?

"Hi, girls," he says. "Hi, Carol. Ready to go?"

Miri makes an I'm-constipated face and disappears into her room. Tigger hisses and follows at her feet.

"You two have fun!" I call down the hallway. "And make sure to have her home by midnight! Kidding!" Kind of. We don't want any hanky-panky just yet. At the moment, two witches in the family are plenty.

The Fountain of Juice

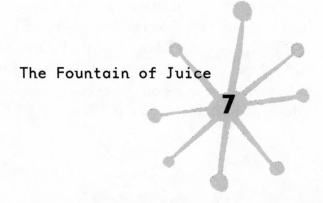

7

"Why do you think he hasn't called yet?" I wonder out loud a few minutes later. Miri and I are lying on the kitchen table, feet up against the apple-patterned wallpaper.

Miri shrugs. "I don't know. Maybe he's just not that into you?"

I gently kick her ankle so that she teeters to the side.

"Now can we focus on my stuff?" she asks. "You promised."

"Yes, let's save the world. What's your plan?"

"I told you, number one on the list. Feed the homeless."

"All of them?"

"Eventually, yes. But my current plan centers around the homeless in Washington Square Park. And I found a multiplying spell. So all we need to do is pick a food, multiply it, and then give it away for free. What do you think?"

"Good idea. When do we give out the food?"

"Tomorrow. If it works. We have to pick a food first."

"Brownies?"

"We want to feed them, not make them fat."

Time to put on the thinking cap. What a lame

expression. My dad uses it all the time. He called today from Hawaii; he and Jennifer were at a luau. Could not understand a thing he was saying over the ukulele music. All I could hear was him reminding me to take my vitamins. Hey . . . "The food should have lots of vitamins. Like spinach."

She pretends to gag. "They're homeless, not taste budless."

"Good enough for Popeye but not for them?"

"Rachel, we can't hand out plates of spinach. We need something that people like. And that's healthy. And that tastes good."

"Orange juice," I say, suddenly inspired. "Or oranges so we don't need cups."

Miri claps her feet together. "Perfect! You're a genius. Very easy. And vitamin C not only nourishes but improves people's moods!"

83

"We can even whip some extras up for Tammy. Maybe then she'll get better and drag her butt back to school."

Miri flips around so that she's sitting upright on the table and leans into A^2. "We need a teaspoon of mint, one-seventh of a cup of chocolate, ten grams of grape skin. And one example of what we want to replicate. So one orange. Okay, you check for the ingredients, and get the measuring spoons. I'll set up in my room."

A half hour later, we're all mixed and set. Miri's sitting cross-legged on her carpet, the orange in her hand, and I'm standing behind her. She uses a silver spoon to coat the fruit in the yummy-looking mixture and then lowers it to the carpet.

"That's so going to stain," I warn. "We should do it in my room—my carpet has seen better days." Once orange, it is now pink due to flea extermination chemicals (Tigger's fault).

"We would if your entire closet weren't on the ground." She takes a deep breath.

"Here is one
Placed on the floor,
I nod three times
And now there are more."

Suddenly, the room fills with cold and the strangest thing happens: the orange starts morphing.

It splits in two, like it's giving birth. And then both blobs begin to regrow to their adult size, giving me the shivers.

84

I don't think I've ever seen anything this creepy.

About twenty seconds pass, and the orange and its clone do it all over again—they each split in half and regrow. And then the four do the same. It's like we're watching a science fiction movie. The next thing I know, there are at least *fifty* oranges covering the floor and it's starting to smell like a grove in here. A hundred oranges. Two hundred. Wow. Coolest trick ever. I take a step back.

"Watch your feet!" Miri warns. Four hundred. The carpet is blanketed in at least two layers of oranges. Her room is flooding with fruit. She stands up and climbs onto her bed.

Eight hundred. "Um . . . Mir? How many are there going to be?" I step onto her desk chair as the pile of oranges doubles in height.

"I . . . um . . ."

Our eyes lock over the citrus explosion and we can't help laughing. But the amusement quickly turns to alarm. We could *drown* in here. "Can't you make it stop?" I ask, and leap over the fruit to stand beside her on the bed.

"I don't know." The oranges are touching the top edge of the mattress. If she didn't have a super-tall pillow-top mattress, we'd have gone under by now. She frantically flips through the spell book's pages.

"Miri, find a stop spell!"

"I'm trying!"

The oranges spill over onto her bedspread. "We're going to suffocate in here!" I say, and get ready to drag the two of us to noncitrus safety. But just as I'm about to leap, Miri mutters something and the multiplying jerks to a stop.

"That was close," Miri says, giving A^2 a grateful pat. She gently steps off the bed and tries to wade through the deluge. "I'm so sleeping in your room tonight."

85

"So tell us everything," I say as I stuff a forkful of poached egg into my mouth. We're sitting in a booth at our neighborhood diner, on Tenth and Broadway. It used to be our favorite brunch spot, but we haven't been here in ages. The fries are extra crispy. My mom always refuses to order any, then eats most of mine.

"It was *interesting*," my mom says from across the table, ripping open a sugar and dumping it into her coffee. Her short hair is tied back into a tight ponytail, which only helps to display her horrible brown roots. Apparently, she needs me to be her stylist 24/7.

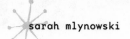

By the time Mom got home last night, Miri and I were already asleep in my bed. Okay, fine, that's a lie; we were wide awake, but we didn't want to explain Operation Orange. We closed Miri's door, hoping Mom wouldn't look in. Mom always checks my room first anyway. I guess that's because she's been doing it longer, since I'm the older child. She crept into my room at eleven-thirty and tucked us in with an "Aw, sweet." Which it was, until Miri rolled herself in the duvet like it was a sari and I almost froze to death.

We are planning on telling her about the oranges. That's why we suggested brunch. We're definitely going to tell her . . . after we pepper her with date questions for as long as possible.

Miri dumps a bowlful of ketchup onto her fries and her tofu omelet. "How so?"

"We went to a place in Little Italy. First we ordered—"

"He didn't do anything stupid like order for you, did he?" Miri asks.

"No, why would he do that?" She steals one of my fries and dips it in Miri's ketchup.

Miri shrugs. "I heard that some men do that."

She's doing an excellent job with our peppering-Mom-with-questions plan.

"We were small-talking about silly things," Mom says, "like the weather, New York, you kids . . ."

"So we're silly?" I ask.

"You know what I mean. Anyway, when the appetizers came, the conversation just dried up. And we both focused intensely on our plates. The goat cheese salad was suddenly

the most interesting piece of food I had ever seen. A minute dragged into two, and then three, and then four . . ."

Oh, no. That's the worst. I've pushed my mom into dating again before she's ready and now I've scarred her for life. She's going to give up dating and get another cat.

"And then I couldn't take it anymore. So I looked into his mind."

"You can do that?" I ask in amazement.

"I read his mind so I could know what to talk about. At first he was thinking that I seemed nice but we obviously had nothing in common. And he was wondering what the score on the Yankees game was."

"What a jerk!" I interject.

"So I blurted out, 'I wonder what the score on the Yankees game is.' "

"Way to go, Mom!" I can't believe it!

"You don't need to be a mind reader to come up with that one," Miri says. "Wasn't he the one wearing the Yankees jersey? On a baseball tour?"

I motion to her to shush. "Brilliant idea, Mom! What did he say?"

"His eyes lit up. And he said he was wondering the same thing!"

Miri shovels her eggs into her mouth. "I hate Yankees fans. He'd be far more interesting if he were a Mets fan."

"*You* don't have to date him," I tell her. I lean across the table. "So what happened next?"

My mom steals a handful of my fries. "We talked about baseball for a while."

"You don't know anything about baseball," Miri says, frowning.

"Right. So I had to do more mind reading. You'd be shocked how much sports trivia this man has in the front of his mind. It's amazing really. Scores, RBIs . . ."

"RBI what?" I ask. My mom can finally explain to me the secret language of boys!

"Who knows? That's all I got. Men think a lot about sports. And about other stuff," she says, and then blushes.

Ew. I want my mom to date, but I don't need the unnecessary details.

"Anyway, I basically kept talking about what he was thinking," she says.

"Mom," Miri says, shaking her head with disapproval, "what happened to wanting a guy to like you for you?"

88

"I know, I know. But it's not like I was in love with this man. I was really nervous, and I saw the night as an experiment. To find out what could happen."

"And what happened?" Miri and I both ask.

"Jinx," I say. "Buy me a Coke."

Mom smiles. "He begged me to see him again. Tonight."

I'm in awe. "Are you going to?"

"No. I told him maybe next weekend."

"Do you like him?" I can't believe this.

"He liked me. I believe his exact words were 'You might be my soul mate.' But I haven't decided how I feel about him. Seeing him tonight seems a bit excessive. But I have to admit, it's nice to feel wanted. Anyway, we'll see. What were you two up to last night?"

Abort topic! Switch gears! I want to avoid this subject

for as long as possible. "Um . . . what did you have for the main course?"

"Fettuccine Alfredo. Now back to you two."

"Wait!" Miri says. "What about dessert?"

My mom smiles. "Lemon sorbet. And what did you two eat? Oranges?"

So my mom saw the fruit. And she wasn't too angry. After Miri outlined her plan, Mom gave us her "just be careful" lecture (whatever, she's using magic to help her dating life; how careful is she being?) and then shocked us by offering to help distribute. "I'd rather be around if you're talking to strangers," she explained.

And that's where we are now. In Washington Square Park, handing out oranges to anyone who looks hungry. The three of us filled two shopping bags each with as many as we could carry. The sun is shining, and my first bag is almost empty.

"Would you like some fruit?" I ask an elderly woman in a sleeping bag on a bench.

She eyes me suspiciously, so I gently place it on the edge of her bed. She picks it up, squeezes it, and then nods. I hand her another one, and the three of us move on.

My hands are starting to chap from the cold, but my insides feel warm, like I just finished a cup of hot chocolate. I don't remember the last time the three of us had so much fun. Once our bags are done, we stop back at the apartment for a refill and then head over to the Lower East Side.

"Oranges! Who wants fruit?" Miri sings, looking happy

89

but determined. Her cheeks are flushed, her hair is wind-blown, and she hasn't stopped smiling all afternoon. Next to her, my mom has the same sun-kissed tousled look. And I bet I do too. I lock my arms through theirs, and we giggle as we skip down the sidewalk, smiling and reeking like a fruit stand.

My good mood lasts until the next morning, when Raf walks past my locker. I wave and our eyes lock and I think, This is it! But then . . . he gives me his half smile, waves back, and walks away. Hello? He's supposed to be under my spell. Why isn't it working? Is his hatred for me that intense?

I don't have time to dwell because we're rounded up for a second all-school meeting in the auditorium. I shuffle inside and find a chair in the front row. Alone. With an empty seat on each side of me. Apparently, my loser status is still intact.

Mrs. Konch, Mr. Earls, and Will Kosravi are back on-stage. "We have some unfortunate news," Mr. Earls says. "The damage to the gym, the cafeteria, the locker rooms, and the downstairs classrooms will cost approximately forty thousand dollars to repair."

The room collectively gasps.

"Even more unfortunate is that the insurance company does not cover acts of cows. Especially since they're sure that this is an act of vandalism, or as some might call it, the senior prank."

I sink lower in my seat. Insurance won't cover it?

Will takes the microphone. "Guys, I'm pleading with

you: if you know who's responsible, turn them in. Because the money has to come from somewhere. Please do the right thing." It's almost as if he's looking directly at me . . . right into my liable soul.

Guilt explodes in my stomach like a bad case of food poisoning. Maybe I should come clean. I'll go to Konch's office and admit it's my fault. My family's, anyway. Yeah, right. I could never turn Miri in. The government would go nuts, and she would be forced to live in a glass box where creepy scientists would study her every move. Poor Miri. I want to wrap her in a warm blanket and protect her, not turn her in. Anyway, she didn't mean any harm. She was trying to save the cows.

Mr. Earls is glaring at the seniors in the back row. It's not like anyone suspects me. I look up at Mrs. Konch. She's eyeing the last few rows with extra suspicion. And Will is . . . still staring at me. Right at me. Intensely at me. I quickly look away. Oh, no. He knows. Gulp. Impossible. He can't have a clue. He's probably not even looking at me. He's most likely admiring some hottie behind me. Why am I such a diva? I twist around, but the block of rows behind me is filled with sophomore boys. Hmm. Slowly, I lift my head back up. Oh, no. He's still staring! I know, he probably hates me because of Raf. That must be it. Of course he doesn't know about the cows. He hates me because I stood up his baby brother. Just as I want to protect Miri, Will wants to protect Raf.

I sit on Miri's spell book to get her attention. "We need to zap up some money."

"I have forty bucks," she says, pointing her chin toward her piggy bank.

"A little more than that." It still stinks like oranges in here even though we gave them all away.

She drops her pen. "How much?"

"Forty thousand."

"Are you crazy?"

"Unfortunately not. The cow damage is expensive to fix. And they don't know where to get the cash."

Her face drains of color. "What are we going to do?"

"Rob a bank?"

She jumps out of her chair and cracks open her piggy bank, which looks nothing like a pig, since it's a plastic slot machine. You press a cherry and it opens up. I know this not because she's shown me, but because I once had to borrow five bucks. Fine, ten bucks. All right, fifty, but I was desperate. She waves a twenty in the air. "Let's do a multiplying spell!"

"I don't know," I say, feeling squeamish. "I didn't mean we need to zap up money literally."

"Why not? It's perfect! We'll whip some up, and you'll mail it to the principal. Problem solved."

"I'm pretty sure that's mega-illegal."

She sits back down in her chair. "Why?"

As much as it pains me, I explain. "We'd be creating counterfeit bills. And each bill has a serial number. So the school would know. And if they didn't know, we could get them into a lot of trouble." When did I become the responsible one?

"I don't think anyone would notice," she says stubbornly.

92

"It's too risky. We've already caused enough trouble. And you have to think of the consequences. In this case, jail." I try to remember what we learned during first semester in economics. "Anyway, you can't just make up your own money. It would cause inflation."

"I don't get it."

"Me neither. But it doesn't matter. We need a new plan. We have to *earn* money."

She drags her spell book out from under me. "I told you my idea. If you don't like it, come up with something else. Anyway, I'm busy. I need to find a way to get oranges to Africa."

"Excuse me?"

"Helping African orphans is number two on my list. You'd know what I was talking about if you hadn't fallen asleep when we were making it. They need the vitamin C even more than New Yorkers do. We could take the broom there, but there must be a faster way."

"There are airplanes. Come up with a way to earn money and we can take a trip." I should really take a look at this list.

Miri snorts. "Airplanes. Please. Don't you get it? I have powers."

Better make it a first-class ticket for her big head.

It's Tuesday morning, and I still have no new moneymaking ideas. I'm stuffing my jacket into my locker, trying to be as inconspicuous as possible, when I spot Will standing like a statue, staring at me. Again, intensely, like he's burning up.

His black hair looks messy, and his big brown eyes are flashing. Come on, Will, it's time to move on. Raf and I are going to be back together as soon as the spell kicks in and then you're going to feel stupid for hounding me.

I pile my necessary books into my arms and march away from him. What a jerk. A sexy jerk, but still a jerk.

"Do not drink from that glass," Tammy tells me, wagging her finger at me in disapproval.

"Oops." I return it to her glass coffee table with a bang. "My mistake."

"That was your third try," she whispers. "I'm on to you."

Tammy has no voice because she's still sick. We're both sitting on the mauve suede couch in her living room, watching a classic-movie marathon. Our heads are at opposite ends, and our feet are scrunched into a ball in the middle. "Trust me, you don't want to get sick. Aaron and I are both miserable. We can't even leave the house! How can a relationship last when the couple doesn't even see each other?"

"If you want it to last, it will last," I say. "And trust me, being at home is better than being at school," I whine. "I can't handle another day. You don't know what it's like. No one will talk to me. Jewel won't look at me. Melissa hisses." At least London has been suspiciously absent. Guess she can't deal with her own revenge, huh? At least she's taken down the freaks Web site. "Raf ignores me. And now his brother hates me too! I told you, he's stalking me! And I had to eat lunch in the library again by myself. No one wants to talk to me!"

"Rachel, I spoke to Janice and she asked about you. She said she always looks for you at lunch."

"Oh. Right." Well. I forgot about Janice, Sherry, and Annie. "I guess I could do that." But they're Tammy's friends, not mine. And they're a little annoying, I'll be honest. "I could sit with them." Or . . .

I make another (unsuccessful) lunge for her water glass.

The final bell just rang, and I'm about to leave the building when I turn and notice Will behind me.

Why has my crush's brother become my stalker? And is he still a stalker if he's so cute? The eyes, the hair . . . just like Raf but with broader shoulders.

I hurry out the door. He follows. I sprint down the street. So does he. I turn onto Tenth Street. Ditto for him. I quicken my pace. He quickens his pace. I make a sharp left at a corner and duck into a magazine store. Seconds later, he walks past. I read *Teen People* and then, ten minutes later, when the coast is clear, head home.

95

"Mom, can you help me take out the recycling?" I ask. "There's a lot to carry."

We've finished dinner and are cleaning up. Something smells like burnt sardines. Must be coming from the recycling cupboard. I grab the pizza box, my mom gathers the empty cartons that have been piling up, and we carry the riches to the dump on the second floor. Now the hallway smells.

"So how's school?" my mom asks.

"Better." Slightly, anyway, since I spent lunch with Janice, Annie, and Sherry. But they're not a reason to get up in the morning.

Dave, aka the hunkalicious fireman, is locking up his apartment. He waves, heads to the stairs, pauses, then shuffles back to us.

"Do you ladies need help?" he asks, giving us his sexy, toothy smile.

"We're fine," my mom says. "But thanks."

"You smell amazing, Carol," Dave says, making me almost drop the glass bottle I'm holding.

What is he talking about? All I can sniff is the sardine thing. Yuck.

My mom blushes a deep red. "Thanks. That's so sweet."

96

"I was wondering, maybe you'd like to stop by sometime for a drink?"

Welcome, ladies and gentlemen. We've officially entered the Twilight Zone. We've been living in this building for a decade. True, my mom has been single for only a few years, but still, the fireman has never shown any interest in her. What is it about the recycling bin that has caused his change of heart?

"Perhaps," my mom says coyly, whisking a strand of her hair behind her ear. She waves good-bye, and we silently return to the apartment.

As soon as she closes the door, I say, "What was that about?"

Blush. "What?"

I can still smell the burnt sardines. Where is that coming from? I lift my nose in the air and inhale. To the right. Closer to Mom. Still closer to Mom. It *is* Mom. I sniff her neck. "Why are you wearing sardine juice as perfume?"

She steps back. "It's a new scent I'm trying."

My mother has not purchased an eau de anything since 1989. Something's fishy here, and it's not just the perfume. "Why would you buy something that smells disgusting?"

She hesitates. "I didn't buy it."

"Was it a sample?"

"Not exactly."

Abracazam! "It's a spell!" I shriek.

Mom turns bright red. "It's an . . . attraction perfume. I was looking through my old spell book, and it looked interesting, so I thought . . . well, I thought why not give it a try? To see. Anyway, judging by what just happened," she whispers, "I think it works."

"Um . . . hello? Can I have some of that?"

"It's too strong for a teen. When you're older. Maybe. If you can prove to me you'll use it responsibly and properly."

I could properly use it right now.

Friday lunchtime! The week is almost over. I'm about to go inside from gym when I spot Will waiting for me outside the door.

I hide behind Janice and sneak into the bathroom. About ten minutes later, when most of my class has left for lunch and I assume senior classes have started, I tentatively

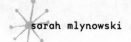

open the door. But there he is, pacing the hallway, waiting for me. "Rachel!" he says, looking relieved. "Hey, hang on. I've been trying to talk to you all week."

The jig is up. I have nowhere left to hide. I'll have to stand here and be told off. "Yes, I've noticed."

"There's something I have to say to you," he says, his voice rising.

I hope this doesn't take long. I'm starving. And Janice invited me to meet her and the girls at the Quiznos down the block. "I know. So just do it already."

He takes a step toward me. He really is handsome. I've never been yelled at by a stud before.

"I think I'm in love with you," he says, and before I die from shock, he steps closer, looks deep into my eyes, and kisses me.

98

Something Borrowed

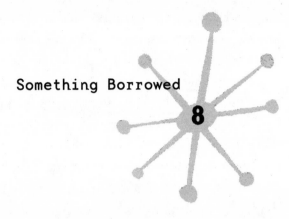

8

If I had died from shock, by now Will Kosravi would have resuscitated me. Because he is kissing me. At first it's like I'm watching the scene from afar: I see Will's hand gently caressing my cheek as his lips press against mine. It's all very romance-novelesque. But then he opens his mouth, and my brain slams back into my body.

My tongue just touched someone else's tongue! And it's squishy!

Oh. My. God. I am kissing Will Kosravi. I am *french-kissing*. And this whole tongue thing makes kissing a real boy far more interesting than kissing, say, my pillow or the back of my hand. I can't believe that after all the many years of imagining what kissing is, and what it feels like, I'm doing it.

Because he's almost six feet tall, my face is tilted up at a ninety-degree angle, which doesn't hurt, because his hand is now very thoughtfully supporting my neck. He smells musky, like aftershave. Omigod, I'm kissing a boy old enough to shave!

I have to admit, this is very nice.

Am I supposed to be doing anything? Besides letting my mouth hang open while my tongue gets pushed around like a grocery cart? Perhaps I should do something with my lips? Jiggle them? What if I bite his tongue by mistake? Am I the worst kisser ever? If I knew he was going to kiss me, I would have spit out my gum. Where is my gum? It was definitely in there before this kissing commotion began. It might be hiding between my molars and gums like a frightened turtle. I don't want to send out a search tongue for it, because what if that's the one thing you're not supposed to do while kissing? Oh, I think I feel it at the back of my mouth. Maybe I should just gulp it. But what if I swallow his tongue instead? And then I choke?

The next thing I know, Will pulls away, signaling that the kiss is over. Now he's smiling at me, saying, "Cool."

"Uh, yeah." I'm mildly unclear as to what planet I'm on. Why did Raf's brother just kiss me?

"I was serious before. I think I . . . love you," he continues, his eyes getting all googly.

What, what, what? Love? How is it possible that the love of my life's brother loves me? When I love his brother? Will leans over to kiss me again, but this time I use my hand to stop him. "What about Raf?"

"I know you two used to be together, but I asked him if I could hang out with you and he said it was cool. Can we do something this weekend?"

"Okay," I say, partly out of shock and partly out of rejection. Raf doesn't care that his brother likes me? *Loves* me? How can that be? No way I'd let Miri date Raf. Unless I was completely and utterly over him.

My heart sinks. Raf must be completely and utterly over me. Not even Miri's love spell could overcome his distaste.

"Another kiss?" Will asks, raising his hand back to my cheek.

"Sure." Well, why not?

"It makes no sense," I say to Tammy via the phone in my bedroom. I'm lying on my bed, my feet up against the wall.

"I don't know what to tell you," she says, her voice still hoarse.

"Should I cancel the date?"

"Do you want to go out with him?"

"I want to go out with his brother! I just don't get it. I never had a clue he had any feelings for me at all!"

"Did he say when he started liking you?"

101

Good question. Did he like me while I was dating Raf? Or maybe he's liked me since the first day of school but didn't feel it was appropriate for a senior to date a freshman. He must have been out of his mind with jealousy when Raf asked me to Spring Fling.

I hear Miri's key jingling in the front door. "Rachel? You home?"

"In my room!"

"Guess what!" she screams at the top of her lungs while throwing open the door. "We're going to Africa! I found a transport spell!"

I hastily attempt to cover the receiver with my palm, but I think it's too late. "Are you crazy?" I mouth. I wave the phone at her.

Her eyes widen and her jaw drops.

I place the phone back against my ear, take a deep breath, and try to sound oh-so-nonchalant. "What was your question? When Will started liking me? I'm not sure. It could have been recently."

Silence. And then: "Did your sister just say that she found a transport spell? And that you're going to Africa?"

Terrific. I shake my fist at Miri. "What? Oh, no, you must have heard wrong." Think fast! "She said the train, um . . . smelled. Like . . . Africa."

Miri rolls up into a ball by my bed, and her lips are quivering with fear.

Another silence. Tammy's not going to buy it. Our cover is ruined. Miri has just ruined everything! I trust Tammy and all, but you never know; this is a big secret. What if she tells her Moms and they call the press, and then Miri and my mom are institutionalized? Oh, no. I'll be forced to live with my dad!

"What does Africa smell like?" Tammy asks.

I exhale. "Um . . . dry? Listen, Tammy, can I call you back? My sister is having some mental issues."

"Sure. Talk to you later."

Miri climbs onto the bed beside me. "Whoops."

"Try not to tell the entire world you're a witch, okay? And excuse me . . . ," I add as I recognize the seat of my favorite jeans hanging loosely over my sister's scrawny behind. "Did I give you permission to borrow my clothes?"

"What's the difference?" she mumbles, face pressed against my pillow. "You weren't wearing them."

And that's when the cold water of realization is dumped

over my head. Stupid, stupid, stupid. Will isn't *really* in love with me. "This is a disaster."

Miri turns her head sideways to look at me. "You're not really mad, are you?"

"Raf's glove," I spit out, "wasn't Raf's. He must have borrowed the gloves from Will."

"Huh?" She sinks her face back into the pillow. "Oh, no."

I start laughing. I can't help it. I recount to Miri the events of the day and finish with a flourishing "Doesn't that suck?"

She nods. "What should we do? Do you want to use the heart-reversal spray? We have one already made and ready to go. Or I can try making a spell reversal, but it's a tough one, a five-broomer. Maybe we should just use the heart reversal."

"I guess." I sigh. It's Raf I want to like me. It's Raf I like. Although Will is a good kisser. But I'm sure Raf is too. "I'll use it on the date tomorrow. He wants to take me out for dinner."

"You're going to reverse the spell at a restaurant? What if he freaks out?"

Good point. New plan needed. What if he deserts me at the table? "Best to get it over with as soon as he rings the doorbell. Like ripping off a Band-Aid," I say. Sigh.

"What's wrong?"

"It felt good to have a guy like Will say he loves me. Even if it seemed weird and over-the-top. Especially since lately everyone else has been treating me like a major loser."

"I can do another spell on Raf if you want."

"Let's focus on one love spell at a time," I say.

103

She shuffles next to me and leans her legs on the wall. "Did it feel good?" She turns bright red. "The kissing part."

"Yeah. It was cool."

"Gross?"

"No, not gross. Fun." But not Raf.

"Hi, guys!" my mom says, popping into the room. I didn't know she was home. "What are you doing?"

"Discussing a magic disaster," I admit. Why not? Maybe she'll have some advice. "We put a love spell on the wrong guy."

She perches on the corner of the bed. "Girls, I warned you to be careful."

We hang our heads.

She sighs. "Why don't you tell me all about it while I make you some pasta for dinner before my date." She retreats into the kitchen.

I'm concerned that an alien has taken over my mother's body.

"Another date?" Miri calls.

"Yes," Mom calls across the apartment. "It's a busy weekend. Dave invited me for a drink tonight. And tomorrow Adam is taking me to a play."

"Two dates in one weekend?" I shriek. Despite my new fake boyfriend, my mom is getting more action than I am. Pathetic.

"Three, actually," she says, and we hear the water turn on. "I'm meeting Jean-Paul for wine and cheese on Sunday."

Triply pathetic.

"Jean-Paul?" At this point I jump off the bed, go into the kitchen, and heave myself onto the counter.

"Who is Jean-Paul?" Miri asks, annoyed, arms crossed, in the doorway.

"Just someone I met this week. He's French."

Bet he *really* knows how to kiss. "Where did you meet a Frenchman?" Where can I meet a Frenchman? I've always wanted to be fed cheese fondue while being whispered to in the language of love.

She opens the cupboard and pulls out the noodles. "It was the craziest thing. I was walking down the street and he bumped right into me. He knocked my purse off my shoulder. At first I thought he was some sort of hustler, like he was going to take off with my money, but he helped me pick up my things, told me I was *magnifique*, and asked me out! Incredible, huh?"

"*Incroyable*." Surely the eau de sardines didn't hurt.

She pulls a wooden spoon from the drawer and points to herself. "Any suggestions on what I should wear?"

"Why don't you whip yourself up some new clothes?" Miri suggests. Somewhat sarcastically, I might add.

Mom hesitates. "I'm trying to use magic sparingly."

Miri snorts. "Right. Well, I'll be in my room."

Mom looks like a wounded bird. "Homework?"

"No. Saving-the-world work. I'd tell you more about it, but you're far too busy." And with that, she stomps off.

"I'm only trying to be a happier person," my mom says sadly. "Maybe this is a bad idea."

"No, no, no, I'll talk to her," I promise. Mom's off to such a promising start; she can't quit now. I adjust her hair so it looks like she has bangs. "Oh, that looks great."

"You think? Time for a new do?"

"Yes. Definitely." I've only been saying that for two years.

"Longer? Or shorter?" She folds strands in half and hides them under her chin. "What do you think?"

I feel warm and girly. "Longer, definitely. You should grow it out. And do your roots!"

When dinner's ready, Miri and I eat while my mom showers.

As I'm doing the dishes, my mom sashays back into the kitchen. "I'll be downstairs if you need anything."

"Have fun," I say distractedly. And then I look up.

Oh. My. God. "Um, Mom?"

"What do you think?" she asks eagerly.

"Don't you think"—how do I put this?—"Dave might notice that your hair grew two feet overnight?"

And it did. Not overnight but in the last sixty minutes. Seems Mom took a trip to the beauty parlor of magic. It's long, and blond, and gorgeous. Roots? What roots? She looks like Barbie. Like Cinderella. Rapunzel.

She nibbles on her thumb. "Did I go overboard?"

"Well . . ." I probably shouldn't burst her bubble. She needs the confidence boost. "You look hot. Smoking."

She gives me one of her big freakish winks, with her open eye not moving at all. "He is a fireman."

Groan.

"Get on my back," Miri says the next morning, barging into my room, holding her knapsack close to her chest.

"Excuse me?"

"Come on. I want you to come with me to Tanzania so we can help the orphans."

There are so many parts to that statement I don't understand. I climb out of bed and stretch my arms above my head. "Explain slowly, pretty please?"

She rolls her eyes. "There are children in Tanzania—"

"Where?"

"Tanzania—it's in Africa, dummy—who don't have enough food, clothes, or books."

"And . . ."

"And we're going to make some for them!"

"How are we going to get there exactly? We are so not taking the broom. That'll take forever. Don't forget I have a date I need to dispose of tonight."

Miri stomps her foot. "Don't you listen? I found a transport spell. I can zap us anywhere we want to go. All I have to do is think of the place, hold two lithium batteries together, positive and negative charges facing each other, say the spell, and off we go."

Fun. "That is so cool. And Mom's letting us go to Africa?"

Miri is suddenly very interested in the zipper on her bag. "Kind of."

"Did you ask?"

"Is it my fault she's still half-asleep? I asked her if I could help the orphans, and she said, 'Bring your sister.' Good enough for me."

Sounds fair. I slip on a pair of sweatpants and a hoodie. "All right, let's go. What do I have to do?"

"I have to carry you on my back, because only me and what I'm holding will get transported."

"Can I pee first?"

She sighs. "Fine, but hurry up."

I use the bathroom quickly and then return to my room. Miri crouches. "Let's piggyback!"

Giggling, I hop on and wrap my arms around her neck. "I'm going to give you a hernia."

Miri groans and stands up. "This is the only way to do it. Grab my knapsack. Everything we need is in there."

"Malaria pills?"

"Ha-ha. We're only going for five minutes. Just try not to get bitten by a mosquito." She tilts her head to the left. "And I wouldn't drink the water either. Now be quiet while I say the spell."

108

This is a bad plan, I know it. "Miri—"

"Shush, I have to concentrate." She makes a tight fist around each of the batteries, twines her thumbs together, and clears her throat.

"Transport to the place inside my mind,
The power of my fists shall ye bind!"

My arms slip, and I'm about to tell her that I'm going to fall off when a jolt of electricity runs through my body. Ouch! I bet that's what getting struck by lightning feels like. Suddenly, my skin feels hot and dry. Instead of my bedroom, all I see are dots and swirls of blue, red, and yellow, as though I'm looking into a kaleidoscope. Even though I'm holding on to my sister, my body feels weightless, like we're swimming underwater. The next thing I know, the blur of colors in front of me is solidifying into a wood and stucco house. The hair-dryer wind turns off, and I can feel gravity again.

"We're here!" Miri cheers.

Dizzy, I slide off her back, and my feet touch the earthy ground. I look around but can't see much besides the one-level building because it's so dark. "Is it already night? The transport only felt like a second."

Miri shakes her head. "It's seven hours later here," she whispers. "Let's try not to attract any unwanted attention. There could be lions, you know."

My arms are covered with goose bumps from the idea of potential killer animals as well as from the cold. "Are you sure we're in Africa? Isn't it supposed to be hot?"

Miri reaches for her knapsack. "Don't you take geography? The seasons are reversed in the southern hemisphere."

This is too much. My head is pounding, although it could be from the supersonic travel and not from the info. I hate how I look when I get a headache. My eyes remain half open like some kind of demented puppet. Miri, however, looks fine. Another benefit to being a full-fledged witch is that they apparently don't need aspirin. "Can we get going?" I ask. "What's your plan, anyway?"

109

"Follow me," she says, and pulls out a flashlight. She approaches a building and finds the door handle, and it opens easily. The people around here must not be too worried about breaking and entering by a criminal lion.

I follow her inside to a small classroom, the floorboards creaking under our every step. The few chairs and tables all look worn out. On the wall is a small rectangular blackboard with numbers and letters scrawled across it. Miri unzips her

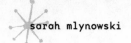

knapsack and pulls out an orange, her math textbook, and—is that my green shirt?

She lays each item on the dusty floor next to the teacher's desk. "These students are all orphans, and they need food, clothes, and books. So we're going to use the multiplying spell." Next she pulls out a plastic container of an already mixed concoction of mint, chocolate, and grape skin. "Ready?" she asks.

Even in the darkness, I can see that her eyes are shining. I feel a rush of pride. My sister is truly a superhero.

She takes a deep breath and begins:

*"Here is one
Placed on the floor,
I nod three times
And now there are more!"*

By the time we transport back to the U.S., I'm emotionally overwhelmed . . . and sleepy. Miri just about filled the school with oranges, books, and tops. In preparation for spritzing Will with the heart-reversal concoction, I shower, diffuse my hair, dress up, and apply lip gloss. The reason I've dolled myself up (including putting on my fave jeans and a sexy new red shirt) is that I cling to the hope that, after the reversal spell freezes his heart, Will might still think I'm cute and convince his brother to like me again. I'm well aware of the power of sibling suggestion.

My mom is equally entrenched in her primping process, and we're having a ball. The radio is blasting, the two of us are singing over the blow-dryer, we're sharing mascara.

Miri wanders into the bathroom as we're in midprimp. "Why don't you let me put some makeup on you?" I ask her. "It'll be fun!"

She rolls her eyes. "I have more important things to do with my time than paint myself. Like number three on my list: ridding the world of land mines."

Mom looks up from lining her eyes. "Have you already done your homework?"

Miri shakes her head. "I'll do it tonight."

"Good. And I made you tofu-and-broccoli potpie for dinner. All you have to do is heat it up in the toaster oven. You know how to do that, right?"

"Yes, Mom. Unlike your other daughter, I know how to use the kitchen appliances."

One little kitchen fire and I'm never going to hear the end of it. How was I supposed to know that marshmallows were flammable?

I don't get offended, because I know she's upset about my mom's new dating dossier and not at me. While waiting for the shirts and books and fruit to multiply, I tried to talk to her about her feelings, but she refused to discuss them. I told her that Mom needs to see other people. And that Miri has to learn to share. She threw an orange at my head.

The buzzer rings.

Yay! What can I say? Even though I know I won't be leaving the apartment, since he'll sprint to safety as soon as the spell hits him, I can't stop chills from running down my spine. I buzz him up. "Miri? You ready? Do you have the heart reversal?"

She joins me in the foyer and hands me the bottle.

111

"Okay. Ready?" I say. "You open; I'll squirt." I get into position. Knock, knock. I mouth to Miri, "Ready?"

She nods. Here goes everything.

My finger is on the trigger, and I'm about to spray when all I see is red.

Will has roses. Three dozen roses. Long stemmed. I can barely see his face because it's blocked by the forest of flowers. I have never gotten flowers from a boy before. (That's a lie. When I was five, on Valentine's Day, my dad brought home a teddy bear for Miri and two wrapped boxes, one for me and one for my mom. One was in silver paper and one was in Barbie wrapping. He told me to pick. I chose the silver, since it was shinier. He laughed and told me to pick the other one, but I refused. A deal was a deal. He agreed. My box had a dozen red roses in it. My mom got a Barbie convertible. We traded.)

"Hi, Rachel," Will says. "These are for you."

Gasp! Adorable! Pretty! Sweet! I drop the spray bottle on the carpet and hug the flowers. "Thank you! Let me put them in water." I retreat toward the kitchen. So sad. The first nonrelated boy/man to buy me roses and I can't even go out with him. If only I could, just for tonight . . . no. That would be a waste of time. I'm not going on a date with him just so I can spray him afterward. Ridiculous. Masochistic. For both of us. And he'd only be left wondering if he'd lost his mind. Taking a freshman to dinner. Insane! There are social norms that need to be upheld or high school society will crumble into ruins!

"How beautiful!" my mom says, intercepting. "Let me take care of those. You go ahead on your date, honey."

"It's a pleasure to meet you, Mrs. Weinstein." Will offers his hand. "I'm Will." He's so adorably grown-up.

My mom takes it. "Nice to meet you, too, Will. But I haven't been Weinstein for a while. It's Carol Graff, but please call me Carol." Is it weird that she's not freaking out that I'm going out with someone so tall? I'm a little freaked out myself. He looks like a man. Instead, she's batting her eyelashes. Is my mother flirting with my date? How embarrassing. "So where are you off to tonight?" she asks. Bat, bat.

"Well, my friend . . . ," he begins as I search for the bottle. I must put a stop to this snowball of a disaster immediately. I must spray. "London"—London?—"is having a party tonight. And I promised I'd stop by before dinner. If that's all right with you, Rachel."

Talk about sweet revenge!

Miri picks up the bottle from the floor and aims. She looks at me for approval.

113

"No!" I practically shout. "Hold on a sec." Heart pounding, I grab the spray bottle from her hands, stuff it into my purse, say, "Be back by twelve," and pull Will out the door.

"What," London says, narrowing her eyes, "are *you* doing here?" Her cheeks are as rosy as her plunging red shirt, red jeans, red boots, red nail polish, and red cast. I have no idea how that last one is possible.

I have just exited the bathroom on the first floor. (Yes, London lives in an insane triplex. I take a minute to enjoy the image of her struggling up and down the stairs in her cast.) The evil one is waiting for me, fuming with anger.

All eyes in the room are on us. "Can you please get out of my apartment, Rochelle?" She stabs her finger at me like it's a sword. Why is she always pointing at me?

Snickers ripple through the room and I want to die. Or at least cry. It seems the party has worked and London has regained her perch at the top of the JFK social ladder. And I'm once again lower than a worm. I'm about to slither back out the front door when Will comes to my rescue. "She's with me. Why? Is there a problem?" How teen-movie sweet is that?

London's mouth opens, but at first no sound comes out. Finally, she growls, "Why would you hang around her? She's a freak!"

"Rachel's my new girlfriend," he replies.

The crowd goes wild. Senior girls whisper to their friends, and the juniors lucky enough to be invited send frenzied text messages to their posses. Oblivious, Will squeezes my shoulder. "Want to see what's happening upstairs?"

I'm still reeling from the G-word. I am a girlfriend. *I am a girlfriend!* I'd love to plaster the slogan on a T-shirt: I, Rachel Weinstein, freshman nerd, am the (temporary) girlfriend of the student council president! Wow. Awesome.

I nod, and Will takes my hand—yes, takes my hand in front of everyone—and we pass a still-in-shock London on our way upstairs. I resist the urge to stick out my tongue at her. (Fine, I do it, but I stick it out only an inch and Will doesn't see.)

When we get to the second-floor living room, Bosh, a

senior, high-fives Will. "Hey, dude." Bosh is on the student council with Will. Even though he's the treasurer, he was definitely not voted in because of his math abilities. He's one of those straight-to-fraternity guys who live in sports jerseys and baseball caps, look like teddy bears, and are loved by everyone. You can almost imagine him growing up to be Norm from *Cheers*. I assume Bosh is his last name, but I'm not sure. That's all he goes by, like Madonna.

"Bosh, do you know Rachel?" As Will introduces us, his eyes stay firmly planted on my face. I'm like a potato chip. He just can't get enough of me.

Bosh high-fives me. "By name only, dude. Will hasn't stopped yammering about you all week."

"Would you like a piece of licorice?" Will asks, and pulls a small package out of his pocket.

"Sure," I say.

He rips off a piece and hands it to me. "I always have it on me. I'm a total sugar addict." He takes a bite off each end of his piece and blows through it like a straw.

He's so cute.

I'd be lying if I said I wasn't loving this. The news of our May-December relationship is spreading faster than the flu. People are knocking me over with their pointing.

"Hey, Rachel," says Mercedes Redding, senior and former cohead of the fashion show with London. "How are you?" Mercedes has not spoken to me since the disaster. But I'm now back on the radar, baby!

Wahoo to the power of two!

I happily meet the rest of Will's posse. (As if I didn't

115

already know who they are. Hah!) There are Jerome, Nelson, and Schumacher. One was in the fashion show, and two are on the basketball team. All three are A-list. Obviously.

As I prance around the room, I'm the queen on the arm of my king. No one will ever be mean to me again. How can they when I have been deemed dateable by Will? I'm finally out of the doghouse!

The tugging of my heavy purse on my shoulder reminds me that it's not for long, though. I'm supposed to spray him tonight and reverse his heart. And then I'll be the girl Will dumped after one day. It doesn't matter. It's Raf I like, anyway, not him. I stuff my mouth with licorice and analyze my dilemma. The sooner we end it, the better.

Speak of the devil. I nearly choke on the red candy. Raf is sitting on the couch with Melissa on his lap.

Are they dating? No, no, no! What on earth does he see in her? She laughs at something he says and throws her long, glossy red hair behind her shoulder. She's wearing a tight sky-colored off-the-shoulder top to reveal her lanky body, big boobs, and baby blues. Show-off.

How did she finagle her way in here, anyway? This is a *senior* A-list party, and she's only a meager freshman.

Will wraps his arm around my waist. Raf looks up. Our eyes lock.

I'm going to be sick. I quickly look away. How can he do that? He knows how awful Melissa was to me. What a jerk. I need to get out of here; I can't watch Raf and Melissa be all touchy-feely. The walls start to close in as images flash through my mind. Raf and Melissa holding hands in the hall. Raf smiling at Melissa the way he used to at me. I'll be watching from afar, alone again. Alone as usual. I wish someone would turn on a fan. The air in here is spongy and too thick to breathe.

"Wanna go eat now?" Will asks, reading my mind.

"Yes! I definitely do." I trail behind him like a depressed puppy as he says his good-byes. I'll spray him as soon as we're outside. No need to waste his time on dinner. What's the point? I might as well get it over with. My heart sinks as we close London's door behind us. I have nothing to look forward to. Raf is falling in love with Melissa, and London will make my life even more miserable when she finds out Will dumped me. It's a return ticket straight back to Loserville.

Will is holding my hand, silently helping me down the stairs. He's probably realized what a pathetic person I am and overthrown the spell all on his own. To add insult to in-jury, he's going to dump me even before I get to spray him. When we're on the street, I reach into my purse. Not that there's a point. He's already all pale and queasy looking.

He coughs twice. "I need to say something."

I don't believe it. My horribleness has actually broken the spell. I'll break up with him first. "I don't think it's—"

"Would you like to be my date for prom?"

Oh. My. God.

Prom? As in the senior prom? A freshman going to prom? That would so make up for all the dances I missed this year, since it's the *mother* of dances. The climax of all teen movies. Crinoline, limo, corsage . . .

I'm going to prom! If I don't spray. But then what about

117

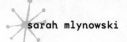

Raf? Raf, prom, Raf, prom. As I weigh the two on my imaginary scale, my hand still gripping the spray bottle inside my purse, Will leans over and kisses me.

Yum. (Three kisses in one week! I'm on a roll.) He looks a lot like Raf. So cute. Only taller. And older. And he tastes like licorice. And Raf wants nothing to do with me. He's probably kissing Melissa at this very second. Maybe, I think, as Will's tongue does this cool semicircle thing, this new relationship will help me forget about my last love.

I drop the heart reversal back into my purse. Well, why not? Prom, kisses, getting off the loser list . . . What else could I ask for? I pull back and smile.

"I thought we could go to Spark's," he says. "Is that cool? Do you eat steak?"

Moo.

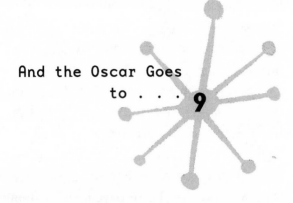

And the Oscar Goes to . . . 9

"Lookin' hot, Rache," says a random junior.

Bosh gives me a high five. "What up, dude?"

"Are we in an alternate reality?" Tammy asks.

I give a half wave to my subjects. I've been working on it all morning. Kind of like a Miss America wave with a touch more flutter in the fingers. "Weird, isn't it?"

It's not even nine a.m. on Monday, and word has gotten around *fast*. Once again, I have reached the pinnacle of high school society. All I have to do is date the king and everyone pretends they like me. It's faker than London's boobs. On the plus side, I'm going to prom! In other good news, classrooms are back to their non-doubled-up capacity. Construction guys have been working overtime—not sure (gulp) where the money is coming from.

But neither the adulation nor the solo desk is the best part of the day. Oh, no, the true prize is that Tammy is back. She surprised me at my locker this morning. I fully attacked her with hugs. Aaron, unfortunately, is still in bed. Seems his case is much, much worse. "I don't even remember what he looks like anymore," Tammy complains. "My moms haven't let me even visit him yet! They're afraid I'll have a relapse."

I feel bad and all . . . but this way I get Tammy all to myself!

Even though I warned her that Will and I are an item, she was not prepared for the sudden worship of our peers. It's like I've just won Best Director and now everyone wants to be in my movies. And this time, I've learned my lesson. I am not, I repeat *not*, ditching Tammy for the A-list. If they want to adore me, they'll have to adore Tammy, too.

Case in point: we walk into math, and Doree and Jewel are sitting in the back.

"Hi, Rachel!" Jewel says. "I saved you a seat."

Doree pats my chair like a throne. "Come sit with us."

I give them the half wave.

Tammy sighs. "Go sit with them if you want."

As if. "Are you kidding?" No way am I giving *those* girls a second chance. Or in Jewel's case, a third chance. "Let's sit here," I say, pointing to two empty seats in the front row.

Tammy gives me her scuba OK and smiles.

"Thinks she's too good for us, does she?" Doree huffs.

Yes. Much too good.

We're on our way out for lunch when two large sexy hands cover my eyes. "Guess who, gorgeous?"

Obviously the spell has made Will blind. Cute, yes. Pretty, maybe. But gorgeous? I wish.

I untangle his hands and kiss his cheek. "Hi, Will." My entire class is staring.

He leans against my locker. "What are you doing now?"

"Going for lunch."

"Want to come hang out with us instead?"

"Don't you have class?" Freshmen and sophomores have lunch from eleven to eleven forty-five; juniors and seniors have it the following period.

"Yeah, I want you to come to physics." He laughs. "No, Sock gets freshman/sophomore lunch period off in order to work."

I must look confused.

"Sock is student council."

"Why do you call it *sock*?"

"I don't know. I guess it's because you can't really pronounce S and C. So we added a vowel. And O is better than *I* or *U*. Anyway, we have an office downstairs. Coming?"

121

I guess it's *soc* and not *sock*. If I were them, I would have gone with *sac* or *sack*. Who wants to be associated with feet? *Sac* at least makes me think of a purse. And everyone likes purses. "I can't. Tammy and I are going for pizza."

His face falls. "Can't you both come? Please?"

Tammy pops up behind me. "He did say please."

"So let's hear your suggestions," Will says to us. "We need to come up with a theme. Prom is May twenty-seventh—in three and a half weeks."

What I need to come up with is a dress. A gorgeous princess, where-did-she-get-that stunner.

I'm lying on a pink sofa, my feet up on the school

president's legs. I'm not sure what's more amazing: my access to school couches or my access to a boy's legs.

The room is small but cozy, filled with couches, posters, and a stocked fridge. Who knew? It's like a college dorm room in the school basement.

"Vampires?" says the soc secretary, River Eugenicks, an über-cool senior. He's the only person ever to be able to get away with having four eyebrow rings yet wearing a bow tie to school every day. I mean, come on. Those two styles just don't go together. Unless, like River, you're A-list, super-smart, and an intern at MTV.

"Black attire only," he continues, munching on a piece of red licorice Will handed out at the beginning of the meeting. "And the lightbulbs in the gym would all be red. All we need is a smoke machine and we're golden."

At least no one has mentioned the possibility that the gym won't be cleaned up in time for prom. Because it has to be. Having the prom in the gym is a JFK tradition, just like the fashion show is traditionally a prom fund-raiser. The ten thousand dollars raised at the fashion show is to be used for decorations, food, and music.

"Shall we call it Night of the Dead?" Kat, the VP, says, laughing. Her full name is Katherine Postansky. Her beige capris and hoodie sweatshirt, pale face, and mop of straight black hair make her look like an ice cream cone. And she keeps a purple pen behind her ear, like a sprinkle. She's about my height, probably five foot one, and a size small. And she smiles a lot—for good reason. She's adorable and A-list. She was one of the few juniors invited to London's party on Saturday. Never mind she's the only girl in the soc (in soc? on the soc?), hanging out with these cool guys every day.

The only other people in the room are Tammy and Bosh, and they're sitting together on the third couch. I've been noticing that every few minutes Bosh inches his way a smidgen closer to Tammy. Maybe he's developing a crush! Imagine if Tammy found a new boyfriend in the soc. How cute would that be? I mean, I like Aaron—he seems harmless—but I can't exactly double with them. The president of the student council wouldn't want to be seen with a lowly freshman. Besides his girlfriend, of course. And his friend's girlfriend. And this way Tammy and I can go to the prom together. We'll go dress shopping, rent a limo, smile at each other as we're locked in our partners' embraces. I can't believe I was considering breaking up with him! Was I crazy? Blind to the possibilities?

Oh, I think I am blind. I just noticed that there is someone else in the room: Jeffrey Zeigster, who's sitting in the corner, doing his science homework. His brown hair looks painted on with gel, and his glasses are so thick that they look like bulletproof windowpanes. Hello, has he not heard of contacts? He's part of the soc but the only person not elected to it. He was appointed by Konch because of his high GPA. Apparently, he sees this meeting as more of a study hall than an opportunity to help improve the quality of student life at JFK.

"Let's just hope the gym is ready in time," Will says. "We've already scored some major donations from alumni for repairs. The administration put the money toward the classrooms first. But the gym and cafeteria have to be *completely* redone and are going to cost a ridiculous amount of money."

Oh yeah. I've been meaning to follow up with Miri about that. Unfortunately, I've been a little preoccupied with the whole Will love spell stuff.

Kat nods along with Will's every word, her head like a bouncing ball. "Until you hear anything, let's hope for the best."

"All right. Any other ideas? Costume party?" Will suggests. "Is that lame?"

"No," says River. "But I doubt London Zeal and her posse will want to dress up."

Most of the room laughs. I perk up. It seems not everyone is her biggest fan.

"Maybe she'll come as a witch," Kat says. "She wouldn't even have to put on a costume."

Funny as that is, witch jokes make me a wee bit uncomfortable.

"She's not that bad," Will says. "She's a friend of mine." Such a politician—he's friends with everyone.

"What would you be?" I ask Kat, anxious to change the subject. But I like Kat. She's funny, and her anti-London politics make her a potential mentor. I resist the geeky urge to beg her to be my friend.

She shrugs. "I don't get to go. I'm just a lowly junior."

"Let's keep brainstorming, people," Will says.

That is so sad. She comes up with the ideas and then doesn't get to go?

"What about Atlantis, dudes?" suggests Bosh. "You know? The lost underwater city. I took some great pictures when I was scuba diving last month."

Tammy's eyes light up. "You dive?"

124

Bosh straightens his posture. "Yeah, dude. Why, do you?"

"Of course! I live for it."

"High five!" he says, and they slap hands.

Did Tammy just blush? They are so going to fall in love, get married, and have scuba babies.

"I hate the water," River says, fingering an eyebrow piercing.

"Whatever you say, *River*." Kat laughs. "Let's think of something else."

Tammy clears her throat. "What about an Oscar night?"

Bosh gives her a scuba OK. "You could have a red carpet leading up to the gym."

"We could give out random mini Academy Awards," River says quickly. "You know, for best mustache."

Weird, but funny. As long as it's not for best beard.

The idea seems to be rolling around Will's brain. "I like it," he says. "We could project old black-and-white movies on the wall."

125

"The photographer could stand outside snapping photos like the paparazzi!" Kat suggests.

"All in favor," Will says. We all raise our hands. All except Mr. Studious in the corner. Will peers at him over the back of the couch. "Jeffrey? You in?"

Startled, Jeffrey drops his pencil. "In where?"

"Oscar theme for prom."

His eyes squint in mystification. "Prom?"

"End-of-year dance. Prom. Oscar theme."

"All right," he mumbles, and then goes back to his work.

"He's shy," Kat whispers to me.

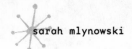

"So we're done," says Will, and squeezes my knee.

Kat raises an eyebrow. "What about Amy?"

River snorts. "If she's too busy with her boyfriend to make it to meetings then she doesn't get to vote."

I forgot about Amy Koppela. She's in the soc too, supposedly in charge of prom. Very tall, very skinny, very blond, and very A-list. Apparently too cool to come to soc meetings. "Who's she dating?" I ask.

"Some NYU guy," Will answers. "She spends both first and second lunches in his dorm. We'll count her as pro-Oscar. So six votes say yes. Oscar theme it is. Thanks, Tammy."

I give Tammy a thumbs-up. I know in underwater language it means something besides good job, but she gets the idea.

126

Tammy and I head to English on cloud nine. If we were floating any higher, we would hit the ceiling. As soon as class starts, I slip a note into her copy of *A Midsummer Night's Dream*, the Shakespeare play about love spells gone amuck. How fitting. Should I be concerned about what's going to happen when I'm a sophomore and we study *Macbeth*?

My note: *Awesome ideas!*

She blushes happily as she reads my scribble and then tosses a note back to me: *I can't believe you get to go. So lucky.*

I write back: *You might get to go too. Bosh was drooling over you.*

And then I get: ☺

Me: *What does that mean??? Do you like him?*

Tammy: *I already have a boyfriend, remember? I can't go to the prom with Bosh! Does he even have a first name?*

Me: *No clue. But maybe they'll let you go since you came up with the idea.*

Tammy: *No way. They won't even let Kat go.*

Me: *Crazy, huh? I like her. She's so sweet for someone A-list. Did you like her?*

Tammy: *Yup. She was nice, considering . . .*

Me: *Considering what?*

Tammy: *Considering that she's in love with your new boyfriend!*

I stare at the note and sink into my chair. Two seconds later I lean over to Tammy and whisper, "Why do you think she likes Will?"

"She kept looking at him. And anytime he talked to her she blushed. I could just tell. Couldn't you?"

I shrug. I didn't notice a thing. My self-centeredness is extraordinary—almost a superpower.

"Don't worry," Tammy says. "He was *not* looking back. He only has eyes for you."

That's one thing I'm not worried about. At least not for another few weeks, before the spell wears off. I'll have to remind Miri to extend it to make sure I get to go to prom. I'll reverse it after that, though. Immediately after. Forcing someone to like you isn't the nicest thing to do. And Will is such a terrific guy, he deserves to be truly in love.

When the bell rings, we pile up our books and head out the door. And that's when I run smack into Raf. And I mean Smack. Into. Raf.

I guess I wasn't paying attention or something, because I swing around and my forehead collides with his shoulder, and my copy of A *Midsummer Night's Dream* and the accompanying notes soar through the air, the covers of my binder spread like a pigeon's wings. Meanwhile, I fly backward and somehow end up lying on my back, my hair all over the dirty floor, wishing I could zap myself to another country. Canada, maybe?

Raf is suddenly on his knees, by my side, hand on my shoulder. "Are you okay?" he asks, his forehead wrinkling into adorable little folds. I look deep into his speckled eyes and feel like I'm being submerged in a warm bubbly bath.

My heart sinks. And not because of my pounding forehead. Unrequited love hurts.

"Rachel?" his yummy lips say. They're red and plump and juicy and . . . "Rachel?" he asks again.

128

"Hi, Raf."

"Hi, Rachel. Did I hurt you?"

"Yes," I say. My heart has been torn into thousands of shards that will no longer fit together. "I mean, no, I'm fine. All good."

He places his hand under my elbow and gently helps me back to my feet. He then lets go of my arm, picks up my binder, and hands it to me. "I think this is yours," he says, and then, after giving my elbow and heart a final squeeze, he disappears out of my life and down the hallway.

"The heart-reversal spell is broken," I tell Miri, pushing open her door.

"What?" She's at her desk reading A² and doesn't look up.

"I tried to use it. I feel sick to my stomach every time I see Raf. I can't deal. So I tried spraying myself but all it did was mess up my hair. Why didn't it work?"

"The spell is only a one-broomer. It's not advanced enough for selfsummie."

I know what a one-broomer is, but self-what? "I have no idea what you just said."

"Selfsummie is when you're trying to trick yourself with an emotion spell. And it won't work unless the spell is at least a four-broomer."

"So what can I do? Nothing?" The pain must end.

She hesitates. "We could try an anti-love spell. That's a five-broomer. Should achieve selfsummie."

Perfect. "Give it to me."

"You sound like a junkie."

I flop backward onto her bed. "I'm serious. Can you make me one?"

She puts down her pencil and tilts back her chair. "Do you—"

"Don't do that. You're making me nervous," I interrupt.

She tilts her chair back farther just to annoy me. "I'll give you a spell if you want. I know the perfect one."

Excellent. I'll no longer feel the pain. Raf who? "I need it now."

Her chair still diagonal, she flips through the pages. "Are you sure?"

"Of course. Why not?"

"Are you sure you want to wipe out your feelings?"

129

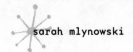

"I feel crappy, so yes."

"Don't you remember all the stuff Mom told us about experiencing the good and bad in life?"

"This is the same Mom who magically bleached her hair blond on Saturday?"

Miri makes a sour face. "She said it way before she dyed her hair, when she still had perspective. She said experiencing the bad makes you stronger."

I flex my bicep. "I'm plenty strong."

She tilts even closer to the floor. "Bad things make you a more interesting person. More profound."

"In that case I must be the most interesting person alive." But maybe she's right. Maybe zapping away my unrequited crush will make me bland and boring. Who cares? I'll be happy instead. "Let's do it!" I scream, and Miri's slanted chair suddenly sails backward and she crashes to the floor. She makes a surprised squeak.

"Told you. You okay?"

She nods and I lunge for the phone, which just started ringing. Maybe it's Raf calling to tell me he's still in love with me, and I won't need the anti-love spell at all.

"Aloha, Rachel!"

"Daddy! You're back!" My father has finally returned to the mainland. "How was it?"

"Rad. The *kaukau* was *ono*. That means the food was delicious. And the surfing was primo. The . . ." I space out a bit, thinking about Raf. I hear a muffle, and I realize a few seconds too late that he might have just said, "My babe new wife, Jennifer, wants to say aloha."

Groan. The truth is during the wedding process I realized that she wasn't as bad as I made her out to be. But does that mean we have to be phone pals now? And what's up with the Hawaiian-surfer-speak? They didn't actually surf, did they?

"Aloha!" she chirps.

"Hi, Jennifer. Did you go surfing?"

"Oh yeah. You had to see me rippin' it up." She continues to tell me about how they "scored some great rides" and really "hung loose." Eventually she offers to e-mail me her "bodacious" pictures and tells me she's "stoked" to see us this weekend, then asks to talk to Miri.

Miri scowls as I hand her the phone and then rolls her eyes, then rolls her eyes some more. Meanwhile, I wonder about the merits of subjecting myself to an anti-love spell. Or any spell, for that matter. Miri's track record hasn't been impeccable. There were cows in my gym.

131

Miri finally hangs up, groaning. "She's e-mailing us pictures! I just finished cleaning out my in-box from all their wedding crap."

"Let's talk about the ingredients," I say.

"You'll need to get a black candle, Dead Sea salts, sunflowers, and a lock of Raf's hair. And then any feelings you have left for Raf will be gone. At least temporarily."

Groan. How on earth will I get Raf's hair? But do I really want *all* my feelings for him zapped into la-la land? "What if I decide I want to grow up to be a writer? Or a painter? Will I still be able to draw on this pain?"

She sits back down in her chair. "What are you rambling about? I thought you wanted to be an astronaut."

Right. I did say that. Or a pilot on an astro-tourism jetliner, because according to 60 *Minutes*, that's so going to be the next big thing. Astronaut. Painter, personal shopper. All sound demanding. Whatever doesn't kill us makes us stronger, right? I decide I really don't want anything unnatural tinkering with my feelings. I mean, let's be honest. My sister isn't all that experienced. What if the spell backfires, and instead of falling out of love, I fall into a well or something? "Forget the anti-love spell. I'll deal. Keeping it real, you know?" And anyway, I'm really way too lazy to try to locate all those ingredients.

She shrugs and flips the page. "If you say so. I bet the real reason is that you're too lazy to get the ingredients. Can I get back to saving the whales now?"

How did she know?

The rest of the week flies by in a surprising haze of happiness. Will drops by my locker after every class and always gives me a quick kiss on the lips. He slides I-Love-You notes into my textbooks. Afternoons are spent hanging out at the A-list in-spot. Lunches are spent with the soc in the lounge. On Tuesday, we order pizza, which is delivered right to our room! How fun is that? On Wednesday, I catch Bosh rubbing Tammy's shoulders. On Thursday, I notice the way Kat blushes whenever Will pays her any attention. But the weird thing is she's nice to me. And not super-over-the-top-nice-but-secretly-bitchy nice. She lends me her purple pen when mine runs out of ink. Laughs at my jokes. Genuinely nice. If I were her, I would hate me.

Even though London Zeal is back at the top of the

A-list, she seems to have forgotten her hatred of me, or at least, she is no longer exacting her revenge. Because of my new girlfriend-of-Will status, I have been forgiven and approved by the freshman, sophomore, junior, and senior A-lists, and therefore by the entire school. Everyone, that is, except Raf.

These days, when he passes me, I don't even get the half smile. Raf is not impressed.

What's his problem now? He doesn't like me, so no one else can like me either? Why are boys so annoying?

On Friday, Tammy and I are sitting in bio when someone knocks on the door. I see Will through the window and I feel warm all over. Special. Chosen. Strange. I used to feel that way only around Raf. Is it possible that I'm starting to like Will, too? To *really* like him? Is it possible to like two boys at once? Two brothers?

"Come in, Mr. Kosravi," Mr. Frederick says.

The cool thing is that no matter which one I marry, I'll be Mrs. Kosravi. If I change my name, which I don't think I'll do. I can't just give up my identity! I see Will's face and block the argument out of my mind. (I guess it isn't something I have to decide on immediately.) He whispers something to Mr. Frederick, who nods and then looks up. "Ms. Weinstein and Ms. Wise, please go with Mr. Kosravi. You're excused for the rest of class."

Wahoo! Tammy squeezes my hand as we excitedly follow Will out the door, passing Doree's envious, longing gaze. I'm sure nothing is really wrong. How awesome is Will? Pretending something's wrong just to get us out of bio!

"Thanks!" I say, kissing his cheek. He smells good.

133

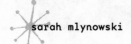
"That was awesome," Tammy says. "It was sooooo boring in there."

Will shakes his head. "Don't thank me. I need your help. We're having an emergency soc meeting. The prom is on the verge of being canceled."

How I Ruined the World

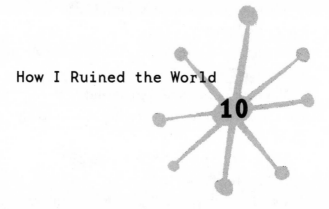

10

"Tell us what happened," Bosh says, shaking his head, his hand gently resting . . . on Tammy's knee? Whoa.

Tammy turns white and then bright red, and then she smiles, then frowns, then slowly shuffles out of Bosh's reach.

Meanwhile, Will paces the room, his arms waving over his head. "The gym won't be ready in time."

My stomach feels like I just swallowed a balloon filled with sand.

"Even once the repairs are complete," Will says, "the floors will be too fragile for the first month to have students dance on them. Same goes for the cafeteria. I'd like to kill the people who pulled that cow prank."

La, la, la.

River groans. "Can't we rent a place?"

Will shakes his head. "That's the second problem. Since Konch is convinced that the cows were a senior prank, she wants to cancel prom until someone confesses."

"What?" we all scream. I may throw up on the floor.

"I convinced her not to. So instead, she's making us fork

over the money the fashion show raised for the prom to help with repair costs."

"What?" Bosh screams. "Dude, how can we afford prom if we do that?"

Will continues. "She recommended we start by canceling the band and the photographer. And possibly the rented tables."

"But where does she expect us to eat?" River asks indignantly. "On the floor?"

"Oh, don't worry," Will says sarcastically. "She suggested canceling the dinner, too. But then she remembered that we already gave the caterer a deposit with the money from advance ticket sales. What are we going to do? The prom is supposed to be in three weeks. But at the moment all we have guaranteed is the meal. And not even the entire meal. The deposit was only seven grand, which means it will cover appetizers and maybe half of the stale chicken plates."

"That sucks, dude," Bosh says. "We can't party in the street. Let's just rent a space and listen to a CD or something."

"We need a band," River argues. "I can listen to CDs at home."

Will shakes his head in disgust. "Ah, man, I'm going to be the soc president responsible for the lamest prom ever."

"We should just cancel it," River says.

No way! Then Will will be the president responsible for canceling prom! "Hold on. What's the total cost of prom?" I ask.

Will sighs. "It's supposed to be twenty-seven thousand

five hundred dollars. Which covered everything. And it worked out perfectly before the cows, because we had almost ten grand from the fashion show, we had a free space, and the prom tickets were fifty dollars a person. And since we're expecting about three hundred and fifty ticket sales, it worked out to . . . well, it worked out."

"You absolutely cannot cancel prom," says Kat, tapping her purple pen. (How does she never lose that pen? I lose about one per day.) "We'll just have to come up with the money. Let's raise ticket prices."

"If you raise ticket prices too high," River says, "people might not want to spend the dough. If anything, you may have to give them a rebate if you don't even have a band. Or dessert."

"We can't raise ticket prices," Will says, shaking his head in dismay. "We've already sold some of them. The price is set." **137**

I do the calculations. "So you're expecting seventeen thousand five hundred dollars in ticket sales. Which means that if we need to reraise the ten thousand from fashion show funds to be able to keep prom as planned, as well as say a few thousand for a location, we're looking at trying to raise twelve to fifteen thousand dollars."

Will nods.

Kat continues tapping. "We can do it. Let's find a new location. Then we'll worry about paying for it. We won't book it unless we have a way to raise the money, but we'll come up with it. We have to."

Will hesitates. "Are you all sure? We only have three weeks. It's going to be tough. And exams are coming up—"

"We can do it, dude," Bosh says. The rest of us nod.

"All right." Will takes a deep breath. "Let's brainstorm. Jeffrey, can you pass me the licorice?"

In the corner near the cupboard, Jeffrey looks up from his notebook. He's like a ghost. Again, I didn't even notice him. He mutters something to himself, reaches into the stock cupboard, and tosses Will a package.

"What we need to do," Kat says, "is find out what clubs or hotels are available."

Will smiles gratefully at Kat. I feel a spark of guilt for causing him all this grief. And a tiny spark of jealousy. "Right," he says. "That makes sense. Let's make a list, and Rachel and I will check them out over the weekend."

Ha! Take that, Kat! Oh, drat. "Oh, um, I'm going to my dad's," I admit.

His face falls. Like, to the floor. "What? You are? I won't be able to see you all weekend?"

I shake my head. "It's only two days. I'll call you." Luckily, I already know his number by heart because of Raf. Not that I've ever called Raf.

He pouts for a few more seconds and turns to Kat. "Kat, would you mind coming with me?"

"Of course not. I'd be happy to."

I roll my eyes at Tammy. And I can't even be mad, because Kat's so . . . nice.

"We ruined the prom," I tell Miri on the train to Long Island. "I don't believe it."

"Uh-huh," she mumbles, slumped in her seat, reading A^2.

"I'm about to make freshman history by going to the prom with the soc president, and I can't even go. Can life be any more unfair?"

"Uh-huh," she repeats.

Hmm. "Is there a rhinoceros on this train?"

"Uh-huh."

"You're not paying attention to me!"

"Uh-huh."

I wave my hand in front of her face.

"What?" she asks, finally looking up.

"We ruined the prom with the cows. Do you get it?"

"Yes, I get it, but is that really such a big deal? It's just a dance. A stupid elitist dance. A dance that you wouldn't even be going to if not for the love spell," she says, whispering the last two words. "There are far more important issues you should be worrying about."

I know I'm normally a little selfish. But I'm pretty sure Miri should be taking some responsibility for this crisis. Not that I'm one to point fingers, but it was sort of her fault. "What are you doing, anyway?"

She whips out a notebook. "Worrying about things more important than prom. Like ridding the world of land mines, number three on my list, and of slave trafficking, number four. Fixing the ozone layer, number five. And there was an oil spill this morning off the coast of France. Do you know how many whales are going to die?" She makes an arrow in her notebook. "The oil just got bumped up to number three."

I squirm in my seat. "Okay, I'm sorry. Sounds serious."

She shakes her head and I notice the heavy circles under

139

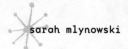

her eyes. "Life is serious," she says, and sighs, then returns to reading, leaving me staring at my hands.

I could so use a manicure.

The whole bronzed family is waiting for us at the train station.

"Aloha!" Jennifer and my dad say.

I need a pair of sunglasses: my dad's blue and red flow-ered shirt is *that* bright. And, oh, no, Jennifer is wearing a lei. I give their honeymoon glow another week, tops. Then they'll get back to being as miserable as the rest of us.

I'm confused. How did Prissy, otherwise known as Priscilla, who was stuck here with Jennifer's parents on Long Island, get so much color? She quickly clears that up when she says, "Am I pretty? I want to be pretty like Mommy and have brown skin too, so I used self-tanner!"

"No, you did not," I say in disbelief. She's five. Is that legal?

She nods happily.

We all shuffle into their Mercedes. Prissy climbs into her booster seat and quickly puts her tiny tanned finger up her nose.

I try to catch Miri's eye so we can secretly make fun of the entire scene, but she's lost in her saving-the-world thoughts.

" 'You will soon discover a treasure!' " Jennifer reads, after breaking open her fortune cookie. "You know what that means," she says, winking at my dad across the booth at Happy Palace, our favorite Chinese restaurant.

"What treasure?" I ask Jennifer as I chomp on an almond cookie. "You buried money in the backyard?" Can I have some?

"No," she says, and then smiles. "I meant the new addition."

"You're adding another wing to the house?" I ask. Now Miri and I won't have to share a room when we stay over.

Jennifer looks at my father. "Well, no," she says.

No? "So what kind of addition?" I ask. And then it hits me. Smack in my face. I choke on the cookie, start coughing, and grab my glass of water.

Miri finally snaps out of her reverie. "Already?" she asks disbelievingly.

She's pregnant? But . . . but . . . but I'm still not used to Prissy. And . . . where are they going to put the baby? Won't they need a nursery? Does that mean we'll have to bunk with Prissy? "When's the baby due?"

"What baby, Mommy?" Prissy asks, sucking on a cookie. "What does *due* mean?"

My dad and Jennifer giggle. "We're not pregnant!" she says, still laughing, her blue-green eyes twinkling.

Then what is she talking about? "Are you getting a dog?"

"Do you know how much work a dog is?" Jennifer says, flipping her gorgeous silky blond hair over her shoulder. "No way. We're *trying* to have a baby. We're just not pregnant yet."

Is that really an image I need?

Prissy slams her small fist on the table, face puckered. "No more babies."

141

Silence.

"Babies are fun!" Jennifer promises in her chirpiest voice. "You'll get to be the big sister!"

"I don't want to be a big sister," she insists, shaking her pigtails. "I want to be the little sister."

I decide to attempt to help. I can certainly relate: rumor has it when I was first told about Miri's upcoming arrival, I spit up in protest. "You can be a big sister and still be a little sister," I explain. "You're so lucky. You get to be both! I wish *I* could be both."

How awesome would it be if I had a big sister? Someone to tell me what to wear, help me with my makeup. Hmm. I've kind of been my mom's big sister lately.

"I don't want to be a big sister," Prissy says calmly.

Miri laughs. "Too bad it's not up to you."

"No more babies!" Prissy screams at the top of her lungs, and reaches for her third cookie.

Everyone at the restaurant turns to stare.

"No more sugar," Jennifer says, moving the cookie plate out of her reach.

The subject comes up again the next morning.

We're sitting, sleepy eyed, in the kitchen, lazily enjoying our poached eggs and toast, when Prissy's question lands flat on the table like a pancake. "Where do babies come from?" Her blue-green eyes are wide with innocence.

Miri starts coughing.

I take a long sip of my orange juice and try to see to the

bottom of the glass. Would it be weird if I climbed under the table?

"Well . . . ," my father begins.

Oh, God. Oh, no. Don't say it. He's not going to tell her, is he? I can't think of anything more painful than having to listen to my dad discuss the birds and the bees. I remember when I first heard about the facts of life: Jewel's older brother told us when we were in the second grade. I went home and asked my mom if the rumors were true. I remember feeling truly appalled. It goes in *where*? Anyway, I have never discussed this subject with my dad, and I certainly don't want to start now. As far as I know, he doesn't even know I know.

"Well . . . ," my father begins again. I look at Miri, and her cheeks are the same cherry red as I imagine mine are.

Jennifer makes a stab. "When mommies and daddies love each other . . ."

Miri and I sink lower into our chairs.

143

". . . they sleep in the same room, alone together," she continues. (The detail on this plate is just amazing. Nice plate. Pretty plate. Pretty white square plate.) "That's when they make a baby."

"Oh," says Prissy. Then her eyes squint into small commas. "But *how* do they make a baby?"

Silence.

"Out of love," my dad says.

Could this get any more painfully embarrassing? I'd rather be writing an exam while a dentist fills my cavities. (Not that I have any; I have perfect teeth, unlike my sister, who must brush her teeth with Kool-Aid. I wonder if Will has any cavities.

He does eat a lot of licorice. I bet Raf has perfect teeth. . . . No thinking about Raf! Better to listen to Jennifer's sex talk!)

Prissy considers the new and extremely vague explanation and slowly nods. Then she shovels a forkful of egg into her mouth and the subject is forgotten—by her. I think I may be scarred for life.

We go to the mall in the afternoon, because Prissy has inexplicably painted Liquid Paper hearts on her black patent leather party shoes. Dad tells Miri and me that we can each pick out one new item for ourselves.

"New jeans! New jeans!" I beg inside Macy's, leading them from the kids' shoe department to the juniors department.

"You have jeans," my dad says. "You're wearing them."

True. I could even use the multiplying spell for more if I wanted to.

"A girl can never have too many pairs," Jennifer says, coming to my defense. I almost pass out from surprise by my new and unexpected ally. Honeymoon Jennifer is awesome! And so smart. I pile ten pairs over my arm and retreat into the dressing room.

Jennifer acts as commentator as I model each one. "Too big. Can we get her a smaller size?" And then, "Too dark. Lighter is really in style this season." She's right! London's groupies are all wearing light jeans.

By the time we've whittled it down to two pairs, Miri, my dad, and Prissy are all asleep on the couch. "Which should I choose?" It's like asking me to pick a favorite parent. I love them equally.

"Ring them both up," Jennifer says. "Let's hang ten! That means go for it."

Viva Hawaii.

If Jennifer keeps this up, I may pick her as my favorite parent.

It's not until we're back in the car that I realize that Miri didn't buy anything. "Where's your one item?" I ask.

"Yeah, honey," my dad says, reversing the car out of the lot. "I said you can have anything you want. And since we bought Rachel two pairs of jeans, you can have two anythings."

"I don't need anything material," she answers. "But you could take my assigned money and donate it to the charity of your choice on my behalf."

Oh, brother.

Jennifer whips her head around. "What?"

My feelings exactly. What a goody-goody.

My father also turns around (which probably isn't that safe). But he smiles at my sister as if she said she'd been accepted to Harvard. "I'd be happy to do that. You choose the charity and I'll double what I spent on Rachel's jeans."

That's not fair. Sigh. I'm horrible. Of course it's fair.

"Thanks, Dad," Miri says.

She's so donating that to the prom.

I prepare to call Will before dinner. This will be the first time I call him; he's phoned me every day for the last week. I close the door, sit on the bed, and pick up the receiver.

". . . bought her the most adorable jeans. I think I might go back and get a pair," I hear Jennifer saying. "Hello? Did someone pick up?"

Foiled! "Sorry. I'll hang up."

"Do you need the phone, Rachel?"

"I can wait."

"Don't worry, I'll get off. Irma, I'll speak to you tomorrow, 'kay?"

I don't know what's come over her. First new jeans, and now she's getting off the phone with her friends so I can use it? We must have put a spell on her by accident. Nah. Is it possible the fairy tales are all wrong? Once a Soon-to-Be Step-Monster officially joins the family, she becomes nice? I should enjoy it as long as it lasts. It could fade along with her tan. "Thanks."

I wait for the dial tone. Then, palms all sweaty, I punch in the number. I don't know why I'm nervous. He likes me. He told me to call. There's absolutely no reason for me to be—

"Hello?"

Heart. Exploding. That's why I should be nervous. It's Raf. I should hang up. No, I can't. He definitely has caller ID. Not that he'd recognize the Long Island number. But he knows that my dad lives out here. And he might call back. But what should I do? I can't ask the boy I secretly still like if I can speak to his brother! This is so awful. Exponentially worse than my dad talking about sex. Why didn't I block my number?

"Hello?" Raf repeats.

Although . . . maybe it's not Raf. How do I know? Their hellos sound identical. It's probably Will. Of course it's Will. "Hello!" I say, attempting to sound optimistic. I

try to use my nonexistent powers of persuasion. Be Will!
Be Will!

"Hello," the voice says again. "Who is this?"

It's not Will. Will would know it was me. Wouldn't Raf
know it was me too? I should hang up. *Don't hang up!* I could
claim I got disconnected. *Be mature!* My palms are now so
sweaty that the receiver slips out of my grasp. "Rachel," I
squeak, pressing it firmly against my ear.

"Rachel who?"

Is he (whoever he is) joking? Which one of them doesn't
know me? "Rachel Weinstein."

"I'm just kidding you, Rachel. It's Mitch."

"Oh, hi." I slap my sweaty hand against my forehead. I
forgot about brother number three. He's not on my daily
radar since he's at NYU. But I thought he didn't live at
home. Why is he answering the phone? Just to make me feel
like an idiot?

"So who do you want to speak to?" he asks, laughing.
"Raf or Will?"

"Raf, please. I mean, Will. Will!" Now I'm confused.

He laughs again and hollers, "Will, phone!"

Glad to be an amusement.

Seconds later Will picks up. "Hello?"

They all sound the same! "Hi, Will."

"Rachel! How you doin'?"

"Headachy." As of now. "You?"

"Good. Kat and I went site hunting and we found
some cool places. I'll bring pictures and prices to show
on Monday."

147

"Great. What are you doing tonight?"

"Wishing I was hanging out with you, but going to some party with Jerome and the boys. Hey, on Friday? I was thinking Patsy's."

Yum. Only the best pizza place in the city. "Sounds delicious." And romantic. I can already see a string of mozzarella stretched between us like the spaghetti in *Lady and the Tramp*.

"Great. My parents love it there, and they want to meet you."

"Your p-parents?" I'm not ready for a meet and greet. Doesn't that happen much later on? Like when we're engaged? What will I wear?

"Don't worry. It won't be just them. My brothers, too."

Really foiled this time.

"Time for all of us to hit the hay," my dad says, turning off the TV. I stand up and stretch.

"I'm not going to sleep," Prissy says, still firmly planted on the couch.

Jennifer laughs. "Oh, really? You certainly are."

"No, I'm not," Prissy says again. She turns around and stuffs her head between two pillows.

Jennifer picks her up by the waist and carries her toward her room. "Yes, young lady, you are."

Prissy begins kicking and screaming, "I want to sleep with you!"

"What is wrong with you tonight? Big girls sleep in their own beds."

Miri and I quickly say good night, leaving them to the parenting trauma, and after washing up, we head to the privacy of our lemon-meringue room. "We have a lot to talk about," I say.

"I know. But let's wait until everyone's asleep."

I don't know why she wants to wait, but I'm too tired to argue. Might as well get in a few winks.

I nod off into dreamworld, and the next thing I know, Miri is shaking me awake. "Are we ready to talk about prom?" I ask groggily.

"Yup," she says. "But let's do it in France." She waves two batteries and some sort of purple potion in front of me. "I found a clean-water spell."

So that's why she wanted to wait. But do we have to do this now, when I'm feeling like a zombie? "Are you kidding me? Don't you think you're going a little overboard on this helping thing?"

She squats on the ground. "Get on. We'll discuss this once we're there."

I sigh and climb aboard the Miri express. I wonder if I'm accumulating any airline points. I'd like a free trip to the Bahamas, please.

A few seconds later, we land on a soft beach. The sunrise is casting shades of pastel pink and orange on the water—if only I had a camera—and the air smells salty and delicious. Excuse me . . . *délicieux*.

Miri goes to work on the oil issue. I make a snow angel in the sand. "I'll be here if you need me," I say.

"Yeah, thanks."

A few minutes later, she's done and I'm in heaven. The

149

lull of the surf is sweet music to my ears. Can I move to France?

"All right, whales saved; let's go home," Miri announces, crouching down beside me.

Already? I pat the spot beside me. "This piece of beach has your name on it, missy. What's the rush?"

Miri shrugs and plops onto her back. "Two minutes. And then I have to get back to work."

I groan and flick a grain of sand toward her. "Stop being such a freak. And speaking of which, I can't believe you didn't get new clothes today."

She sighs. "How could I take home clothes when there are people in the world who are freezing?"

I don't want to sound selfish or anything, but what she just said makes absolutely no sense. "Whatever. What charity are you going to give your money to?"

"I don't know yet! That's the problem. There are so many causes. The homeless, peace in the Middle East, AIDS, animal rights . . ."

Wrong answer. "The prom! We need the money for the prom! Remember our discussion about how we had to help earn money? This is it! So help!"

She props herself up on her elbows. "The prom is not a charity."

"Actually it is. JFK alumni have shelled out thirty thousand dollars for school repairs. Because of the cows. *Your* cows. The school is using the prom money to fix the gym, so we need to raise money to rent a ballroom."

"I'm not giving up peace in the Middle East for a stupid prom."

Hello? Does she feel no accountability here? "But you ruined prom! You should feel responsible!"

Miri bursts into tears.

Oops. I sit up and put my arm around her. She starts sobbing silently, as though afraid that any sound she might make will . . . scare the whales?

"What's wrong?" I ask.

"I feel"—sob—"so"—sob—"awful. That I ruined p-p-prooooooooom." Snot dribbles along her upper lip. "And I"—sob—"don't know how"—sob—"to fix it. And there are so many bad things in the world. And I have to fix them, too. And I know I'm supposed to be happy that I'm a witch and that I have all these powers, but I feel so"—sob— "responsible for everyone. There's this huge weight on my chest, like someone's sitting on it all the time."

My poor, sweet sister. I need to make her laugh. Not knowing what else to do, I sit on her stomach. "Like this?"

She giggles but quickly starts crying again. Then snorting. "You're hurting me," she says, and I roll off. I got sand all over her shirt.

"I know what will make you feel better," I say.

"What?"

"The Eiffel Tower! Let's go to Paris!"

She shakes her head. "I'm tired. Can we just go home and go to sleep?"

Party pooper. "All right, but can we at least get a baguette?"

She squeezes the batteries in her little hands and motions to her back. "Another time."

151

When we return to Long Island, I climb straight back between my sheets.

"What are we going to do about the prom?" Miri asks, getting into bed.

I think for a minute before I answer. "We need to raise money. And we can definitely use your help with that. So stop worrying. We'll figure something out. Now, about your feeling responsible for the entire world—"

Suddenly, we hear the door next to us open, followed by little feet scampering down the hallway, then my dad and Jennifer's bedroom door opening.

"Prissy?" my dad says. "What are you doing in here?"

"No more babies!" she declares. "From now on I'm sleeping with you. I don't want a sister."

Miri and I start laughing. After a few minutes of debating with my dad and Jennifer the merits of her staying, Prissy tires them out and wins the argument.

My eyelids feel heavy. "Let me just rest for two seconds and then we'll continue talking." I close my eyes for two seconds, but the next thing I know, the light is streaming through the blinds, Miri is at the desk making lists, and it's morning. All this globe-trotting is definitely exhausting.

"Hello?" I say, turning on the hallway light. "Mom?"

"It doesn't look like she's home," Miri says, dropping her weekend bag onto the floor.

Huh? She's always here when we get back. Always. "Maybe she's sleeping," I say. I open her door and flick on her bedroom light. Nope. Her unmade bed looks a lot like mine, covered with clothes.

"This is weird," I say. "It's eight o'clock and she's out? Did she have a date tonight? It's Sunday! She should be home to greet us." With cookies and milk and . . . Oops, been watching too many retro shows.

We decide to watch TV until she gets home. By ten Miri is asleep on the couch. "Go to bed," I say, nudging her. "I'll wait up."

I'm starting to worry. What if something happened to her? What time should I start panicking? Why hasn't she called? I try her cell phone, but it goes right to voice mail.

At ten-thirty I'm pacing. At five to eleven I'm about to start calling—well, not the police, but at least the fireman downstairs—when I finally hear my mom's key in the door.

"Hi, hon," she says, casually hanging her jacket on a hanger. She notices my scowl. "What's wrong?"

"Where," I spit out, "have you been?"

"I am so sorry," she says, unzipping a pair of stunning new leopard-skin high-heeled boots. Where did those come from? "I didn't realize how late it was."

"Next time, Mother, you call home when you're going to be late." I'm about to add that I'll have to ground her if she pulls a trick like this again.

She hangs her head. "I am really sorry, honey." She gives me a hug. "Where's your sister?"

"Asleep. It's *eleven*," I say.

She gasps. "I really didn't realize it was so late. Want to tell me about your weekend? I'll make some tea."

153

Sighing, I follow her to the kitchen and slump into a chair. "How was *your* weekend? Busy?"

"Oh, boy, yes. I went out—a lot."

"How many dates did you have?"

She smiles as she fills up the kettle. "Four."

"Four!" I didn't even know she knew four men! Who are they? "There's the fireman, Adam, Geriatric Lex . . . Who else?"

She shakes her head. "I had to reschedule with Lex. By the time he called on Friday to confirm, my weekend was booked."

I raise an eyebrow.

"I fit him into the schedule for cocktails next Saturday from five to seven." She unwraps two herbal tea bags and drops them into two chipped mugs. She picks up the wall calendar to confirm. "Yup, five to seven." The entire month is covered with red scribbles.

"Pass that to me, please." I don't believe it. There are men's names and locations written down for every night of next week. Two on Friday. Three on Saturday. Yes, three. Has my mom gone crazy? When did she become Crazy Dating Mom?

How can I get my calendar to look like hers?

154

My Mother, My Headache

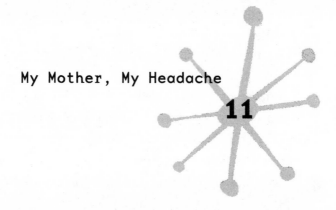

11

On our way to homeroom, Tammy stops me in the middle of the stairwell, looks around to make sure no one can hear, and whispers, "Bosh called me last night."

"What? No way."

"Way." Her eyes sparkle mischievously. "We spoke for three hours. I told him I have a boyfriend, but he wouldn't let me off the phone!"

"Tammy, what did you possibly have to discuss for that long?" I wonder how many times he said *dude* during their conversation.

"Everything. Life. Movies. The diving in France. He went with his family last year, and he's so relieved that the oil spill didn't damage any of the sea life or underwater wrecks. Can you believe that story? That the oil just disappeared? I mean, one day it was there, and the next day there's no trace of any—"

Enough with the stupid oil! "But back to Aaron," I interrupt. The results of our France adventure have been all over the news. Every possible explanation and conspiracy theory has been suggested, my favorite involving Oprah,

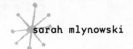

Bill Gates, and a vacuum cleaner–like submarine. "What are you going to do about Aaron?"

"Can you stop clogging the stairs?" I hear.

I look up to see Melissa glaring at us.

I roll my eyes and lead Tammy to class, to two empty seats in the back row. I wave her on to continue. "So? Your current boyfriend? Go on."

She slides into her chair and her shoulders slump. "I spoke to him, too. For two minutes. I don't think we have as much in common as I thought we did."

"What do you mean?"

"Well, he doesn't like movies, or diving. All he seems to care about is fantasy baseball. He got off the phone so he could make a trade or something."

What is it with guys and baseball? "But do you still like him?"

She hesitates. "I mean, he's a nice guy. I like him . . . but as a friend. Not like . . . you know. The stomach butterflies are gone."

"It's not fair of you to lead him on if you don't feel the same."

"I know, I know. But how can I dump someone who's sick in bed? It's too mean." Her eyebrows droop. I never noticed what expressive eyebrows she has. "When I bring over his chicken soup, do I just blurt out 'By the way, I'm dumping you'? I don't think I can do it."

She knows how to make chicken soup? Impressive.

It's four-thirty and I'm in Raf's living room.

Impossible, you scream. How can that be?

156.

Will made the shocking decision to move the soc meeting from lunch to after school at his town house in the West Village.

Obviously I had a total panic attack when he casually mentioned the development.

"I won't leave you," Tammy said, trying to reassure me, which didn't work, because it's not being alone that's making me hyperventilate. It's seeing where Raf lives. And sleeps. And eats.

Unfortunately, Raf doesn't seem to be home. Perhaps he's out gallivanting with Melissa. Or more likely, he's at Stromboli's or whatever locale the A-list has decided to make today's after-school hangout.

Besides us, the town house is empty, since Will's parents aren't home yet either. I was kind of hoping to meet them— then maybe we could cancel Friday's Get to Know Each Other Dinner, otherwise known as Sure to Be the Worst Night of My Life. What if I can't hide my true feelings for Raf? And then the entire family hates me?

Will and I are sitting on the white carpet in the center of the living room. Hotel and club brochures are spread in front of us.

"These are the only places that still have our date available," Will explains.

"Can't we change the date?" Bosh asks, on the couch with his head on Tammy's lap. Someone's moving in quick, dude.

"Unfortunately no," Will says. "The caterer is already partially paid for, and the band is all booked up. Actually, we're lucky JFK always has prom on a Thursday, because the

157

places are *mucho* more expensive on the weekend." A JFK tradition—seniors get the postprom Friday off. "Anyway," Will continues, "I think we found the right place. I just wanted you guys to run the numbers. It's called Penthouse Fifty and the room will cost us four thousand dollars. But as opposed to hotels, they'll let us bring in outside food. And there are wraparound terraces with panoramic views of the city, since it's on the fiftieth floor of a tower uptown. Kat and I thought it was cool."

Bosh nods. "Sounds good, dude."

"Fine with me," River says. "Jeffrey?"

Jeffrey peeks over from behind the couch. Where did he even come from? I swear he didn't walk over with us.

"All right," he mumbles.

We begged Amy to come too, but she just laughed at us. Way to go, head of prom.

Will calls Penthouse 50 to confirm. "We're in," he says after hanging up. "I'm going to delay giving them a deposit as long as possible. But we seriously need to come up with some fund-raising ideas. Any suggestions? We only have a few weeks. Rachel, Raf said you're like a human calculator. How much money do we have to raise to pull this off? Exactly?"

I know my heart should not be swooning, but . . . Raf still talks about me? I am so pathetic. Now, let's see. "Twenty-seven thousand five hundred was what it cost before, plus four thousand for the room. Minus the profit if we keep the ticket prices at fifty dollars a head . . ." Now I'm just showing off. You can just add four thousand to the missing ten thousand. "Fourteen thousand." Of course, if there were more cool guys like Will and Bosh, guys who date nonseniors, we'd get more kids to come to the prom. Nah. Scratch that idea. I'm looking forward to my special status.

"What do you think, Rachel?" Will asks. "Can we raise that kind of money in time?"

I cannot ruin the prom. I cannot ruin Will's reputation. I look deep into his eyes. This boy is so in love with me that he will listen to anything I say. "Yes," I answer in my most assuring voice, "we can."

"All right," he says. "Let's brainstorm."

Kat twirls her purple pen in her fingers. "Open prom up to nonseniors?" she asks hopefully.

"No way," River says. "Our class will revolt. We don't want a bunch of freshmen cramping our style."

I give him the evil eye.

"It wouldn't help," Bosh adds, head still in Tammy's lap. "We'd have to order more tables and more food, and our costs would go up."

Kat shrugs. "Sell chocolates?"

"That's a whole lot of chocolate," River says. "Why don't we have another fashion show?"

Please, no. I've barely recovered from the last one. "Car wash? That's what people in the movies always do," I say. I envision water fights and lots and lots of suds, Raf wiping a smudge of soap off my cheek, looking deep in my eyes, kissing me . . . I mean Will. Will, Will, Will.

"That's a lot of cars," Bosh says, popping my fantasy

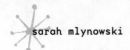

bubble, "considering most people in our school don't drive. This is Manhattan."

"We need to leverage the skills we have," River says, fingering an eyebrow piercing.

What do I have that no one else does? A sister for a witch, that's what. How can I best use Miri's magic? Maybe we can sell oranges? Maybe Miri can whip up something even better to sell, and all the money can go to the school. Like a flying broom! Okay, not that, but something more feasible. And then we can have—"An auction!"

Will lights up. "That's a great idea. We can ask people for donations. Theater tickets, gift cards, that kind of stuff. Get parents to donate."

"I bet I can get free CDs from MTV," River says.

"I work at Borders," Kat says. "Maybe they'll donate some books."

"Cool!" Will rubs his hands together like he's starting a fire. "I'll try for some leather coats. My dad's in the leather business. We can put up signs all over school asking for donations. And we can ask local businesses. I'll ask Konch if we can hold the auction after school one day so all the underclassmen can bid too. We'll even invite parents. It'll be wild."

"I like it," Kat says, "but we need some big-ticket items. We're not going to sell fourteen thousand dollars' worth of books and tattoos."

Will looks concerned.

"I can come up with a big-ticket item," I blurt out with a confidence I don't feel.

Tammy's eyebrows go nuts.

"Like what, dude?" Bosh asks.

"I—I don't want to say yet. But I have some pretty incredible resources. So don't worry," I say vaguely, and then instantly feel queasy. "Where's the restroom?"

"Up the stairs, then follow the hall to the third door on your left," Will says, and then starts writing out ideas.

I excuse myself and begin my journey down the hall. Or down the museum. Every space of wallpaper is covered in family photos of the three boys at every stage of their development. Will dressed as a pirate for Halloween. Think it's Will. Could be Raf. Or Mitch. I take another step. Raf as a five-year-old. Shock of midnight hair (in a bowl cut, ha-ha!), adorable dimple in his left cheek, big grin with missing baby teeth. Tiny plaid jacket, mini corduroy pants.

And this must be—

Raf's room. I stifle a gasp. I know it's Raf's room, because the door is open and from my position outside I can see our fat green freshman *Biology: Understanding Organisms* textbook on the desk. I wonder what the rest of his room looks like. Is he messy? Neat? Does he have any pictures up? Any photos . . . of me?

I shouldn't.

I should!

I mustn't.

I must!

I do. I take a deep breath and plunge straight into Raf's room. All my senses are overwhelmed at once. Blue paint! Boy smell! Walls of books! Silver laptop! Gray bedspread that has sailboats and . . . Raf on it!

Oh, no. Please no.

161

"Hi?" says a voice. Raf's voice.

Raf is sprawled on his stomach across his bed, writing in a notebook. I am a deer frozen in an SUV's headlights. If only I were a witch. If only I could zap myself back downstairs. Or zap myself into a fly on the wall. Or fly around the world like a superhero and turn time back three minutes. Then I could calmly find my way down the hall and not be caught in this more-painful-than-a-needle-in-the-eye situation.

Heart. R-r-racing. Calm down, calm down. "Oh, hi, Raf," I say in my most composed voice. "This isn't the bathroom."

Please tell me I didn't just say that. *Please*. Now he's associating me with a toilet. How is it possible I managed to make this impossibly bad situation worse?

He places his notebook facedown on the bedspread and arches his left eyebrow. "It's on the other side of the hall."

I begin backing out immediately.

"Rachel, hold on," he says suddenly.

I stop in my tracks. The tingles that have been rushing down my spine are already in my toes. "Um, yeah?"

He spins around so he's now sitting up against the headboard. "How's . . . you know . . . everything going?"

In life? In love? I miss you, I think before I can stop myself. I lean against the doorjamb. "Good."

"Yeah? What are you guys busy doing down there?"

"Trying to save prom."

He nods and looks at his hands. "Are you going? Did my brother ask you?"

My cheeks burn. "Yeah."

"Whatever," he says, and shrugs. Then he looks back up at me. Our eyes lock. "Have fun."

"Right," I say. "Thanks. I should get back." No! Wait! I want to stay with you!

"Can you close the door?"

I back out of the room, confused, feeling like I've been slapped. Does Raf still have feelings for me? Does he care that I'm dating Will? Why does he seem upset? He's the one who broke it off. I said yes to Will only because Raf wanted nothing to do with me.

So why do I feel like I've made the biggest mistake of my life?

"I'm just off to MOMA with Jordan," my mom declares as I walk into her room when I get home. "Finish your home- 163 work before you watch TV. And make sure Miri finishes her reading in A². She's been falling behind in her training. I left you money to order Chinese food on the kitchen table—"

Again? And who's Jordan?

Mom slaps her hand against her open mouth.

"What?"

"I forgot the laundry in the washing machine. Do you think you can— Oh, never mind."

She closes her eyes and purses her lips, and the next thing I know, a heap of our clothes is dry and folded into neat piles on her bed.

All the folding and sorting I've done over the years be-comes a distant cruel memory.

"How do I look?" she asks, twirling. She's wearing chocolate-colored pants (new), a white blouse (new), and her heart-shaped necklace.

"Gorge. Have fun," I say, and kiss her on the forehead.

She takes off in a flutter, and I try to block out my Raf-induced confusion and focus on the task at hand—figuring out what I'm going to auction off. I find Miri at her desk. "I'm really busy," she says without looking up. "Did you hear about the bushfires in California? What are we going to do?"

"Not much," I say, lying down in my usual position, my feet propped up on her wall. "Can we take a few secs to discuss the prom debacle?"

She closes her notebook and turns to face me. "Go ahead."

"So it seems that alumni have donated most of the money to repair the school, right? But since this whole screwup is partially your fault, I still need your help. Like you promised. To raise prom money instead. And we're having an auction. So I need you to poof up something that I can donate. Something that we can sell. Something cool and expensive."

"Such as?"

"I don't know. What can you whip up? Let's brainstorm."

She heaves a sigh, then opens her notebook to a clean page. "What do teenagers want?"

No more acne, no more rules. "To be older."

"Not sure I can do that." She scratches her nose with the wrong side of her pen and draws a blue line across the bridge. I try not to laugh; I don't want to interrupt the flow of this brainstorming session. "What about a trip some-where?" she suggests.

"How would we do that? Fly the person plus guest there on your broomstick?"

"Ha-ha. Maybe I could zap up some airline tickets to Cancun."

"Yeah? That sounds more like computer hacking than witchcraft." I take her pillow and balance it on my feet.

"Can you stop? I sleep on that, you know."

"It helps me think. Maybe we could get Mom to help."

"Are you kidding? She's way too busy lately."

"No kidding. She needs a clone of herself just to meet all these guys. Hey, that would be cool. Can you make clones?" I would get mine to go to school for me. What would her name be? I think of London and grimace. Definitely not Rochelle.

"I don't think so."

"An iPod?" I could really use one. I kick the pillow over to Miri and she catches it in her lap.

"A laptop?" She tosses back the pillow.

"A TV?" I kick it right back to her, like we're playing hot potato.

She throws it right back. "A flat-screen TV? Lots of flat-screen TVs!"

I catch it with my hands and then lie down on it. "Per-fect! A fancy TV will get us at least a few grand. We poof one up, then use the multiplying spell, and presto, the prom is saved! Is there a spell for TVs?"

"I doubt it, no. But I have a ton of stuff to do this week.

165

I'm going to try that cleaning spell on the Hudson River, and maybe the Mississippi. So let's make Saturday spell day. And we'll figure it all out."

"Perfect! I have nothing to do Saturday anyway. Will is working and Tammy is babysitting Aaron." I realize how selfish that sounds. Here I am asking Miri for a favor and expecting her to fit it into my schedule. Still, there's no reason we can't be efficient with our time, is there? And as far as the prom is concerned, time is of the essence!

"I thought she didn't like him anymore."

"She likes him as a friend, but that's it. But because he has mono, she feels too guilty to break up with him." I really shouldn't gossip with Miri so much about my friends. She never tells me anything about hers. Hmm, I'm not sure she has any. "So Saturday will be a sister day. Maybe we can watch a movie on the new TV!" Maybe I should stay home and watch TV on Friday, too, instead of going out with Will and Raf. How can I deal with both—correction: *all*—the Kosravi brothers simultaneously?

I need a clone. Rochelle, where art thou?

"Oh, will you do me one more favor?" I ask. "I need you to extend the love spell on the glove."

"Extend?" Miri says, shaking her head. "You can't renew a love spell. It isn't a library book, you know."

"What?" I scream. "Are you kidding me?" What am I going to do? Will's feelings for me are going to wear off and I'll be left with nothing! Unless Raf starts to like me again . . . Yeah, right. It looks like I've lost Raf for good.

Miri leans back in her chair again, laughing hysterically. "I'm just kidding. Of course I can do it again. You can sleep on it tonight. Wow, you should have seen the look on your face. It was so funny."

Hilarious.

Operation Save the Prom, aka the Auction, has been approved by the principal and scheduled for Monday, May 24, which is only three days before the prom.

I'm in the school bathroom trying to get the no-touch auto-dryer to work when Jewel and Melissa saunter in. They start flicking their hair excessively when they see me.

"Hi, Rachel," Jewel says, catching my eye in the mirror. I feel the familiar tug of my heart. We used to be best friends. Before she joined the dark side.

"Hey," I respond, and stop waving my hands like a weirdo. I wipe my hands on my new fabo jeans. This room is too small for the three of us.

"So, Rachel," Melissa says, sliding up next to me. She reapplies her lipstick. "Looking forward to dinner tonight? Patsy's is my fave. Love that white pizza."

What?

Not only do I have to deal with my boyfriend, my quasi ex-boyfriend and love of my life, and their parents, I also have to deal with my archenemy? Are Melissa and Raf *that* serious? Are they a full-fledged couple? Maybe I'll stab her with the pizza slicer. Maybe I'll stab myself. Waiting for hours in the ER waiting room has got to be better than enduring an entire evening at the restaurant, as fave as it is. (And I know about waiting for hours in an ER. A person has to be run over by a steamroller before a doctor will see her.

167

When I was five I got my finger caught in the car door, and I had to wait six hours before someone finally came out from somewhere in back, and then all he gave me was one lousy stitch and a lollipop.)

Melissa's green eyes are twinkling with evil.

You know what? I'm not going to take her intimidation any longer. She should be nicer to me; I'm practically her sister-in-law. So what if Raf and Melissa are an item? It doesn't matter. Raf doesn't want me? Well, I don't want him. I'm dating someone older and wiser. Someone who *wants* to date me. Fine, maybe his feelings are a bit enchanted, but that's irrelevant. I have a boyfriend. Raf is history. "I am," I say in my loudest, bring-it-on voice. I stretch myself up to my full five foot one. "See ya." With that, I exit the bathroom.

Not my best closing line, but at least this time I didn't trip over a bike rack.

168

It's Friday night, and once again my mom and I are acting like wound-up toy cars, running all over the apartment. She's in a bathrobe, blow-drying her long, perfectly blond hair, as I struggle to find the right outfit for my potential night from hell.

When the buzzer goes off, I kiss Miri on the forehead and go into my mom's room to say good-bye. "Have fun tonight!" I say over the sound of the blow-dryer.

She's tilted upside down and smiling, so it looks like she's frowning. "You too! Where are you going?"

It smells like smoke in here. That had better be her hair burning and not a cigarette. "Patsy's!" I say.

"What?"

"Patsy's!"

"Barbequing? Have fun! Can you open the . . ." The blow-dryer drowns out her words.

"What? I can't hear you."

"Never mind!" she says, and with a purse of her lips, she opens her bedroom window with a bang.

I grab my purse and I'm out the door.

This is a disaster.

No, really. I know I've called things disasters before, but this qualifies as an eleven on the Richter scale. Here is the seating arrangement at our round table: Will is on my left. Next to him is Mitch. Next to Mitch is Louise, his girlfriend. Next to her is Mr. Kosravi ("Call me Don, sweetie," he says). Next to Don is Mrs. Kosravi (who keeps giving me the evil eye, most likely for ditching her baby boy and then promptly taking up with her middle child). Next to Mrs. Kosravi is Melissa. Which means guess who's sitting to my right? (Drumroll, please.)

Raf.

How did this happen? It was like a game of musical chairs gone wrong. And now anytime Raf or Will moves his legs, his shoes accidentally bump against mine and shock waves go through my body. My left foot—Will. Right foot—Raf. My brain sensors are in overdrive. And Melissa is

169

ignoring me entirely, laughing and joking with Mrs. Kosravi (she calls her Isabel) and Louise. Melissa's parents, Louise's parents, and the Kosravis go way back. How quaint.

Isabel and Louise let out peals of laughter and my back stiffens. Who knew Melissa had anything funny to say? I stare into my plate of Caesar salad.

Okay, it's not *all* a disaster. The fried calamari is pretty awesome. And the truth is listening to the three boys tease and joke with one another is pretty adorable.

"Do you wanna play some ball tomorrow?" Mitch asks Will. Mitch is, not surprisingly, as hot as his younger brothers. The three of them all have the same sexy dark hair, dark eyes, and lean athletic bodies. Mitch's hair is the longest, his face the most angular. Will's hair is the shortest and I think he's the tallest. Raf has the widest smile. And a curl to his hair that the others don't have.

"I can't," Will says. "Unlike you, I have a job on Saturdays."

He is so responsible, my boyfriend. How many eighteen-year-old boys work just to be independent?

"Why do you work so hard?" Mitch asks.

Raf rips a roll in half and dips it into his bean soup. "It's called money. You know, that green stuff you keep milking from Mom and Dad?"

Funny. Fine. But *he* doesn't have a job. So there.

But he does have a drop of soup on the corner of his mouth. He licks it off. Must stop staring at Raf's lips. Must stare at Will's instead.

"You're a comedian, Lobes!" Mitch reaches clear across

the table and tugs on Raf's ear. "Doesn't he have the floppiest ears? Raf, does your girlfriend give you mooshies?"

Me? What? Oh, right. I'm *Will's* girlfriend.

Raf squirms and turns a deep shade of red.

Melissa stops her conversation to beam a smile across the table, as if she's accepting an award. The Snob of the Year Award.

"You should have seen him when he was younger," Mitch says. "He had the biggest ears in the world. Dumbo ears. Will and I used to tape them to the back of his head. We still think you should have had that surgery." He polishes off the remainder of his salad.

"He was freaky looking," Will says teasingly.

"Lucky he grew up to look more normal," Mitch says. "More like us than Dumbo."

Raf winks at Melissa. "If I looked like either of them, I'd never leave my room."

Why doesn't he wink at me?

"Oh, tough love from Lobes!" Will says, and laughs.

I give Will a wink. He winks back. Ha!

"What's a mooshie?" annoying Melissa asks.

"Pulling his earlobe," Will explains. "Go ahead, try it."

Raf is still blushing, but he's smiling, too. Adorably. And the little-brother thing is so cute.

Not cute! Not cute!

Melissa pulls on his earlobe and the entire table cracks up. "Very soft," she says.

The waiter comes to clean off the table, interrupting the love fest and saving me from intense stabs of jealousy.

171

"Any news on the Columbia scholarship?" Don asks Will.

"What scholarship?" I ask.

"No big deal," Will says dismissively. "The political science department is considering giving me entrance money. Nothing major—just some money for books."

My boyfriend is modest, too! Take that, Raf. And political science! My boyfriend probably wants to be president—which means, one day, I could be the first lady. If I kept the spell up that long, which I wouldn't, of course. But he might have fallen so deeply in love with me by prom that even without the spell he will still adore me—and I him—and we'll live happily ever after, or something like that. That is so cool. *So cool.* I would make the best first lady ever! I could wear tailored suits and say, "Air Force One, fly me to Bermuda!" And I'll have bodyguards. And, of course, do lots of charity work and stuff. Fix health care and social security . . . Would I have to cut my hair short? All the first ladies have Grandma Hair. I wonder if that's a requirement. I could always cut it and then grow it out as soon as he's elected. First lady for thirty seconds and I'm already shirking my duties.

Anyway.

"I should have gotten a scholarship to NYU," Mitch says.

"For what?" Will asks.

Mitch grins. "My good looks?"

The whole table groans. "I think your head might need its own chair. It's getting fat," Raf says, smirking.

I stifle a laugh.

"I thought the youngest one was supposed to be the ham," Melissa says.

Isabel smiles at her three sons. "Not mine. My baby is the introvert. My oldest can't stop talking, and my middle one is on a quest to run the world."

Melissa touches Raf's hand. "Raf? Are you going to run for student council president too?"

He shakes his head. "Not interested."

"Really?" Her face drops in disappointment. Someone wants access to the soc lounge. "You'd be so good at it."

"I doubt it. I can't suck up to so many people."

"Hey!" Will says, obviously offended. "I didn't suck up to anyone."

"Kidding, kidding."

How rude. "If you're such an introvert," I blurt out, "why did you try out for the fashion show?"

173

Our eyes lock. "I didn't," he says. "Will signed me up."

"I knew it would be good for you," Will says. "You needed to make friends besides T. S. Eliot and Dylan Thomas."

Oh. I tear my eyes away from Raf and smile at Will. How sweet is he? Worrying about his little brother.

"Are you going to be in the show again next year?" Melissa asks Raf.

He shrugs. "Maybe."

"And what about you, Rachel?" Melissa asks, the evil glint back in her eyes. "Are you going to try out for the show again too?"

"I might," I say, and pick up my glass of water. Maybe I should dump it on her. How could Raf like someone so awful? It shows poor character. Will is definitely the better brother.

"Mom," Mitch is saying, "will you sew on my camp labels for me?"

Camp? What camp?

She nods and takes a sip of wine. "Sure, dear. Bring over whatever you want labeled."

"Don't you think twenty-one is time to get a real summer job? Or at least sew your own name on your T-shirts?" says Will.

Isabel smiles patiently. "Oh, come on now. There's nothing wrong with a little help from Mom. I'm helping Raf with his camp labels again this year. And I'm happy to help you, too, Will."

The tips of Raf's floppy ears turn pink. I resist the urge to give him a mooshie.

"I didn't know you worked at a camp!" I say to Will. I've never understood what the appeal is. Tents? Mosquitoes? Forced swimming lessons? Not my cup of tea. If my parents had been inclined to send me somewhere for the summer, I would have opted for Club Med.

"Yup. Wood Lake. It's up in the Adirondacks. Didn't I tell you I was going back this summer? My *last* summer," he says to Mitch.

"You're just jealous of all the power I'm going to have as a section head," Mitch says.

"I can't believe they're making you the boss of anything." Will makes a face at his brother and puts his arm around my shoulders. "Rachel, what are you doing this summer? Why don't you come too?"

I almost spit out my water. "No thanks, camp's not for me." As much as I like Will, I'm too much of a city girl.

Raf nods. "I can't really see you there," he says.

Excuse me? I stew silently. How dare he comment on my camp potential!

"May I take that plate?" asks the waitress, and our pies are suddenly in front of us. Who does Raf think he is? From now on, I'm all about Will. Raf who?

After Don pays the check (Will tries to pay for our share, but his dad laughs him off), Melissa suggests that the six of us go to a movie.

"I've already seen it," I say quickly. This painful night must end. I've never felt more confused. I can't stop thinking about Raf.

Melissa laughs snarkily. "We haven't decided on one yet."

"I've seen a lot of movies lately. And it's already ten-fifteen, and I told my mom I'd be home by twelve. Maybe another time."

We push our chairs back and head toward the door in a single line. And that's when I can't help staring at the world's best cleavage.

I don't often stare at cleavage. But the woman's dress is so low cut and her cleavage is literally spilling over and—

That silver heart necklace looks familiar. That neck looks familiar. That chin. That face. Oh. My. God. It's my mother. My eyes whip back down to her cleavage. That is not my mother's cleavage. Well, it wasn't my mom's

175

cleavage yesterday. My mother is sitting at a table for two, wearing a low-cut black dress I've never seen before, chewing on a piece of crust. Across from her is Adam.

Mitch bumps into me from behind because I've stopped short. He follows my line of vision. "Sweet," he says, and then whistles, which causes my mom to look up.

At first she smiles, but then awareness washes over her face and her cheeks drain of color. She folds her arms across her chest. Too late! Then she pretends she didn't see me and looks back at her date.

My mouth opens but no sound comes out. Did the woman who gave birth to me just ignore me? "Mom?"

She doesn't look up. Is this not my mother? Maybe my mom has a doppelganger too.

The woman bites her thumbnail. Oh, it's my mother all right. "Mom?"

She looks up, feigning surprise. "Well, hello there!" Is she kidding me? "Adam, you remember my daughter Rachel."

"Nice to see you again," I say weakly.

"I thought Rachel just called you," Adam says, looking confused.

"Did I say that?" my mom asks. "I meant Miri. I'm always doing that. It's *Miri* who needs me to come straight home after dinner."

Huh? What? "There's nothing wrong with Miri. When we left she was—"

My mom gives me a please-shut-up look and I realize that she used my suggested make-your-cell-phone-ring-magically-when-you're-bored trick. And I just totally busted her. Oops.

"That's your mom?" Mitch says, poking his head over my shoulder. "Nice."

Will, who's already a few tables ahead, comes back. "Hi, Mrs. Graff. We were thinking of going to a movie. Is it cool if Rachel's home a little later tonight?"

I try to shake my head without actually shaking it. Why can't I project my thoughts? Why why why?

"Of course, Will!" she says with a great big smile, obviously thinking she's doing me some sort of favor. "And I told you to call me Carol."

Will takes my hand and squeezes. "Thanks."

"Terrific," I mutter, giving her and her breasts the evil eye all the way out the door. I wanted a friend for a mother. When am I going to learn to be careful what I wish for? **177**

It's One A.M. Do You Know Where Your Mother Is? 12

Miri's light is still on, so I pound on her door. "You up?"

No answer. I open the door to find her room empty. Where in the world is she? Oh, no. She might actually *be* anywhere in the world.

I'm about to panic when there's a blast of cold and light, and a soaking-wet Miri materializes in the middle of her room. "Hi," she says, blinking furiously, startled to see me. "When did you get home?"

"Two minutes ago. Where *were* you?"

"Arkansas. De-polluting the Mississippi. How was your night?"

"Lame." I could not concentrate on the movie. First of all, it was one of those action extravaganzas consisting of seven car chases, one after the other, which made me dizzy. My larger problem was that we were all sharing one super-sized popcorn, which Raf was in charge of. So even though I wanted nothing more than a handful of buttery delicious-ness, I couldn't exactly reach my hand into my ex's lap. How would it have looked?

Melissa was giggling and whispering to Raf the whole

time, which I found annoying and infuriating. How could a guy who liked me like her? But the most distracting part was Will's fingers, which were drawing circles in my palm. See, I'm so over Raf. Will is just amazing. Smart, handsome, ambitious. A senior. What more could I want in a boyfriend?

Miri strips out of her wet clothes and leaves them in a lump by her door.

I cover my eyes. "Mom isn't home yet, is she? I ran into her at the restaurant. Can you say *embarrassing?*"

"Nope, she's still not back." We both silently mull this over.

I sit down on her desk. "Do you think she's gone a wee bit off the deep end? She used magic to do laundry."

Miri sighs. "Yesterday she pretended she made those Mexican tofu tacos from scratch. But I so saw her zap them up."

"What is up with her?"

"She's been acting weird ever since Dad got married. Dating, letting me do magic. And then you convinced her to use a spell or two. Or a million. And I found an empty pack of cigarettes in her room. On top of everything, she's smoking again."

She has gone a bit overboard. My mother obviously doesn't know the meaning of moderation. Speaking of which, the waistband of my pants is digging into my stomach. I ate too much pizza. And tiramisu. And Will's licorice at the theater. Good thing I didn't partake in that popcorn; I wouldn't be able to breathe. A yawn escapes my lips.

"You look exhausted," Miri says. "Why don't you go to sleep?"

"I will. What about you?"

"I just have one more spell to find tonight. The bushfires are seriously endangering lives in California," she says. "Remember last year? How many people were hurt? I need to stop them now."

I pat down her soggy and tangled hair. "Moderation? Hello?"

She gives a small shrug. "At least I know where I get it from."

"Ready to work?" asks my irritating sister as she yanks the covers off my half-asleep body. This is known in our apartment as the Wake Up by Freezing Technique. She discovered it way back when she was three and has been using it to torture me ever since. I mumble a very bad word into my pillow.

"We have lots to do today!" she sings.

I pull the covers back over my head. "Come back later. Go bother Mom."

"Get with the program, deary. Mom is already long gone on today's breakfast date. And from there she goes straight to her lunch date. It's just you and me. All day."

I groan. Think fast. "I have to—"

"Don't go making things up."

I roll into a sitting position. "What are your plans for us, precisely?"

"First we're making a TV for your auction. Then we're making rain in California."

Sounds fair. "One project for me and one for you?"

"If you mean one for the pathetic prom and one for the betterment of humankind, then yes."

After a shower and a bowl of cereal, I'm ready to work. I sit myself down on her desk, swinging my legs. "Zap it up, baby. Give me a whopper of a TV."

She pushes me off her notebook. "I found the perfect spell. It's called the incarnate spell."

"Creepy sounding. How does it work?"

"We need a picture of what we want to create, a half cup of broken mirror, a half cup of crushed peanuts, and two cups of dirt."

"I can find that."

"Good," she says. "Go to it while I work on the rain spell."

My first stop is the apartment building's mail room off the lobby downstairs. There I search through the recycling bin for one of the millions of flyers and catalogs that get tossed out daily. Win a Million Dollars! Yeah, right. Free CDs! Sure. Carpet Cleaning! No, thanks. Circuit City electronics! Ding, ding, ding, we have a winner! I carry the catalog back upstairs, plop myself onto the couch, and search for the perfect TV. Hmm. There are an awful lot of terms that sound like a foreign language. Like plasma. Composite video. S-Video. Aspect ratio. And many acronyms that I don't know the meanings of. Like LCD. HDTV Non-CRT. RGB+H/V. How about T.I.V.C? This. Is. Very. Confusing.

"Miri, what kind of TV should I chose?" I scream.

"Busy saving California!"

I flip and flip and flip through pages. Finally, I find a TV

181

I like: 50" HDTV Plasma Display Wide-screen. It looks larger than our apartment. Possibly the size of Times Square.

I like this one the best because the image on the screen is a scene from *The Sound of Music*, and most of the others feature football. In the picture, Maria (aka Julie Andrews) is sitting on the green grass with her guitar, singing to the dressed-in-curtains von Trapp children. I love that part! This must be a good omen. And the blue of the Austrian mountains and the green of the grass are quite vivid; I bet this TV is top-of-the-line. "Doe, a deer, a female deer," I sing happily. "Ray, a drop of golden sun. Tee, a television, I found myself"—ha-ha—"far . . ."—hold the note, you can do it!—"a long, long way to run . . ." I run, giggling, into my sister's room. "Found it!" I say, shoving the catalog under her nose. "You like?"

182

"Well done. Now find the other ingredients."

No fun. "How do you solve a problem like my Miri-a?" I sing all the way back to the couch. Next! A half cup of broken mirror. That sounds sketchy. Am I supposed to break a mirror? Won't that give me lots of bad luck? "Miiiiiiiiiiiiiiirrrrrriiiiiiiii?"

"I'm wooooooooooorking. Figure it out!"

What is luck, anyway? I bet my mom has a hand mirror somewhere. Ten minutes and a large mess later, I find a small one under the sink. Now, where best to break it?

Kitchen table? Nah, don't want to eat glass shards by mistake. Bathtub? Don't want to bathe in them either. Hmm. I'd better do it out in the hallway. (Though if anyone comes off the elevator as I'm in midshatter, they might have me arrested; is this vandalism?) I lay out the remaining catalog papers on the floor and place the mirror on top. I'm about to give it a good heeling when I realize I'm not wearing shoes. Brilliant. Back inside I go.

Oops. A key would be so helpful. Ring. Ring. *Ring! A drop of golden sound* . . .

Miri opens the door, scowling.

"Sorry. Just need a shoe. And a key. Wanna watch me break the mirror?"

She hands me a pink sneaker and grumbles, "Fine."

"Not that shoe. Give me one of Mom's." She hands me a high heel (another new shoe? Mom is unbelievable), and I slip it on. Very nice. I should wear these things more often. They're so glam. "Ready? Set . . . go!" I smash my foot down. Crunch. "Yay! See? I have everything under control; no need to give me that look." I bend over to pick up the large shards. Oh. "Can you pass me something to put these pieces in too?"

By three o'clock, I have collected all the necessary ingredients. "Operation Wide-screen TV for the Auction, known in TV lingo as OWSTVA, is primed and ready to be turned on. Tuned in. Booted. Energized. Channeled . . ."

"Can you stop with the bad TV puns, please?" Miri begs as she dumps the soil I harvested from the dead kitchen plant into the cauldron.

"But it's fun. Try it. Are you ready for prime time?"

She throws a peanut at my arm. "Why don't you help?"

I sit cross-legged next to her. Tigger rubs his face against my knee. "What should I do?"

"Crush the peanuts, shred the image, and mix 'em together with the mirror pieces. Then plant that concoction like a seed in the earth. Then I'll add water, say the spell, and wait for the TV to grow. And can you take Tigger out so he won't attack our TV tree?"

Wow. "That is the coolest spell I have ever heard. Will it grow *anything?*"

"I guess."

The possibilities are endless. Where to start? What are my favorite things? *Raindrops on roses?* I lift Tigger up and try to carry him out. He tries to scrape my chin with his need-to-be-cut claws. *Whiskers on kittens?* Those I can do without. "Can I have a new prom dress?"

"Can't you wear the dress you bought for Spring Fling?"

Duh. "It's not fancy enough."

184

"Why don't we raise money for the prom first and then worry about what to wear to it?"

I drop Tigger outside, slam the door shut before he can sneak back in, stick out my tongue at Miri, and start crushing peanuts. This is going to be so awesome, as long as we don't somehow screw it up, which I'm sure we won't. The spell seems pretty straightforward. What could go wrong? I'm about to give the page a solid rip in half when I freeze. If the spell creates whatever is in the image, I should check what's on the back! I am so clever that it kills me. I flip the image over to find a picture of a man's hand holding a remote. Good save, Rachel! Imagine if we grew someone's hand! And what if it attacked us? Strangled us? Tickled us? "I'm going to color this hand in with black marker, to avoid conjuring up severed body parts."

Miri giggles. "Nice catch."

Nice catch, indeed. What would she do without me? I find a permanent marker in the kitchen, and then as well as getting ink all over my fingers, I manage to cover up the hand. "Let's do it," I say. I rip up the image, drop the pieces into a plastic bowl, and add the shards of broken mirror. Then I crush the peanuts with a tablespoon and add them to the bowl. Using the same spoon I mixed the stuff with, I scoop up the mixture and dump it into the cauldron of earth.

"*A mirror's reflection*
For your own detection
Planted in the depths of the earth
Solidify, congeal to a birth."

Miri sprinkles a few drops of water on top and I feel the familiar rush of cold.

Yes! Wide-screen TV! When we do the multiplying spell, I'm so keeping one for us. "Hey, why don't you split the lump into two so we can have one for the living room?"

She considers the idea, then shakes her head. "What if that only makes half a TV? Or two twenty-five-inch ones instead of a fifty?" She carries the bowl to my room, places it carefully on the floor under my window, and opens the blinds. "It needs sunlight," she explains. "And I think we should let it grow here, because your room is bigger."

Yeah, sure. She's trying to avoid a repeat performance of what happened with the oranges. Her room still smells. "Never mind," I say. "One will do." For now. I poke the cauldron with my big toe. "How long does it take to grow?"

"Two moons. Forty-eight hours."

"Then on to the next spell!" I wiggle my fingers in the air. "Rain, rain, go away, come again some other day."

"Rachel, we're trying to create rain in California, not banish it. And we have to concentrate. This one's hard. It's a five-broomer."

Rolling up my sleeves, I follow her back to her room. I'm ready to rumble. "What do we need?"

Miri flips to her sticky note in A^2. "A glass of water, pepper, and a pot. As soon as the water starts to boil, we say the spell."

That's it? Puh-lease. "No problemo. That's all it takes to make it rain? We could do that one with our eyes closed."

"Except we have to do the spell in California. We'll have to build a bonfire."

"I'm bringing marshmallows!"

Miri frowns. "At least we won't be taking a toaster oven for you to burn down the entire state."

I hoist myself onto her back. "Where exactly are we going in California? Can we go to Rodeo Drive? Wait! Let's go to the Kodak Theatre."

"Where?"

"Where the Oscars are! Maybe we'll see a star!"

"Can you be quiet?"

Humph. I cling to Miri as she does her stuff, and the next thing I know, we're in—

The sky is blue. The air is hot. And I smack my elbow against a red minivan. Are we in a parking lot? "Where are we?"

"Disneyland," Miri says sheepishly. "It was the only place I could think of in California."

"We couldn't go to Rodeo Drive, but we could come here?"

"It has to be something I can picture!"

"But how are we going to light a fire in a parking lot?"

"We'll have to find an empty spot. I brought along a reflective shield we can use so no one can see us."

We walk around aimlessly until we find the most deserted area. Miri pulls a newspaper out of her bag, shreds it up, and lights it with a match. When the flame catches, she fills the pot with the glass of water and pepper, puts on an oven mitt, and holds the pot by the handle over the flames.

Her technique concerns me on many levels. "Let me hold it," I say, grabbing it from her and holding it far above the flames. "Put up the shield!"

She reaches into her bag, then pulls out and opens what appears to be an umbrella. An enchanted one, I'd guess. Four seconds pass. Miri stands on tiptoe to peer into the pot. "Is it boiling yet?"

I don't see any bubbles. "Nope."

Thirty seconds pass. "Now?"

"Nope."

Twenty seconds. "Now?" she asks, exasperated.

"Miri, if you keep asking, it won't boil."

"That makes no sense. It's going to boil regardless. And I have to say the spell at the sign of the first bubble."

"Get ready," I say, watching the water. "I think it's about to pop."

She jumps closer, picks up the book, and recites the spell:

"*Sweet expansive sky,*

Dress yourself in clouds that cry.
Let the heavens shower a tear,
Over yonder by and near."

Cold blows against my cheeks. Yes! "I felt it; it must have worked."

She peers into the blue sky. "But I don't see any clouds."

"It probably takes a few minutes."

"But most of the weather spells work immediately," she says. "We should have brought those marshmallows to pass the time."

"Whoops. But I have a better plan. Let's go on Space Mountain! By the time we're done, it'll be pouring."

"Well . . ." She hesitates. "Okay. Since we're here."

Wahoo! "Can you zap us to the front of the line?"

Miri shrugs. "I can try."

188

Two Space Mountains, three Mad Tea Parties, and one Big Thunder Mountain later, it still hasn't rained, so we decide to monitor the weather from home.

While I study for a bio test, Miri writes an English essay, taking breaks every few minutes to check AccuWeather. But so far—nothing. The sun is proudly beating over California, fully mocking us.

"I hope I didn't mess anything up," she says nervously. "It *was* a five-broomer. Maybe it sent the rain somewhere else?"

I open the blinds. It's a gorgeous day. "It's not raining here, either."

"I have to pee," Miri says, and disappears into the bathroom.

"I'm going to check on the wide-screen!" Unfortunately,

the cauldron of dirt and broken glass hasn't morphed into an electric appliance yet. "Nothing?" Miri asks when she joins me.

"Nope. Now I have to pee."

"Me too," Miri says.

"You just went!"

"I didn't get it all out." We size each other up and then race to the bathroom. Luckily, because I'm taller and therefore have longer legs, I make it there first.

I don't notice the hot steam until I'm sitting on the toilet. The shower sounds like it's on full blast. Did I leave it on? Is my mom inside? "Hello?" I squeak.

No answer.

I pee quickly, wipe, flush, and open the flowery shower curtain.

The water is on with no one in the stall. Weird. I must have left it on by accident. Ouch, it's hot.

189

I reach to turn it off and attempt to revolve the handles. And attempt.

Hmm. The water is off. But then . . . why is it on? "Did you do something to the shower?" I yell.

She pounds on the door. "Don't shower! You are so mean. I said I had to pee again so you take a shower? What do you want me to do, pee in the sink?"

A splash of hot water scalds my hand. Ouch. I unlock the door. "I'm not showering, you doofus. The water is stuck. Did you not notice how hot it was in here?" How can someone with so much power be so clueless?

"Are you sure?" She pushes me out of the way and proceeds to burn herself on the handle. "Owwww. The shower is busted."

No kidding. *Let the heavens shower a tear* . . . Oh, man. "I think the spell worked. It just took the word *shower* literally."

Miri's fingers go straight into her mouth. "Uh-oh. I knew it was a tricky one. I can't believe I screwed it up! What do we do? We're going to use up all the hot water in the building!"

"Call the super?" I suggest.

"What for? It's not like he can fix it."

It's getting seriously steamy in here. "Do you have any clothes you want de-wrinkled?"

"Very funny."

"Rain, rain, go away, come again some other day?"

She sits on the closed toilet lid and rests her head in her hands. "I don't think that will work."

"I thought you had to pee."

190

"It got scared away." She looks at me miserably. "Maybe we should just let the water run out. It isn't going to rain forever, right?"

"Can't you do a spell reversal?"

"Perhaps, but I told you, it's a five-broomer. Plus I don't have any of the materials. . . . I guess I can if I have to."

"Let's give it a few minutes. Eventually the sun comes out again." It feels like the sun is beaming in here right now, it's so hot. "I have to get out of this room; I'm sweating up a storm."

I close the door behind us. "What do we do now? More homework?"

"I guess."

We open our respective assignments and take our respective places (me on Miri's bed, Miri at her desk) and are about to dig in when Miri sprints back to the bathroom.

"Still running," she says, sitting back in her desk chair. "Or raining."

The downstairs buzzer goes off. Miri jumps up again. "Expecting anyone?"

"Nope."

We both approach the buzzer. "Hello?" she says.

"Hi! It's Lex! I'm here to pick up Carol."

Too bad Carol is MIA (Mom in Absentia). And it's not like Lex has time to waste. He's already, like, a hundred.

"What do we do?" Miri whispers.

"Why are you whispering? He can't hear you. Audible range lowers with age. And you're not pressing the buzzer. Call Mom. I'll buzz him up."

"Hi, Lex!" I say a few seconds later, opening the door.

He's holding a bouquet of daisies. "For you and Miri."

"Thank you!" As I gather the flowers from his arms (second bouquet in less than a month! New record!), I notice that he has nice hands. Long fingers, filed nails. Big palms. I would have expected them to be old and wrinkled, but they're not. Last year I bought my dad leather gloves for his birthday. When he put them on, he was swimming in them. They were at least two sizes too big on him, but on Lex? I bet they would have fit like a glove. Oh, yeah, they *are* gloves. Lex is taller than I remembered too. Although maybe his cowboy hat gives him an extra few inches.

"So how've you been, Rachel?" He gives me a warm smile. "How's school?"

"Great, thanks." My sister and I destroyed the gym, but now I'm dating the soc president, so all is good. "And you?"

"It's been a busy few weeks. Baseball tourism kicks up again in the spring, so I've been leading a whole lot of tours."

Miri returns from the phone call and crosses her arms in front of her chest. "She's not answering," she says, ignoring Lex.

He gives her the same warm smile and tips his hat. "You must be Miri."

She rolls her eyes. "Brilliant assumption."

Terrif. My mom's not answering, so I have to dump Lex for her. I've never dumped a guy myself, so how am I supposed to dump one for someone else? I rack my brains for the excuses I've heard in the movies. It's not you, it's me. Can we be friends? It's not a good time emotionally for me right now.

Not that my mom deserves my creative excuse-making. Forget her; I'll just be honest. "We don't know where my mother is," I explain. "I don't know what to tell you. She could be on her way home. You're welcome to come in and wait."

Lex's brow wrinkles in concern. "Did she have to go into the office this morning?"

Yeah, right. The office of love. "I think so," I say instead.

"I can hang out." He looks from Miri to me. "As long as you two don't mind."

"Not at all." My heart sinks in sympathy. He brings us flowers and my mom can't even bother to show up? "Can I get you something to drink?"

He removes his shoes, lines them up, hangs his hat on the coatrack, and follows me into the living room. "Water would be terrific."

That's something we have lots of. Lots and lots and lots of. Would he like it boiling? As I'm fetching a glass, I hear, "Is it all right if I use the bathroom?"

"Of course," I say over the running water in the sink. As soon as the words leave my lips, I realize my mistake. "Wait!" I scream. Too late.

The door is open and the steam is rushing out. "Is someone inside?" he asks, obviously confused.

I'm about to say "Miri" when she appears next to me.

We're putting in a spa? Trying ashtanga yoga? "Shower's broken."

He squints into the haze of steam. "Do you want me to take a look at it?"

That could be a recipe for disaster. On the other hand, "Why not?"

He steps inside, and his face is immediately dripping with sweat. I hope he's not too old for this type of activity. A heart attack would be very bad. I don't even know CPR. But I have always wanted to learn it. I've also always wanted to learn the Heimlich maneuver. I once saw a woman pop a chicken bone right out of a man's constricted throat. I bet Miri would be up for that since she's so into lifesaving these days. "Mir," I start, but then stop myself. Maybe this is not the time.

Miri is hitting me in the thigh with the back of her hand. "What if he realizes that the shower is cursed?" she mouths.

193

I wave her away and step into the bathroom after Lex. Come on. It's not like he's going to make that leap. Shower's broken, one of these girls must be a witch!

"Just watch him, please," Miri grumbles, and returns to her room.

"This is odd," he mumbles from somewhere in the steam. "I'm going to try taking apart the valve handle. If that doesn't work, I'll try the water source in the basement. Do you have a wrench?"

Blink, blink.

He laughs. "Where's your toolbox?"

That we have. Somewhere. I return a few minutes later and carry the toolbox into the sweatbox. "You know what you're doing?"

"Yup. Don't worry about me."

194

"Don't burn yourself." We don't want a lawsuit on our hands.

"The hot ran out. It's just cold water now, which makes it easier."

"Good." I'm sure everyone preparing for Saturday evening plans appreciates it.

"So what are you up to? Entertain me with stories while I fix this."

"We're having an auction to raise money for the prom. My boyfriend is the president of our student council . . ." I go on and on, and he actually seems interested, nodding and asking questions. After ten minutes his shirt is totally damp and what's left of his gray hair is all wet.

"This should do it," he says as he makes one quick turn of the screwdriver. And then, the water stops coming.

Oh. My. God. He's like a magician. Okay, not exactly, since his skills have successfully reversed magic, not provided more, but still. Wow. "Thank you so much," I say, quite amazed. "Miri! He did it!"

Miri comes into the foggy bathroom. "That's imposs—" She stops talking when she sees that the water is no longer running. "Oh. Thanks."

How did he do that? Maybe magic *was* involved. Maybe he's a witch too. Or a wizard. Warlock? Weirdo? Nah. If he were, he wouldn't have two massive sweat stains under his arms. How cute is that? Mortal, anyway. And nice. Even though Mom is MIA, he still messed himself up to help us.

Perhaps encouraging Mom to date other guys was not my best plan.

Lex glances at his watch. "It's been a real pleasure, girls, but it seems your mother has forgotten our plans, so I guess I'll take off. Please tell her I stopped by." He heads to the door, steps into his shoes, and plants his hat firmly on his head.

Awwwwwww. He's so nice! Much nicer than Adam or the fireman. They're cute, but they've never given us anything or acted remotely interested in us. Why did I butt into Mom's private business? And he's so handy. If I had only encouraged Mom to date Lex exclusively, by now they'd be practically engaged. And that hard-to-reach bedroom lightbulb would be long changed. And Mom wouldn't be running around like a chicken with five heads.

"Hope to see you soon," Miri says, her voice sounding sad. Apparently, even my I-want-Mom-to-be-miserable-and-alone-and-all-ours sister has been charmed by Lex.

195

He reaches for the door handle and gives us his warm smile. "Take care of yourselves, girls."

"Thanks," we say, choking back tears. Okay, not really, but almost.

The closing of the door echoes throughout the apartment. I sigh. "Mom just stood up the nicest man in the world."

Miri shakes her head in disgust. "I know! What are we going to do with her? Do you think she's having a midlife crisis?"

"Yes."

"She should just zap herself up a Corvette and get it over with."

When she finally calls us back at seven-thirty, I'm furious. "Where are you?" I can barely hear her, she's surrounded by so much noise.

"Everything all right, honey?" she yells.

"You missed your date!" I yell back.

"What? I can't hear you! I'm on my date!"

"No, you missed it! With Lex!"

"I can't hear you, hon. Reception is terrible. I'll try not to be home too late. I left money for takeout! Make sure you do your homework!"

This. Is. Absurd. Miri and I spend the rest of the night pacing. And complaining about our mother. And pacing some more. We take a break for *Saturday Night Live* but continue pacing during the commercials.

We fall asleep on the couch. When the clock says two a.m., I'm awakened by the clink of a key in the door. Then the lights zap on. Yes, zap. Miri is still unconscious, but I'm quickly on my feet, ready to attack.

"What is wrong with you?" I growl, hands on my hips. Sniff. Sniff, sniff. And Mom reeks of smoke. Like she was *bathing* in cigarettes. "You're smoking again."

Her face falls. "Bars," she mumbles. "People smoke in them."

Gasp. She just lied right to my face. There's no smoking in bars in the city! "Mother, you're smoking again. You're using magic like crazy. You're going on more dates than you can handle. You're home too late. You stood up Lex."

She grimaces.

"Are you having a midlife crisis?"

Her face cements into an unreadable expression. She slowly removes her shoes and leaves them in a mess on the floor. She walks past me and into the kitchen. "I forgot about Lex." 197

I follow her. "I know. It was rude."

She waves me away and pours a glass of water. "You didn't even want me going out with him!"

"I was wrong. I admit it. He's very nice and you've probably ruined your chances with him. I hope you're happy."

She shrugs. "There are lots of fish in the sea. But frankly, Rachel, I don't appreciate being told what to do by a fourteen-year-old."

"Well, someone has to tell you. You're acting crazy." I make a cuckoo motion with my finger. "Why do you have to be so extreme? You went from *no* magic, *no* dating, and *no* smoking to drowning in magic, dating, and smoking. Don't

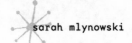

you know how to ease yourself in? First a pinky toe, then a foot, then a leg—"

She slams the glass onto the table, sending water flying everywhere. As if I haven't had enough waterworks for one night. "Are we not clear? I'm the mother. You're the daughter. I tell *you* what to do."

I feel like I've been kicked in the stomach. "Then act like my mother," I snap. I run into my room, slamming the door behind me. She'd better come apologize. She always comes to talk to me when I slam the door. Slamming the door = I need to talk.

Five minutes pass. What is she doing? I peek into the hallway. The nerve of her! She's taking a shower. I hope the water is still cold.

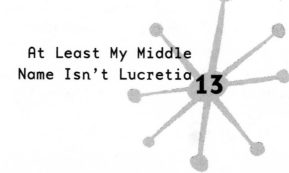

At Least My Middle
Name Isn't Lucretia 13

My mom and I ignore each other on Sunday. Not that she's around to be ignored. She has a lunch date with Nick, pops home in the afternoon, takes a nap, and decides to make us a cheese soufflé for dinner (out of remorse, I bet) but then forgets it's in the oven while she showers and lets it burn to a crisp. She zaps up a new one for us, along with a salad and apple cider, and then goes out with Tony for dinner. I refuse to eat her guilt dish out of principle, and make macaroni and cheese instead. The microwave kind. I accidentally add too much milk and it ends up being macaro-mush.

Miri spends most of the day trying and failing to find a better rain spell. I spend most of the day on the phone with Tammy.

Her: "Bosh invited me to prom!"

Despite my sympathy for poor Aaron, I shriek with joy, "We can double!"

Tammy: "I can't go to prom with someone while I have a boyfriend! And anyway, there might not even be a prom."

"There will be," I say. "I'll worry about that. You worry about dumping poor Aaron already."

Meanwhile, I stare at the potted TV, which still looks like a bowl of dirt and nothing like a television. "Shouldn't it be growing?" I ask for the sixteenth time.

Miri pokes it with a pencil. "It takes time."

"But it hasn't done any developing." And I know. I've been lying on my carpet watching for the last eight hours.

"Give it till tomorrow."

"It had better work. I have no backup plan."

She opens the window to let in some fresh air. "You have to think positively! If you don't believe in it, it won't work. Like the tooth fairy."

"You sound like Mom."

"Well, she was right, wasn't she? As soon as I said that I didn't believe in the fairy, that I knew it was Mom, she stopped putting money under my pillow. And where did that leave me?"

200

"Five dollars poorer?"

"Exactly. So don't worry. Until tomorrow, anyway. Then you can freak out. Has my magic ever let you down?"

Uh, yeah. The phone rings, distracting me.

"Hi, dear!"

"Hi, Dad," I say, and stretch out on my bed. "How are you?"

"Long week. You know. Getting back to the office after so much glorious time off." He yawns in my ear.

"Tired?"

"A little."

We chitchat for a few seconds and then he passes the phone to Jennifer. "What's up?" I say.

"It's a madhouse around here," she says. "You wouldn't

believe what my daughter is doing. She refuses to sleep in
her own bed. Absolutely refuses. How are we supposed to
conceive if she won't leave us alone?"

Ew. I'm not sure why she thinks I'm the appropriate person to discuss this with. Gasp—does she think we're friends?
Buddies? Does she think I'm someone who wants to hear
about her marital relationship with my dad? That is so gross.
I can't stand it. I close my eyes, trying to shut out the repul-
sive images—which makes it worse. "I don't know what to
say." Except, please stop talking.

"I am so depressed! I don't have time to waste. I'm already thirty-six. And Priscilla is acting like a child."

"She's only five."

"Almost six. It's her birthday next weekend, remember?
She's too old for this! I'm too old for this!"

"I'm sure she'll snap out of it."

201

A loud sigh. "I know. You're right, Rachel. You know exactly what I'm thinking."

What is going on here? Why am I her new best friend?
She's my stepmom! She should be acting her role—mean
and bossy. And my mother should be acting like a mother.
Why can't everyone behave properly?

"It's just that I spent so much time worrying about the
wedding that now I'm behind on all my other projects. Like
finding a summer rental in the Hamptons. And my car has
been giving me trouble—"

Beep!

Thank goodness, it's my call waiting. "One sec," I say,
and click off. "Hello?"

"Hey, gorgeous," says Will's deep, manly voice.

Ah. See? No role confusion on his end. Me = girlfriend. "Hi! How was the rest of your weekend?"

"Cool. You? What did you do last night?" he asks.

"Oh, I wasn't feeling so hot," I say. I can't exactly tell him I stayed home doing nothing on a Saturday night, can I?

"Are you better?"

A concerned boyfriend. Cuteness. "A-okay. What's up?"

"Penthouse Fifty needed a deposit. So I gave them two thousand dollars."

Don't panic. "Where did you get the money? From ticket sales?"

"No, I had to use the advance ticket sales to give the caterer a deposit. I just took it out of my savings."

My stomach free-falls. "Are you kidding me? The money you've been saving for college?" Doesn't he know the first rule of business: never use your own money?

"No worries. You said you're bringing in a big-ticket item, right? Any hints as to what it is?"

He's basing his future on my promises? What if I can't deliver? "It's, um, a secret. Until tomorrow." I forgot about Jennifer! "Will you hold on? I'm just getting off the other line." Click. "Jennifer?"

"—you know? And my tan is already fading. And all the good rentals are gone."

I don't think she realized I was gone. "That's awful, Jennifer. Really. But I have to go. Will and I have to work on the prom auction. We have to raise fourteen thousand dollars."

"I love auctions! Are you selling any good stuff?"

Gulp. "Hopefully."

"Can I come?"

"Sure, parents are invited." Did I just use the word *parent* in association with her? "Can I tell you more about it next weekend?"

"Sure, sorry. Have fun with Will. Are you going to invite him to the Hamptons for a week?"

"I thought you didn't have a house yet."

"I'll find one. So will you?"

My finger is eagerly hovering over the Flash button. "No, he's going to camp for the summer."

"He is? What camp?"

"Wood Lake," I say.

"Really? Hey, that's an idea."

"Jennifer, I have to go. Emergency school stuff, re-member?" I say good-bye and switch back. "So where were we?" Eight days till the auction, and eleven days until prom, that's where. And I still don't have a TV or a dress.

By Monday morning, the TV has yet to grow even an an-tenna. I walk to school with a heavy heart. At lunch, I buy a muffin in the caf and head straight to the lounge. Will and Kat are already there, sitting on the floor, cutting out pad-dles for the auction.

I plop down beside Will and he kisses me on the fore-head. "So are you going to tell me the big secret? What are you bringing in?" He looks at me with those puppy dog please-feed-me eyes.

"Wide-screen TVs," I blurt out. Oops. Think positively, don't speak positively. "I'm working on it," I add quickly.

The puppy dogs light up. "They go for like four grand! That would be *so* cool. Where are you getting them?"

"Family connections," I say as nonchalantly as possible. "I'm still working out some of the details."

Kat nods. "Awesome. When do you think you can bring them in?"

"I . . ." That's an excellent question. Even more excellent, *how* am I going to bring them in? Am I planning to carry them on my back? No worries. Miri must know a moving spell. Maybe she'll put them on her back and do the transport spell. Not.

204

Will smiles at me. "We should send out an e-mail with a list of the stuff that's being auctioned off, so students know to bring lots of green. Or their parents' credit cards."

"I'm thirsty," Kat says, putting down her scissors. "Anyone want a drink?"

"No, thanks," Will and I both say.

"See you in five." Kat removes her wallet from her backpack and closes the door behind her.

Will immediately wraps his arms around my waist. "Finally, we're alone."

My heartbeat speeds up like I just ran to class. He gives me one of those perfect kisses. Soft, sweet, warm. How lucky am I?

After a couple of minutes, I pull away. "We need to get

back to work," I say, smiling. "These flyers aren't going to make and hang themselves."

"Very true. But we need more paper. Can you check in Kat's binder? She said she brought orange cardboard."

"Sure." I skip over to the pink couch and take Kat's binder out of her backpack. "Here we go," I say, pulling out the paper. And that's when I see the neat blue ink writing on the inside wing. First her address and then:

Kat Kosravi

Kat Postansky-Kosravi

Mrs. Katherine Kosravi

Mrs. Will Kosravi

Mrs. Katherine Lucretia Postansky-Kosravi

I slam the binder shut. Without the proof staring me in the face, it's easier not to care that Kat likes Will. Is it possible that beneath the spell Will has feelings for Kat? "Will," I say, handing him the orange paper, "if we hadn't gotten together, who would you have asked to the prom?"

He lies on his stomach and pulls the cap off a black marker. "Probably Kat."

Oh, no. "Really? Did you two ever go out?"

The apples of his cheeks turn red. "Me and Kat? No. She's, like, my best female friend."

"And you never thought about asking her out?"

He shifts on the floor, starting to look uncomfortable. "I thought about it. But then you came along, and I realized that it was you I wanted to go with. And be with." He blows me a kiss. "Don't be jealous."

It's not jealousy that's creeping up my spine. It's guilt. I feel bad for her. Not only is her middle name *Lucretia*, but I stole her boyfriend. As soon as prom is over, I have to set him free.

I head straight to my room when I get home. Mom's out, of course. And there's still no TV.

Miri is already sitting in front of the cauldron, staring. "If it's not there by morning, we'll try something new."

"Uh-huh."

I spend the night tossing and turning, and turning and tossing. Every time I turn toward the bowl, I can't stop myself from opening my eyes and staring at its barrenness. I don't even remember falling asleep, but the next thing I know, the sunlight is spearing my eyelids. I open them slowly. Please let there be a TV. Pretty please?

Omigod. Right in front of my eyes is the largest TV ever. It stretches across my window, from my bed to my desk. I don't believe it. The spell worked! I am overwhelmed with awe. It's gorgeous. Amazing. A metallic fixture of true beauty. Long, rectangular, black, and sleek.

"Miri! Come look!" I scream. But a quick peek at the clock tells me that it's only six a.m. Oops.

A second later, she's at my door, dressed in shorts and a tank top—and covered in soot. "It grew?"

"Where were you?"

Miri yawns. "Back at the bushfires, trying to blow them out. But it didn't work."

She's really starting to worry me. "Do you even sleep anymore?"

She rolls her eyes. "I can't waste time sleeping, Rachel. I have too many important things to do." She approaches the TV and taps her fingers on the screen. "This is cool."

"Isn't it? Let's do the multiplying spell right away! Let's make five for the auction, then one for you and one for me!"

She raises an eyebrow. "Mom doesn't get one?"

Humph. "Not these days." I haven't spoken to Mom since our fight. "I can't wait to show the soc. Can we do the multiplying spell right after school?"

"We could. But I have to figure out how to control it. If we make a few hundred, like we did with the oranges, we could have a real space issue." She stands on tiptoe, as though measuring its length. "I'm not sure where even two are going to fit. We don't want the TVs to break."

"We can do it in the living room." Whatever. We'll figure it out. Cha-ching! Even if for some inexplicable reason the multiplying spell doesn't work, I have one TV to donate. A TV that's worth at least four thousand dollars! I rock! I want to test it out immediately. I find the plug and squeeze between the TV and my bed to locate the socket. "And now," I say in my radio-announcer voice, "the moment of truth." I insert the plug and squeeze back onto my bed, where my sister has already made herself comfortable.

"We probably have to turn it on," the know-it-all says.

I have to get up again? "Is there a remote?"

"I've got it," she says, and presses Power.

And nothing. "Press the Power button on the TV," I instruct.

She does, and still nothing. "Maybe it's warming up,"

207

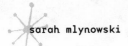

she says. "I bet you it will work by the time we get home from school."

I yawn. "Maybe. I'm going back to bed."

"And I'm going to pop over to Antarctica. You wouldn't believe what's going on with the ozone layer down there."

I sigh. "You'd better put on something warm."

"Rachel, where are you getting the TVs? And when are they coming?" Will asks during lunch. We're all sitting around the soc lounge, finishing the paddles for the auction.

I ignore the first question. "They're almost ready. I just have one *tiny* problem left to fix." Which I'm sure we'll be able to do.

Bosh gives me a high five. "Awesome, dude. Let's make up a new poster advertising them!"

"Whoa, wait," I say, suddenly nervous. "You know, in case I can't get them to work."

Tammy raises an eyebrow.

"They'd better work," River says quickly. "We need some expensive stuff. Otherwise the auction is going to be a wash."

Oh, God. He's right. I push the concerns out of my head. It will turn on. It has to.

"Don't worry. The TVs are new, right?" Kat asks.

"Yeah." Brand-new.

"Then they'll be fine. And if not, my uncle has an electronics repair store on First Ave. He can fix anything."

I doubt that.

"Um, guys?" whispers a voice from the back of the room.

"What was that?" River asks.

"Guys?" the voice says again. Ah, it's Jeffrey. "I was thinking," he mumbles. "If it's all right with you, on the big day, I'd like to be the auctioneer."

Will scratches his head. "Do you know how?"

"Yes," he answers.

Will looks to me for advice. I shrug. "All right, then," he says. "If you know what you're doing."

I hope I know what *I'm* doing.

I run straight back to my room after school and holler, "Let's take our baby out for a spin!"

"Huh?" asks Miri from the other side of the wall.

"Let's watch some high-definition television!" I drop my jacket onto the floor and dive onto my bed. Miri joins me on the bed. I pick up the remote and press the Power button. Come on, come on.

Suddenly, there is a jolt of color, and the blankness on the screen morphs into a swirl of blues and greens.

Yay! Pretty! There are mountains and hills and grass . . . and Julie Andrews singing to the von Trapp children.

"Far . . . a long, long way to run . . ."

"It works! It works!" Miri cheers. "I rock!"

It does work, but it's Julie Andrews who's rocking. Uh-oh. "It's *The Sound of Music.*"

"I know!" Miri squeals. "I love that movie!"

"But that's the exact scene that was on the image I cut out from the catalog. Isn't that odd? What channel is this?"

"Three." Miri chomps her thumbnail. "Let me change it." She squints at the TV and presses the Channel Up button. A church comes into view.

Thank goodness. I exhale. "At least it's not—"

"*How do you solve a problem like Maria?*" the nuns on the TV screen are singing.

Right now, Maria's not my problem. "Change the channel again," I order.

"*I am sixteen, going on seventeen . . .*"

Beads of sweat drip down my forehead. "Again?"

Miri flips through ten more channels and all are showing various scenes from *The Sound of Music.* Eventually we return to channel three, back to "Do-Re-Me."

I flop my face onto the comforter and moan. Wait a sec. I lift myself up on my elbows. "Do we need cable?"

Miri nods. "Let me get a hanger." Miri is a cable superstar. Seriously. Before we got cable she hooked us up with many channels. Now that she's a witch, maybe we can hook up to every station in the universe.

When she returns, she unravels the hanger and adjusts it on the television. A few minutes later, she sits back on the bed. "Let's give it a try." She changes the channel.

The Sound of Music.

The Sound of Music.

The Sound of Music.

"Just turn it off; it's too freaky," I say. I feel like spiders are creeping up my back.

Miri presses the Power button. But it doesn't turn off.

"What's wrong?" I ask.

210

"I don't know. It isn't working," she says, panic seeping into her voice.

"*That will bring us back to Do, oh, oh, oh,*" the TV tells us.

Before I'm the second person in this apartment to have a nervous breakdown, I squeeze behind the TV again and yank the plug out of the wall. I exhale with relief. That should do it.

"*Doooooe!*" Maria and the children sing.

I close my eyes in pain. "What do we do?"

Miri shakes her head in bewilderment. "I have *no* idea."

"Maybe you should do a reversal spell."

"I'm scared of that spell. Maybe it's like paint and needs time to dry."

That's true. It might just need to set. Like a cake. We check on it again after dinner, but it's still singing away. "Okay, let's let it sit for the night, then." I grab my pillow. "Sleepover at Miri's!"

She groans. "If you steal all my covers, you and the von Trapp children can sing duets all night, you hear me?"

"I don't think it's a duet if there are seven of them."

"You know what I mean."

The next morning, I open my door with trepidation. Unfortunately, I find the hills still very much alive. Guess we won't be doing the multiplying spell just yet.

"Dudes, we're running out of space here," Bosh says.

It's after school, and we're trying to make room for all the loot we've collected. There are CDs, books, dinner cer-

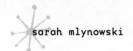

tificates, a cactus (no clue who brought that in), designer clothes, spa visits, airline miles, rounds of golf, gift cards, shoes, dishes, and iPods, all new. It's amazing how much stuff people are willing to give for a good cause. And it's amazing how hooked up JFK students are.

"I'm trying to figure out the best place to put all this stuff. Maybe in the cupboard," Bosh says, pointing to the massive storage area on the left side of the room. "Tammy, you want to check it out with me?"

River, Will, Kat, and I laugh. Tammy turns a deep shade of red. Bosh has been using every technique in the book to put the moves on Tammy, but she's not budging. She IMed me last night that she absolutely can't break up with Aaron. He's still home sick in bed. And when he does get better, she still won't dump him. She's been doing a lot of research and she read that stress suppresses the immune system, and if he gets too upset, he could have a relapse. And if he has a relapse, he won't be able to take his exams, and he'll have to retake the entire year.

TamTam: I can't be responsible for that!

PrincessRachel: You're never going to break up with him? Are you going to get married?

TamTam: I just have to wait till he finishes exams in June.

PrincessRachel: But UR gonna miss prom! It's next week.

TamTam: It's just the prom. Not the end of the world.

Tammy is way too nice. Anyway, it's driving Bosh crazy. Every time she turns him down, he seems to want her more. He decorates the outside of her locker with pictures from his last scuba trip. He brings her seashells. Tells her she's prettier than a tropical fish.

"Rachel," Will says, snapping me back to reality. "How

big are the TVs? Are they going to be delivered? Where do you think we should put them?"

In a fun house? "Um, I'm not sure yet. I'll let you know tomorrow."

Evade, evade, evade.

I almost pull out my hair on the way home from school. With the auction, stress, and my recent frequent sightings of Relissa (that's what the kids are calling Raf and Melissa these days), in addition to my mother, I'm surprised I'm not bald yet.

Oh yes, my mom and I are *still* not talking to each other. It's been four days! We've never been mad at each other for this long. She hasn't even commented on the singing TV. And I know she's heard it. How could she not have?

At home, I find the TV still singing, and with a sinking feeling, I head to Miri's room, which is a mess. There are papers all over the floor, notes and lists are taped to her walls, and Tigger is lounging in her still-unmade bed. She's sitting in the center of the disaster, dumping the contents of her backpack onto the mess.

"What happened here?" I ask.

"I'm just figuring something out."

"What are we going to do? Do we get rid of the TV? Can you find a new spell that will work? Am I supposed to sleep in your room forever because that movie will always be playing—" The phone rings, and I grab it. "Hello?"

"Is Miri there, please?" squeaks a tiny voice.

Miri has a new friend! Finally! "Sure. Who's speaking, please?"

"It's Ariella from school."

"Hold on one second." I smile and pass Miri the phone. "Ariella?" I say.

Miri shakes her head violently. "Tell her I'm busy," she mouths.

"Why?" I mouth back.

She shoves the receiver away.

"Can I take a message?" I ask, perplexed.

"Yeah," Ariella says. "I wanted to know if Miri wanted to come over this weekend. I'm having a sleepover."

"I'll let her know. Does she have your number?"

"Well, I've given it to her before, but she never calls me back."

As she recites her number, I glare at my sister. "Why won't you call her back?" I ask after hanging up.

"I don't have time for sleepovers," Miri says. "You know that. I can barely keep up with my homework and saving-the-world stuff. I haven't even been to Tae Kwon Do in weeks."

I wondered what happened to Tae Kwon Do. "You're being crazy. And why are you wearing one white sock and one black sock?"

She eyes her mismatched feet. "Oops. I told you, I have a lot going on." Now back to my questions. "No, you cannot sleep in my room again. You sleep with your mouth open and your breath stinks. And I haven't found a new TV spell. I'm working on it, but I also have to figure out how to make it rain, and I need to get back to Antarctica to work on the ozone problem. And my head hurts."

"Tell me about it." I sit next to her and hear paper crumpling.

"Careful!" she says, annoyed.

"Sorry." I pull the paper out from under me and am about to hand it to her when I see the red writing in the top right-hand corner: *D-*. What is this?

1. 8x - 2 = 14

And underneath Miri wrote: *x = 1.5*

Which, of course, is wrong. It's 2, Miri. The answer is 2!

I don't believe it. "You failed a math test?"

She grabs the paper from my hand. "I did not. *D-minus* isn't failing."

"Miri, what happened? Didn't you study?"

"I didn't have time, okay? What's more important, a math test or the ozone layer?" She opens her mouth to say something else but yawns instead.

I start rummaging through her papers. "Are you having problems in all your classes?"

"Stop it. I'm fine." She tries to lie across her papers so I can't get to them.

I grab what looks like a book report. "C-plus? Miri, you've got to be kidding me." I find a French test. An F. "Oh, Miri, come on. You have got to promise me you'll start paying attention in school."

She waves her hands above her head. "I'm trying. But I have a lot to do!"

"Miri, an educated witch will solve more global problems than a middle school dropout witch."

"I'm not going to fail, all right? I'm doing my best. But I'm tired! So can you stop wasting my time? You're in my way and I have lots to do."

She has lost it.

215

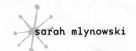

We hear my mother's key in the front door. So nice of her to come home.

"Girls?" she calls. "Can you come to the kitchen, please? I'd like to talk to you."

Terrific. Now what? Miri follows me silently to the kitchen, where we find our mother already sitting at the table.

"Girls," she begins, "I know that seeing me move on with my life is scary for you. Watching a parent date can be difficult for kids of any age."

Just what I need on top of all my troubles: the Divorced Parent's I Have a Life Too Talk. Well, at least she's talking to me again.

Click, click. Click, click. My mother is tapping her fingernails on the table. My mother is tapping her long red fingernails on the table. When did my mother get long red fingernails?

I grab her hand to take a good look. "What *are* these?"

"My nails," she says, coloring.

"No, you bite your nails. Like Miri." I hold up my sister's left hand. "It's disgusting. But it's you. So where are *your* nails?"

She pulls her hand away. "I fixed them, all right?"

"You went to a salon and got acrylics, or you poofed up a new set of hands?"

"Rachel, what does it matter?"

Doesn't she get it? "It matters to me. You're turning into a crazy woman."

"I am not," she says, and then, right before my eyes, she zaps up a cigarette and an ashtray. "I understand that my dating scares you. But I need you two to grow with me. I'm still your mother." She taps her claw against her forehead. "There was something else I was supposed to talk to you about. But I can't remember what. I have too much on my mind these days. It was something to do with your father—"

"At least he acts like a parent," I mumble, squeezing Miri's hand. "More than you, anyway. Do you know that Miri is failing school?"

Miri takes back her arm and scowls at me.

My mom leans over to Miri while magically lighting her cigarette. "Honey, I guess that's your way of getting back at me for my dating—"

"It has nothing to do with your dating!" I say. "Miri has also gone crazy. I'm living with two loons!" And with that, I storm out of the kitchen and into my room. I don't leave until I hear the front door slam two hours later. Guess my mother has another date. Miri's door is closed, so I make myself a grilled cheese (I'm all egg-rolled out), do my math homework, and get into bed.

What am I going to do? My mother and sister are going crazy, and there's no way we're going to make enough money at the auction to save the prom. If we don't make enough, my boyfriend's reputation and savings account are officially ruined. And—sob—if there *is* a prom, I don't even have a dress.

I blink back tears and try to fall asleep.

A difficult feat when my lullaby is a thunderous rendition of *The Sound of Music*'s "The Lonely Goatherd."

License to Thrill

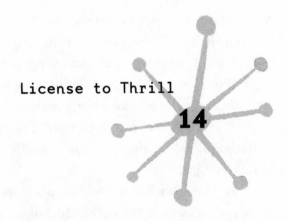

14

Aaron is back. Now that he's healthy, and around, Tammy can no longer spend her entire day with Bosh.

"Just dump him!" I beg her during bio.

"I can't!" she says miserably. "He's very fragile. Did you see him? He's so pale and skinny."

She's right; I spotted him before homeroom and he looked pretty waifish. "But prom is in one week! And you don't even like him anymore!"

"I know, I know, but I can't do it. It's just prom. Bosh understands."

Again with the *just prom*? What an oxymoron.

When I get home from school, I find Miri right back in the center of her disaster, dressed in a tank top and earmuffs. She must have done a Cali-Antarctica combo. I decide to forget about our fight. "How was your day?"

No answer. Apparently, she's decided not to forget.

"Hel-lo? What are you doing?"

"I'm not talking to you. You called me a loon."

Because you've been acting like one? "I'm sorry. But I want you to do your homework. And study for your tests."

"What, now you're my mother?"

"Well, someone's got to be." I sit down next to her. "Do you have any tests coming up that I should know about?"

"No."

I tickle under her arms. "I don't believe you."

"Get off. Stop it," she says, laughing. "Fine, I have a math test tomorrow. Happy?"

"Yes. Did you study?"

"I will, as soon as I finish doing this global—"

"Enough saving the world," I say sharply. "For tonight, anyway. Right after dinner, we're working on equations and inequalities."

She sighs. "We're on our own for dinner again. Mom has another date. She zapped us up a pizza, but it looks a little rubbery."

"Surprise, surprise."

She leans back, smiling. "But I'll let you help me. You owe me anyway."

"What for?"

"Do you hear anything?"

I listen intently. "No. Should I?"

"Yes. The sound of silence. I did the five-broomer reversal spell to get rid of your TV. So it's gone."

I throw my arms around her neck. "Awesome! You figured it out! Thank you! I only slept for five minutes last night."

"No kidding. I heard every toss, turn, and sigh," Miri says. "Rachel, the spell-reversal charm was so cool. I had to buy a clear crystal and bury it in a tub of salt for an hour. Then I put it on a silver chain and wore it around my neck while I circled the TV backward. And finally, the TV disappeared." She snaps her fingers. "Just like that."

"Thank you, thank you, thank you!" But panic creeps back in. "What am I going to bring for the auction? I have nothing. Nada. Zilch. Zip."

Maybe we could try one of the football TVs. At least that wouldn't be a musical. Although I'd have to listen to annoying sportscasters all night.

"Don't worry, I'll find a new spell so you can make a TV. I just need some time."

"We don't have time! We're going to Dad's tomorrow and the auction is on Monday! We need to get cracking."

"I don't really need to study for math anyway," she says, looking relieved.

I remember her D-. "I think you do. Math tonight, the spell tomorrow." Sigh. What's another day? It's not like we're cutting it close or anything.

"I found a transformer spell," Miri whispers on the train to Long Island. "You basically change something into something else of the same family."

"Huh?"

"Like a radio into a big TV."

I heave a sigh of relief. "Sounds perfect."

"So what do you want to zap? A TV again?"

"I guess. And then, if it works, we'll use the multiplying spell to make a whole bunch. We need to raise fourteen thousand dollars, remember?"

When we get off the train, we can't find my dad's car.

"Where is he?" I wonder aloud. And that's when I spot Jennifer in the driver's seat of a brand-new Mercedes-Benz convertible. It's slinky. It's silver. And Jennifer is honking like a deranged woman, smiling and waving. Guess she's feeling better. Funny how a brand-spanking-new car can do that. "Hi, girls," she sings. "A present from your dad. You like?"

I like.

"Shotgun!" Miri screams. She climbs into the front, and I slide into the small backseat. It smells yummy, like a hundred new leather purses. The seats feel soft, like the skin on the inside of my arm.

Jennifer reverses and pulls onto the road. And even though the wind has a field day on my hair, blowing it every which way, making me look like a singer in an eighties cover band, I don't care.

Because I have a new plan. Who needs a TV? We're going to zap up a car.

221

*

"Happy birthday to you, happy birthday to you! Happy birthday, dear Priscilla! Happy birthday to you!"

Prissy takes a big breath and blows out all seven candles (one for good luck) perched on her chocolate cake. "Do you want to know what I wished for? I wished not to have any more sisters or any brothers. Do you think it'll come true?"

Jennifer and my dad squirm in their dining room table seats. "We hope not," Dad says.

All I want is for this dinner to be over already. Miri and I have *lots* to do tonight.

Jennifer smiles across the table. "Do you want your birthday present now?"

Prissy claps excitedly. "Yes! What did I get? A Princess Barbie castle? Is that what you got me? Please, please, please, please. Where is it?"

"Here it is!" Jennifer says, and hands Prissy a fancy envelope with a pink bow in the corner.

What on earth is that? A restraining order?

Prissy shakes it and then rips it open. She pulls out a photograph. "Huh?" she says, staring at it. "What is it?"

The photo is of some kids canoeing. Across the sky in bubble letters, it says *Wood Lake*.

Excuse me?

"For your birthday, we signed you up for two weeks at sleepaway camp! It's a very special place for girls and boys. You're going to get to sleep in a bunk and play all day!"

Prissy looks confused.

"What about visiting Daddy?"

Jennifer smiles. "You'll get to spend a few weeks with him in L.A. this summer. But first, camp!"

"Are you going to be there too?"

Jennifer shakes her head. "I won't, but your sisters will! We signed Miri and Rachel up too! And they're going for the whole summer!"

"What?" Camp? Hello? *Raf and Will's camp?*

My father walks over and kisses me and Miri on our heads. "I remember how much you two always wanted to go to sleepaway, so I figured this would be the perfect birthday gift for all of you."

"But my b-birthday isn't until December," Miri stutters.

"And mine's not until August," I protest.

"It's an early present. Surprise!" Someone wants Prissy out of the house. Badly.

"But I never wanted to go to camp. Club Med! That's where I wanted to go." On the other hand . . . moonlit sailboat trips and campfires with Raf? I mean *Will*. Moonlit sailboat trips and campfires with *Will*. My boyfriend. Raf . . . and Will?

My dad looks momentarily confused. "Oh. Well, you should have told me that before we paid in full. And wasn't it you who suggested the idea to Jennifer? Anyway, I promise, you'll love it there! Even your mom thought this was a good idea."

What? I bet that's what she wanted to talk to us about but was too busy to remember. My back stiffens. I guess she wants us out of the house too.

Dad lifts his wineglass. "You three are going to have the best summer ever!" He takes a big gulp and starts cutting the cake. "Small piece or big piece?" he asks me.

I can't believe my mother would okay this without even mentioning it to us. But you know what? I don't even have time to properly worry about this. My plate is that full. Although it could use a piece of cake. "Big, please."

"Do you have everything?" I whisper.

"I hope so," Miri says. "We're so going to get caught," she adds.

"No, we're not! Think positively."

If anyone on my dad's street opens their blinds, we will

definitely be spotted. Somehow I think two girls flying on a tricycle might attract attention, even though it's three a.m. on Sunday.

"Ready?" Miri asks.

"Yup." Before I know it, we're airborne.

"I can't believe they're forcing us to go to Wood Lake," Miri says as we pass over a neighbor's roof. "How am I supposed to save the world if I'm at camp?"

Tell me about it. "I don't understand where we're supposed to go to the bathroom. Are they outside the tents? Are we supposed to pee in the bushes?" Grossness overwhelms me, as does guiltiness. I was planning on stopping Will's love spell after prom, but now I'll have no choice but to extend it through the summer, will I? How much would it suck to be stuck at camp with two ex-boyfriends? And anyway, dating Will has been fun. And it's not like Raf wants to get back together with me anytime soon.

"What I can't believe is that Dad asked Mom, and she allowed it," Miri says.

"She probably just wants us out of the way so she can date twenty-four seven."

"No kidding. Okay, no more talking; I need to concentrate."

Our new plan is slightly adventurous, if I do say so myself. We've decided to zap up a new Mercedes with the transformer spell. This way we won't need to worry about controlling the multiplying spell. So that's why we're on my tricycle (which I handed down to Miri, which she handed down to Prissy), which we've discovered flies just as well as a broom. That is a good thing, because we couldn't find a single broom in the house—Jennifer is far too glam—so instead we would have had to use her high-tech vacuum cleaner, which weighs at least a hundred pounds.

We're flying all the way to JFK. The school, not the airport, although we will pass the airport. I hope they don't pick us up on their radar. We don't want to get arrested for breaking the no-fly zone. We tried to use the transport spell, obviously, but for some reason it refused to move the tricycle with us (perhaps it has a weight maximum?), which is an integral part of our plan, so we had to use the more primal technique of flying. It's not the most comfortable for me, I'll admit, since I'm squashed in front of Miri between the handlebars and the seat. *E.T.* made it look much more fun. Anyway, we're wearing all black in an attempt at camouflage. (Not that the canary yellow bike will give us away or anything.) Once we get to JFK, we're using an open-door spell to get inside. The spell totally works. We tested it before dinner on the garage. It's made of oil and—wait for it— sesame seeds. The spell actually includes the phrase *open sesame*. I'm not kidding.

225

After dinner, we tested the transformer spell. How? We made me a prom dress. A beautiful, long, emerald green silk gown. We borrowed/stole one of Prissy's Barbie outfits and transformed it into a perfect prom dress. And the best part of the spell is that it works immediately: the cloth stretched itself into a size four and grew taffeta right before our eyes. The dress fit me perfectly. If I were ever in another fashion show (which no one would ever let me do), I would want to wear this.

This plan might actually work. The lights of the

Queensboro Bridge are twinkling below us; the full moon is glowing overhead. The wind in my face is warm, the helmet itch is minimal (Miri packs these babies wherever we go), I have the best prom dress ever. . . . I think I might be happy. I know I complain a lot, but the truth is, I'm one of the luckiest girls in the world. I live in an amazing city, I have two (plus one) parents who love me, and I have a younger sister who not only adores me but is also a witch. I do well in school, and I have a boyfriend and a fantastic best friend. So I have to spend the summer as a mosquito snack. I'll deal. At least Miri will be with me.

Suddenly, the tricycle swoops a few feet, and my stomach shoots into my throat. But then we stabilize.

Did I mention I'm happy I have my health?

As we fly high over the city and above the buildings, I peer down at the miniature taxis and people, who look like game pieces on a Monopoly board. And then, before I know it, the ride is over and we're landing on the home plate of the JFK baseball field. (It's a miniature field; we're in Manhattan, after all.) No matter how much fun flying is, it's always nice to feel the grass under my shoes. By the time I take off my helmet and shake out my hair, Miri is already at the door working her magic.

I roll the tricycle and meet her at the gym entranceway, just in time to watch her toss the sesame seeds at the door handle and say,

"Slack to slick,
Talk to tick,
Believe and see,
Open sesame!"

226

The door springs open. "Good work!" I say, and happily skip into the building, the tricycle trailing behind. It's very dark in the hallway. We don't want to turn on any lights for fear of attracting attention. Why did I take off my helmet? I could really use the night vision.

"Where should we put it?" Miri wonders out loud.

"In the auditorium. Follow me." As I creep through the empty hallway, every sound makes me jump. Being in the school alone at night is super creepy.

I open the doors to the auditorium and see the rows and rows of seats. Now, where do we put the car? "Let's do the transformation on the stage," I say, and climb up the steps and pull back the curtain. It'll be the grand finale! This is really the best plan I've ever had. From the Mercedes Web site, we learned that Jennifer's car cost sixty thousand dollars. So even if the highest bidder offers only a quarter of the money, fifteen thousand, I save the prom almost single-handedly (with the help of Miri and her magic, of course).

227

Miri climbs onto the stage and removes the ingredients from her satchel: sunflower seeds, raisins, flour, and lemon juice. She tosses them into the purple plastic container we borrowed/stole from the house. Once the ingredients are mixed, she says, "Ready? I have to pour it on the tricycle."

"Go for it!" How cool is this going to be? She's going to whip up a Mercedes. And some lucky person is going to buy it and drive the car right out of the— "Wait!"

She stops in midpour. "What?"

"How will someone drive the car outside?" I point to the four walls. "There's no garage door."

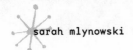

She places the container back on the creaking stage floor. "Oops. I guess we have to do it outside."

"We'd better wish up a car alarm, or the Mercedes will be gone by Monday."

A few minutes later we've dragged the tricycle and the ingredients back through the hallway and outside and set up the bike in the outfield next to the school gate. Miri then begins to pour, chanting:

"Transform this being,
With the cycle of life,
To become its destiny.
Like a caterpillar into a butterfly
("This is the part I added," she says, smiling.)
A Mercedes from this tricycle."

Her lips purse, the air gets cold, and I take a giant step backward so I won't get run over. Good-bye, sweet bike! You served me, Miri, and Prissy well. We had a fantastic time together in Central Park. But now you're being turned into your destiny. Or at least something that could get a higher price at the auction.

Nothing happens for the first few seconds, but then my front tire expands, like gum being blown into a bubble. When it's fattened to car-tire size, it suddenly splits in two and separates. With an earth-shattering squeak, the metal frame of the bike starts expanding into the body of a car. Cool! The small triangular seat transforms into five seats of plush black leather, and the handles grow into a steering wheel. As the interior completes itself, the car's exterior grows upward in liquid form and then hardens into finished, shiny steel.

Thirty seconds later, a complete canary yellow Mercedes roadster convertible is assembled in front of us. "It worked! It worked, it worked, it worked!" I can't stop myself from jumping up and down.

Miri jumps up and down with me, equally amazed. Wow. A prom dress is one thing, but *this* is a car. My baby sister just built the world's coolest car from practically birdseed. The hood glistens in the moonlight, and I give the side mirror a pat.

"Let's make sure it works before we get too excited," Miri says with caution. "I don't want this to be another fiasco."

She's right. We've had a lot of fiascos lately. I'm barely able to contain my excitement. I hop toward the front seat. "I'm driving!" I've always wanted to say that. "But you can have shotgun," I add.

I jump over the side window, like they did in the fifties. Ouch. They must have made the cars shorter in the fifties. Yes! The keys are lying on the seat. Magic is so clever.

"Where are we going?" Miri asks, opening the passenger door. "You know you don't know how to drive, right?"

I fasten my seat belt. "Back to Long Island?"

She starts biting her fingers.

"I'm kidding! I thought we would just spin around the field. How hard can it be? Millions of morons do it." Now if I can only figure out how to start the engine.

"Put the key in the ignition," Miri advises.

Obviously. I lean toward the ignition and insert the key. Done. Still not on. "Do you think it's broken?"

She laughs. "You have to turn it."

Right. I turn the key and the car roars to life. Fun! Now,

229

let's see. Hit the gas? How do I know which is the gas? I press down my right foot. The engine revs but nothing happens. "It must be broken," I say, deflated.

"I think *you're* the moron," Miri says, still laughing. "You have to take the car out of park. Put your foot on the other pedal." I do as I'm told. "Now move your foot back to the first pedal. Gently. I said, gently!"

We tear a few feet forward before I slam on the brakes. Yikes. "I declare the car working!" We check the reverse, the air-conditioning, the heating, the windshield wipers, the convertible top, the power seats and windows, and of course the CD player. Céline Dion's voice blares from the speakers.

"It's perfect!" Miri says. "And it smells so new and leathery. Just like Jennifer's car. Too bad she already bought hers, or we could have made her one for free."

"Oh, how you've grown, little tricycle," I say, like a proud parent.

We get out of the car, taking the keys with us. (I'll leave them in the student council lounge on Monday morning.)

"Perfect," Miri says. "Let's get back to Long Island."

I climb on her back, and away we go.

"It's gone! It's gone! We have to call the police!"

That's what wakes me up the next morning.

Miri and I both jump out of bed and run to the two-car garage, which is where my dad, Jennifer, and Prissy are standing.

My father's car is still there. But in the spot where Jennifer's car used to be is my old tricycle. At least, I think it's my old tricycle. It looks exactly the same except it's ... silver?

Tears are streaming down Jennifer's cheeks, and her hands are flailing above her head hysterically. "Someone stole my car! Right out of "—she lets out a loud wail—"my garage!"

My eyes lock with Miri's. This is not looking good. If my bike is here and Jennifer's car is gone, does that mean that on the school baseball field is Jennifer's car?

"Did anyone hear anything last night?" my dad asks, scratching the bald spot on his head.

"No," Miri and I say simultaneously.

Jennifer sobs, shaking her head.

"I did!" Prissy chirps. "It was after I climbed into your bed, and you were both sleeping. There was a noise, and I tried to wake you up, but, Mommy, you told me I was being a big baby and I should go to sleep. When am I going to camp?"

"I'm calling the police," my dad says.

"At least I hadn't put a car seat in yet," Jennifer says.

"Was anything else in the car?" Dad asks.

"Just my Céline Dion CD," she sobs. "I love that CD."

It's official. We stole our stepmother's car. And to add insult to injury, the spell reversed the colors.

Miri and I retreat back into our room as our father files a complaint.

"I knew it looked like her car," Miri says.

"How did that happen?" I murmur. "We have to transport ourselves back to school right away and switch it. Now."

"We can't disappear in the middle of the day," Miri says. "Don't you think Dad will wonder where we are?"

"So we'll tell him we have to go home. *Now.* I'll pack up. You tell Dad that you forgot about an assignment due tomorrow and you have to get back to the city. And that I've offered to go home with you. Go."

Six hours later, we've taken the train back to the city (Dad insisted on making sure we were on), stopped at the apartment for the spell reversal, snuck back onto the school baseball field, and reversed the spell. By the time the police arrived at my dad's, the car was back in their garage, causing, I'm sure, much confusion.

The thing is, it's Jennifer's car—they could tell by the serial numbers—but it's still canary yellow.

"I kind of like it this way," Jennifer said.

I didn't dare ask about the tricycle.

At the moment I'm pacing up and down my room. I failed. All I had to do to save the prom was come up with something to auction off, and I have nothing. And now we won't make enough money on Monday and Will is going to lose his deposits and there won't be a prom and it's all my fault.

But that's not what's bothering me the most. What's scratching at my brain is how Jennifer's car ended up at JFK. Isn't magic creating something from scratch? What about all the other stuff we zapped up? Like the oranges?

I pace right into Miri's disaster of a room. "Have we been stealing?" I ask.

She continues writing without looking up. "I screwed up a spell. Get over it."

"Nothing comes from nothing, you know? Remember when you zapped the cows to safety? And they ended up in the gym? If everything has to go somewhere, it's only logical that it has to come from somewhere."

She adamantly shakes her head. "You're wrong. Can you stop wasting my time, please? I have real people to help. Starving people." And with that, she stands up, pushes me out of her room, and slams the door in my face.

I turn on my computer. I type *orange shortage* into the search engine. Two hundred and thirty thousand hits.

I click on the most recent. Maybe no one would notice a few oranges missing.

233

"Tristate Grocery Stores Missing Fruit." Oh, no. It's dated Saturday, April 24. The same day we zapped up the oranges. How weird. And reportedly, all the crates of oranges in the tristate area inexplicably went missing. Did we cause the shortage? I feel sick to my stomach.

Funny that the oranges went missing from the stores and not a grove. Maybe because Miri's an urban witch?

What about the clothes we gave away?

I type in *clothing disappearance* and am horrified to read that after a hundred shirts disappeared from Bloomingdale's Soho on Saturday, May 1, a staff member was fired, even though she claimed she hadn't taken them.

Is magic just stealing from someone else?

If I went to Circuit City, would a salesperson tell me that

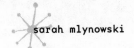

a fifty-inch wide-screen TV had disappeared one day and then reappeared shortly after?

Instead of saving the day, are we taking from the rich to give to the poor? Are we not Batman and Robin, but Robin Hood and a merry man?

Going Once, Going Twice, Going
Fourteen Thousand Times 15

I am hiding in the student council closet.

The first bell just rang and there's no way I can be seen in the hallway, because then everyone will ask me where my TV is and I will have to admit failure. Admit that there is no TV. No car, no *anything*. I have nothing to auction off. Will is going to dump me, spell or no spell. We're going to raise only a measly few hundred dollars, and Will is going to lose his deposit and be known as the worst JFK soc president ever. And I'll be known as the worst girlfriend ever. No wonder I've never had a boyfriend before. I am a hazard to men.

He will probably be so upset that he'll need to spend some time rethinking his life, and he'll put off going to college for an entire semester. And in that time he'll get some random job. Like as a limo driver. Every day he'll pass the Columbia campus and feel a heaviness in his heart, and then one day he'll pick up some crazy client who will yell at him for no reason, and he'll get distracted and veer into a pole and then spin the other way, drive straight off the Brooklyn Bridge, and plunge to his death.

Sob. I've killed my boyfriend.

I came in early today with the hope of being inspired by the donations. Unfortunately, the donations are thousands short of true inspiration. If only we could auction off broom rides. Although, after what I discovered on Sunday, I'm not sure I ever want to use magic again.

I stiffen at the sound of the door opening. Clomp, clomp, clomp. I'm about to be found out. Discovered. The person is opening the closet. He/she must smell my desperation. The light spears my eyes and I blink twice.

"What are you doing here?" asks Kat. "What's wrong?"

Terrific. She'll expose me to Will as a complete fraud and he'll dump me. I know she's always acted nice, but surely she'll use my failure to her advantage. Before I can stop myself, I burst into tears. "I don't have the TV!" I snivel. "I have nothing to sell. The auction is going to be a big flop and it's all my fault."

Kat's creamy vanilla forehead wrinkles in concern. "It's *not* your fault. You didn't put the cows in the gym."

I hiccup. Little does she know. "But I promised Will I would have something to auction off."

She climbs into the cupboard beside me. "Let's brainstorm. What do you have that's sellable?"

Doesn't she listen? "Nothing, that's the problem."

She pulls her purple pen out from behind her ear and taps it against the closet. "Aren't you a math genius? Exams are coming up. Why don't you sell blocks of tutorial time?"

Well.

Why, that's a good idea. I could tutor. I realize something else: there are lots of smarties at JFK. I'm not the *only* one. What about help in essay writing? Biology? My heart races with excitement. "We can ask all the smart people to auction off tutoring!"

"There you go," Kat says, smiling. "Problem solved."

My mind is whirling. "And not only tutoring. There are a million things we can auction off. Like . . . a date with the hottest senior?"

Kat's pen is tapping in overtime. "Locker cleaning? Slave for a day? Tennis lessons?"

I reach over and give her a big hug. "You're a genius!"

She backs her way out of the closet. "I'm going to beg Konch to let us take the morning to prepare. You start making a list of all the services." She tosses me her pen. "Let's hope this works."

I'm already scribbling as the final bell rings.

237

"I can't believe she said no," Tammy says, shaking her head. "We're trying to save *her* prom!"

"She's horrible. What did you expect?" I ask.

It's freshman lunch, and Tammy and I are washing our hands in the girls' bathroom before returning to the lounge. London has refused to auction off dance lessons. And it's not because she can't—her cast came off at the beginning of last week—it's because she just doesn't feel like it. (Who knows? Maybe she doesn't have a date!) Not that it matters; we've lined up fifty students who are willing to volunteer their services.

We're so busy complaining about London that we barely even notice Jewel, Melissa, and Doree spilling into the bathroom.

You know what? I'm no longer afraid of them. In fact . . . "Guys," I say bravely, "I have a favor to ask you."

The three of them freeze in shock. "What?" Melissa snarls, crossing her arms.

"I was wondering if you three, and Stephy, would be willing to be part of the senior auction today and sell a dance lesson. Since you four were so good in the show. What do you say? We would really appreciate it."

Tammy, Doree, Jewel, and Melissa are all looking at me as though I should be institutionalized.

Melissa shakes her head. "Have you not noticed that Stephy hasn't been here for, like, a month?"

Oh. Not really. I lean against the sink. "What's wrong with her?"

"Duh," Doree says. "She has mono."

Tammy snaps to attention. "She does?"

Melissa gives her evil grin. "Yup. She got it from your boyfriend. They had a little make-out session over spring break."

"What?" Tammy and I both scream.

"Sorry to be the one to break it to you." She smirks. "But your boyfriend's a cheater."

At first Tammy doesn't speak. Her lips form a shocked O.

"You're not going to start crying, are you?" Melissa says, thoroughly enjoying this.

Tammy's O slowly turns into a huge smile. "Fantastic! He's so history!"

238

I laugh. Melissa, Jewel, and Doree give each other a what-weirdos! look.

"So how about the three of you, then?" I ask. Might as well.

Melissa tosses her long red hair behind her back. "As if."

Oh well. Didn't hurt to ask. I shrug and am about to head out the door when I hear: "I'll do it."

I turn back and realize that it was Jewel. She's looking me right in the eye. "You will?" I ask. My heart skips a beat. Is it possible? Is this Jewel's way of . . . making amends?

Doree and Melissa are scowling at her.

"Yeah," she says, smiling hopefully at me. "Why not?"

"Sixty, do-we-have-a-sixty-five? Sixty-five to the young man in the red sweatshirt. Do-we-have-a-seventy?" says Jeffrey. I've never seen an auctioneer, but I bet Jeffrey is the best one ever. Who even knew he could talk?

The auditorium is packed with students, teachers, and parents. We've raised more than eight thousand dollars so far, which is great but not nearly enough. We've gone through most of the items—clothes, books, CDs, picture frames, dinners. We're almost done auctioning off the students' services. Kat and I are sitting on plastic chairs offstage, keeping track of the income. Bosh and Tammy are suspiciously absent. I'm pretty sure they're making out in the soc lounge. Right after we left the bathroom, Tammy found Aaron in the finally fixed cafeteria and dumped him.

"Last call at seventy dollars for ten hours of biology tutoring? Come on, boys and girls, chemicals are confusing! If you fail bio, you're not getting into a good college. Seventy to the guy with the goatee in the back row. Do-I-hear-seventy-five? Seventy-going-once-going-twice-going-three-times. Sold!"

Hah. My five hours of math tutoring went for eighty. Never mind. Jewel's dance lessons went for two hundred.

Jeffrey holds the next item above his head. "Two prom tickets for nonseniors. Price starting at a hundred dollars for both. Do I hear a hundred?"

Where did those come from? Will must have slipped them in.

A sophomore raises her paddle.

Kat nudges me with her foot. "Maybe I should buy them," she jokes.

"Do I hear a hundred and twenty? A hundred and twenty to the girl in the back! Do I hear a hundred and thirty?"

"You're going to come for a bit, aren't you?" I ask.

She shakes her head. "I can only go if a senior asks me."

"That's insane. You worked on it all year. The prom wouldn't be happening without you."

She shrugs. "That's the way it works. Don't look so horrified," she adds, giving me her big smile. "It's not the end of the world."

"A hundred and thirty. Do I hear a hundred and forty?"

"Buy the tickets!" I urge. "Then you can go."

"I don't have anyone to go with," she says. "Really, it doesn't matter. I'll go next year." Her head stays straight, but I can't help noticing that her eyes trail to the other side of the stage—where Will is now standing, holding four jackets.

I feel a dipping in my stomach. Will would have asked Kat if it weren't for Miri's love spell. As with the oranges, and the clothes, and the car, I stole his affection.

"Sold for three hundred dollars to the pretty redhead!"

My head snaps up at the word *redhead*. I peer out from behind the curtain to see who's cheering. Melissa. Groan. Melissa is going to prom? That means Raf will be at prom too.

"Maybe the four of you can double," Kat offers.

Double groan.

"Next up, donated by the generous Kosravis from Kosa Coats and Goods, we have classic men's high-grade leather jackets, in the color camel, sizes small, medium, large, and extra large. Retail value six hundred and thirty-five dollars each. We're starting off with size small. Do I hear a hundred?"

241

My heart lurches. Now I'll be thinking I'm seeing Raf everywhere. Definitely a potential problem.

But not the only problem. Will's jackets are our last items. That means that after these products, we're out of loot to auction off. And we've raised only ten thousand dollars. We're still four thousand dollars short! Even if the coats earn their retail value, that's only two thousand five hundred and forty dollars!

I watch with a sinking feeling as the size small goes for four hundred and fifty, the medium and large go for six hundred apiece, and the extra large goes to Mr. Earls for only three hundred fifty. We're two thousand dollars short.

We didn't make it. After all that, we're still going to have to cancel prom.

I'm about to cry when Will walks over to River with a final bag. More coats?

"And for our final item tonight, also from Kosa Coats & Goods, we have a brand-new limited edition Izzy Simpson leather hobo bag, retail value one thousand five hundred dollars."

Yes! One more item to go! A gorgeous item, if I do say so myself. Izzy Simpson is my all-time favorite designer. Not that I would *ever* spend so much money on a bag. But if someone buys it, we're almost saved.

"Bidding starts at five hundred! Do I have a bidder?"

At this point, both Kat and I have pushed the curtains aside and are eagerly watching to see if there are any buyers. Even *I'm* biting my nails. Come on, come on.

A paddle goes up from Ms. Hayward.

"Five hundred dollars to the math teacher in the front row. Do I see seven hundred? Come on, people, it's for a good cause!"

Wow, go, Ms. H! Who knew she was a fashionista? You so wouldn't be able to tell from her boring gray pants and sweaters.

Amy Koppela raises her paddle. So nice of her to show up.

Then Ms. Hayward raises hers again.

London Zeal raises her paddle. Boo!

"One thousand three hundred dollars," Jeffrey says. "Do I see fifteen hundred?"

The room is silent. Please don't tell me we're going to be short by seven hundred dollars!

Come on, Amy, you're the worst soc member ever! Can't you at least buy the purse?

And that's when a paddle goes up in the back of the room. "Two thousand dollars," the person says in a familiar voice. Who is it?

All of us backstage are in shock. Is it possible?

"Two thousand going once. Twice. Sold to the blond woman in the back!"

I step on tiptoe and see Jennifer waving at me. Oh my God!

As soon as the crowd begins to disperse, I run right up to my stepmom. "I can't believe you bought it."

"Why not? It's gorgeous and a fantastic deal. It's a limited edition, you know. I'm already on the waiting list at Henri Bendel. Plus, because I bought it here, it's tax deductible."

243

"But how did you know that we needed two thousand dollars?"

She shows me a notepad that's covered in numbers. "I was keeping track. You said you needed to raise fourteen thousand, right? So that's what you had left."

"Wow" is all I can say.

"I was an accountant before I had Prissy, you know."

I didn't, actually.

She pays for her purchase and then waves good-bye.

"We did it!" Will says, picking me up and spinning me around. "We raised fourteen thousand dollars! Prom is going to be amazing. And it's all because of you, Rachel. This auction was your idea."

He puts me down and looks into my eyes. "I really love you," he says.

And you know what I wish? At this moment, what I wish more than anything is that I never used the love spell. I wish that his words were real.

All anyone can talk about for the next two days is prom, prom, prom. It's on! After school on Tuesday, Tammy and I go shopping to get her a dress and me some shoes. When I get home, I spend an hour walking around the apartment, hoping to break in my new two-inch heels. At least neither my mom nor my sister is around to make fun of me: Miri is locked in her room doing God knows what (she'd better not be ignoring her schoolwork), and my mom is out as usual. *Not* that we're talking. When she arrives home at nine, looking tired and out of it, she zaps her shoes off and goes straight to bed. I go to bed less than an hour later, counting the hours (forty-four!) till prom.

By the time I get home on Wednesday, I can barely contain my excitement. I slip on my new heels right away to continue breaking them in. When I hear my mom's television, my good mood convinces me that it's time to make amends.

I hop over to her room. The door is ajar, and I gently push it all the way open. I find her in her bed, surrounded by a huge mess. Clothes and food cartons are piled on the sheets, and the room stinks like an ashtray.

"Are you sick?" I ask.

She shakes her head but doesn't move. I sneak over to her bedside and see that her bed isn't the only thing that's a mess. Her hair is in knots, her skin looks pasty, and her nails have been bitten down to the quick. I immediately climb into bed beside her, pushing over a wrinkled cashmere sweater. "What's wrong?"

"I'm fine," she says, and zaps on the light. "It's the men. I've gone on all these dates, and I know they all like me, but I don't really like them. Do you want some cheesecake?" she asks, and then zaps one up. "Or pie?" and then zaps that up too. "I want a cappuccino." Cappuccino appears on a tray on her bed. "Never mind. I think I want a cup of tea." The cappuccino is replaced. "Or maybe—"

"Stop. Just stop," I say. "Are you feeling okay?"

She shrugs. "Actually, I'm a little depressed."

245

No kidding. "Why don't you go fix yourself up?"

Mom nods and does a little waving thing with her hand.

"No!" I say, sternly grabbing hold of her wrist. "I meant, take a bath."

She blinks. "Oh. But it's easier this way."

"I know it's easier. But a bath feels good."

She considers the possibility and decides to do it. As my mom runs her bath, I start cleaning up her room. A sweater here, a jacket there . . . What is all this stuff? Why did she zap it all up? Because it was easy? Maybe that's why she's so depressed. When you get what you want so easily, it doesn't mean anything.

Like an empty I-love-you, I realize sadly.

After I finish cleaning, I check on Miri, who looks

equally exhausted. She's sitting on her floor, surrounded by three binders with labels: *Saving the Whales*, *Bushfires*, and a new one, *The Evil Circus*.

Another head case. But one problem family member at a time. "Mom is having a crisis," I say.

At first she looks confused, and I'm worried she's going to say "Mom who?" but then the clouds clear and she says, "What's wrong with her?"

Do these people live in the same house? I'm beginning to wonder if anyone pays attention besides me. "Just back me up," I say. And a half hour later, when we hear the bath draining, Miri and I are waiting on my mom's bed.

"What's going on?" my mom asks.

"This is an intervention," I say. "Mom, you shouldn't be using magic at all if you can't use it in moderation."

"But I . . . ," she begins, and then trails off. She sinks onto her bed. "I can't believe this is happening. Again."

Huh? "Excuse me?"

"This is why I stopped using magic. Why I became a nonpracticing witch. When I was a kid, your aunt and grandmother and I used magic for everything. Clothes, tests, school, boys, friends. But I was never happy. Nothing meant anything. And it wasn't just me. My mom and sister were never truly happy either. So I decided I would stop using magic. Just stop. In college, I studied for my own exams, bought my own clothes, and met my own boyfriend. Your father. And it made me happier."

"Not for long," Miri says. "He left you. It didn't work out."

"If I hadn't married your father, I wouldn't have had the

two of you. I wouldn't trade my situation for anything in the world. I'm not saying everything was perfect, but I experienced life."

"I get it," I say. "Keep going."

My mom takes a deep breath. "When your grandmother saw how at peace I was, she decided to do the same. We both realized that our powers were more of a curse than a blessing. We vowed that we would never use magic again. Of course, when Sasha realized what we were doing . . . when I let it happen . . . when I didn't use magic even when . . ." She chokes up, and tears spill over her cheeks.

I lean toward her. Is she finally going to tell us why she doesn't speak to Aunt Sasha? "When what happened?"

She shakes her head.

I guess not.

"I should have realized that this would happen this time," my mom says finally. "That I couldn't just dip my toe in. That it's not in my nature. I can't live like this. I have to quit." She nods slowly. "Cold turkey."

"Are you sure you need to cut it all out?" Miri asks.

"Yes," she says. "I didn't plan on being so extreme this time. But I'm an all-or-nothing kind of witch. I'm sorry, girls."

I hug my mother tightly. "I promise to support you any way I can. We both do. Right, Miri?"

But my sister is already lost in her own thoughts. I elbow her in the ribs, and she quickly snaps out of it and nods. "What? Oh, yeah, I'll support you. But I don't have to give it up too, do I? I have a lot of stuff I need to take care of. Important stuff."

"We all have to do what we all have to do," my mom says. "It's your decision."

Miri looks relieved. "Good. Because I'm still working on that rain spell for California. And, Rachel, I just found out that the circus is in town, and I absolutely have to take care of that first. Do you think—"

How insensitive is she? "Miri, I think Mom has enough to be concerned about without worrying about your next scheme." I mean, come on. Do you smoke a cigarette right in front of someone who's trying to quit? I give my sister my best stop-being-an-idiot eyebrow lift and say, "Why don't we get Mom into bed and make her dinner?"

"But I'm really—"

I give her my don't-mess-with-me look.

"Oh, okay."

My mom touches my cheek. "When did you become so mature?"

Mature? Me? "Good question."

After we tuck her in, make dinner, and clean up, I follow Miri to her room and close the door. "Okay, what's all this about a circus? You planning to become an acrobat or something?" Now, that's a cool job. I've always wanted to try a real trapeze. When I was younger, I pretended the curtain rod was one, and I'll admit that didn't end happily for me, Miri (she was the catcher), or the living room.

She thrusts a flyer at me. "The Faher Family Circus is in New York!"

I read the photocopied yellow paper. "So? You want to go?"

She grabs the flyer back, rolls it, and hits me over the head. "No, I don't want to go. Don't you know how cruel circuses are? They chain the animals to the ground! Lock them in cages! Make elephants, lions, and monkeys perform acts that are totally unnatural!"

"I like the circus," I say. Our parents took us when we were kids. Hmm, now that I think about it, I remember that Miri spent most of the trip crying while I spent most of the time eating cotton candy. Yum.

"We have to save them! It's our responsibility! Animal circuses are already illegal in most other countries. Sweden, Austria, Costa Rica, India . . ."

"Let's sit down and discuss it." I make myself comfy on her bed.

"I don't want to sit down!" she screams, sounding a wee bit hysterical. "We need to go. Now."

"Now? As in tonight?" My plan for the night involves lots of sleep. "It's been a stressful few weeks, and prom is to-morrow, and now I'd really like to chill."

She narrows her eyes. "The elephants don't get to re-lax. They're too busy having metal hooks slammed into their feet."

Gross. "That's pretty graphic."

"You can't just pretend these things don't happen." She disappears from the room and returns with the lithium bat-teries. "I'm going. Are you coming or not?"

She's out of control. "Let's just take the night to think this through. We'll make a plan. Why don't we have a rally? Or a protest? We don't have to do it tonight. I did lots of

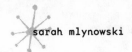

research on the Internet and the consequences of our spells have been—"

"I said, I'm going. Guess you're not." She puts her fists together, scrunches her eyes shut, and says, "Transport to the place inside my mind."

Oh, drat. I jump on her back.

"The power of my fists shall ye bind!"

I close my eyes in preparation for the screaming light.

"It didn't work!" Miri says angrily.

I open my eyes. Indeed, we are still in her bedroom. I slip off her. "What happened?"

She places her fists on her hips. "Did you gain weight?"

"No!" The nerve. "Maybe the batteries died. Do you have spares?"

She pouts. "Noooo. Guess we'll have to fly. I'm changing into camouflage!" she says, stripping. "And bringing the reflective shield in case."

"Can we just pause for a second and discuss this like rational people?"

"There's nothing to talk about. I have to help. It's my responsibility."

"Not everything is your responsibility!"

"You don't understand," she says as she pulls on my black sweatpants. "You're not a witch."

Ouch. "You're right, I'm not." Maybe she has a point. I don't understand how she feels. I don't know the pressure of having the capability of doing so much good. Of feeling like the entire world's health and happiness is in my hands. I don't know the fear that comes with magic. I don't know anything.

She fetches our broom, then pulls a black sweatshirt

over her head and fastens her helmet. "Are you coming?" she asks.

The only thing I do know is that it's my job to support my sister. "I'm coming," I say, and dash back to my room to change. "Do I have a choice?" I scribble a note for our mom.

Miri joins me in my room, the broom in tow. She yanks open the window and the cool air breezes in.

"Time is of the essence," she says, straddling the broom. "Hop on!"

I fasten my helmet, climb on behind her, hold up the umbrella shield, and duck as the broom jolts toward the open window.

Here goes nothing.

Should Have Taken a Taxi

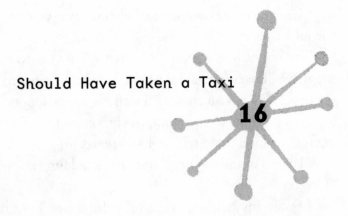

16

"What's your plan exactly?" I say over the sound of the wind.

"Huh?"

"Plan? What? Is? Yours?" I yell directly into her ear.

"I can't hear you!" she says back, obviously ignoring me. Funny, I can hear *her*.

We're flying high over the buildings in Chelsea, my two-inch heels dangling beneath me. Unfortunately, in my rush I forgot to put on something a little more appropriate.

Miri does a few circles over the massive convention center as she scouts a landing. When she sees a side entrance that appears empty, she nose-dives toward the pavement and quickly lowers the broom to the ground. We topple onto the cement. I wish she'd learn to land this thing better; one day I'm going to break an arm for sure.

This is obviously the worst plan she has ever had. We're in a sketchy part of the city, all the way on the West Side. We could easily be mugged. By the time I regain my balance, Miri is already at the convention center's side door, chanting her open sesame spell. I hand her the broom and she props it against the brick wall.

The door opens, and Miri rushes inside. I'm reluctant to follow. "There are going to be trainers here," I whisper. "What are you going to do? How are you going to save the animals exactly?" I'm afraid to lose her, so I step inside.

"Don't close the door," Miri tells me. "In case we have to make a quick exit," she explains. Not exactly encouraging words.

Great. My heart speeds up as I enter the dark building. At least we have on our night-vision helmets. I hurry to catch up with Miri, which isn't easy in these heels. Maybe tonight isn't the best time to break them in.

"ROWRRRRRRRRRRRRRRRRR!" A wild, animal noise echoes through the room. I'm pretty sure that was a lion. Or a tiger. Very possibly a bear. Oh my.

We both freeze. "Miri. This. Is. Not. Safe," I hiss through a clenched jaw.

"Don't worry. It'll be fine."

And that's when I see it.

A massive lion licking her massive paw.

And she sees us.

I jump back about twenty feet before realizing she's in a cage. A locked cage. There are two lions in there, and they're both beige and maneless and lying in the corner. It's kind of sweet, actually. One of them is resting her leg against the other's leg. They're kind of cuddling. I wonder if they're sisters and—

"ROOOOOOOOOOOOOAAAAAAAAAAAAAAA AAAAAAAAR!" The cranky younger sister, obviously. I jump back about ten feet.

How secure is that lock?

"Poor little lions," Miri murmurs, tiptoeing toward the animals. Little? "See how claustrophobic they look in that tiny cage?"

I grab her shoulder so she won't get any closer. I like my sister in one piece, and those lions look hungry. Fine, they look sleepy. But maybe that's just a trick.

"We should start here," she says, reaching into her satchel.

I begin to panic. "Start what?"

"Freeing them, what else?"

That's it, she's losing it. *I'm* losing it. I shake her by the shoulder. "Are you insane? What are you going to do? Open the cages and set the sister lions loose on New York? They'll have us for appetizers and then chomp down all of Manhattan for the main course!"

You know what? It smells in here. A lot like JFK after the cow invasion.

She struggles to remove my hand from her shoulder. "Do you think I'm stupid? Manhattan is no place for them. I'm sending them home. Where they can run free. Now, let me go!"

I step back and take a good look at my angry, red-in-the-face, disheveled-haired sister. She's definitely out of her mind. I think my entire family needs a vacation.

She removes a Tupperware container from her satchel, opens it, then sets the spell book in front of her and chants:

"Be free of reins
And drop your chains,
By tomorrow's morn

You'll be back where you were born!"

She tosses the concoction on them, and I feel the familiar rush of cold as I ask, "Can't you just get them to click their heels together three times?"

The two lions begin to fade. They get lighter and lighter, and then they're gone.

"Cool," Miri says.

I really hope they're not going to reappear behind me. I carefully turn my head. Nope. I let out a long breath. "Where do you think they went?"

"Duh. Africa. Let's see who's next," Miri whispers. But she stops walking when she spots a trainer at the end of the room rattling about outside a cage. "Wait for him to go," she whispers. We freeze, and I start to panic. What if we're caught? How would we explain the animal disappearances? Would we be arrested for animal-napping? Even if they couldn't find the evidence?

As the trainer comes our way, we duck behind a pole. "Don't move," Miri whispers.

About five minutes later, the trainer disappears into a back room out of view, and we move on to the next cage. Camels. I love camels. How cool are they that they don't need any water? How cute is that hump? Not that I would want a hump like that or anything. I snap back to attention as Miri chants the spell.

And away they go!

Next we hit the tigers, elephants, zebras, horses, alligators, and llamas, which takes forever. Finally we're at what I think is the last cage.

Where there are two goats. A mama goat and her baby.

Once again Miri goes through the whole spell, the throwing, yada, yada, the cold, the fading. Well, the big goat fades, but the little one doesn't budge.

Miri approaches the cage. "What's wrong, baby goat?"

"Try again," I tell her, already bored. I'm now sitting on the floor, too tired to care about what's been on the floor before me.

Miri tries again. *"Be free"*—blah, blah, blah—*"born!"*

The goat still doesn't budge.

"Something's not working," Miri says. "I'm going to check it out." She looks around for a lock, finds it, recites the open sesame spell, and opens the cage. "Isn't he cute? Hello, adorableness. Why won't you go home?" She gently pats his head.

256

I approach the door. He *is* cute. Small, too. He's all white, with a small wet gray nose and two triangular floppy-looking ears that are pointing to the high ceiling. I bet he'd be great to mooshie. He looks like a teddy bear. Teddy goat. Billy the Teddy Goat. He looks so cuddly, probably only a few weeks old. "Maybe he was born here," I say. "That's why he didn't disappear."

Billy looks up at us and widens his big dewy eyes.

"Aw," Miri and I both murmur.

And that's when it happens.

Billy bolts. Right out of Miri's arms, right between my open legs, and out of the cage, galloping at a speed I would never have believed possible for a goat. A baby lion, maybe. But a goat? This one is faster than a speeding bullet. As Miri and I watch him in disbelief, Billy the Supergoat runs straight for the door. The open door.

"Get that goat!" Miri screams, and we take off. Fine, I'm laughing a bit. I can't help it. But I run after the goat anyway, right through the convention center, until I'm outside, wondering which way he went.

"Billy's gone," I tell Miri.

"Who's Billy?" she says, panting. "We should fly. That will make the goat easier to—"

The broom is no longer where she left it. "What the—"

"What did you expect to happen on an isolated street in the city?" I scream. Someone is in for a rude shock when they try to sweep their floor. "There's Billy!" I say, pointing at the small creature currently licking his hoof.

We bolt after him. And he runs. And we chase. We chase him all the way down Thirty-ninth Street, cringing every time he crosses an avenue, praying he doesn't end up goat cheese. We continue chasing him right to Forty-second and Eighth, and then right into the—

Oh, no. Not the subway station!

Miri freezes at the landing. "We're not allowed to take the subway so late at night," she whimpers.

We're allowed to go hightailing over Manhattan but not to take the subway? Does this make sense? I ignore her and take the stairs two at a time, trying to catch up to Billy the Bolting Supergoat. "Come here, Billy," I call, but he doesn't stop. Instead, he runs right under the turnstile. Of course I don't have my MetroCard. Why would I? It's two in the morning!

257

"Zap it around," I tell my ashen-faced sister. She's almost the same color as Billy, who's now calmly licking himself in a very inappropriate way on the other side of the turnstile.

Miri does as she's told, and I push through and lunge after Billy. He's faster and takes off as soon as I'm an inch away from grabbing him. Luckily, there're only two other people waiting for the train.

And then Billy the Supergoat takes a flying leap—"No, Billy, no!" we shriek—directly onto the subway tracks.

Our jaws drop in horror, and we peer over the edge. Billy seems to have realized that he might have made a mistake, because he is now bleating loudly, and his little legs are quivering.

"We have to get him," Miri says, and takes a step toward the track.

I give her a power block with my arm. "Over my dead body are you stepping onto a subway track."

"But . . . but . . ."

And then we hear it. Oh yes, the rumble of the swiftly approaching train.

"Oh, no," Miri whimpers. My heart races almost as fast as the oncoming car. As the headlights glare toward us, I see poor Billy, eyes wide and wet, begging us to help.

Miri shrieks, reaches her hands toward the train, and yells, "Stop!"

Her lips purse, I feel the rush of cold, and the subway grinds to a sudden halt.

The station is silent. Until Billy bleats.

The conductor pops his head out his window. "What the

hell?" he says. "We just lost power." He spots Billy. "All this because of one little goat?"

"One little goat," I say. "That my father bought for two *zuzim*."

Miri starts to cry.

I lead my blubbering sister and the sleeping goat she's cradling up the pitch-black stairs. It seems Miri blew out the power in the whole station. Thank goodness for our night-vision helmets. "I almost killed you," Miri tells the goat between sobs.

"Yes, you did," I say as I finally step into the night. I'm furious. We have no broom, no batteries, no money, and no working subway, and my feet are killing me. Not only are my shoes broken in, but my feet feel broken too. "You have to think about the ramifica—"

Oh, no. I look around.

The entire city is dark. As in cloaked in darkness. As in all the sparkling lights that normally illuminate the city have either burnt out simultaneously, or—

"Uh, oh," Miri squeaks. "Did I . . . ?"

"Yes, Miri. Apparently you did. Apparently your little stopping-the-train tactic blew out all the power in Manhattan." I am so mad, I'm fuming.

"Well, what else could I do? What about poor little Billy?"

We arrive home two hours later. I won't even discuss the bloated, deformed shape of my feet. I'm too angry to talk to my sister, so I leave her and Billy to figure out their sleeping

259

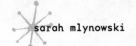

arrangements. I throw the itchy helmet onto the floor and feel my way toward my mom's room. After making sure that she's sleeping soundly, wrapped in her covers, oblivious to the world, I kiss her on the forehead and feel my way back to my room, drop my camouflage outfit on the floor, and slip under the covers. I need to get some sleep! Prom is tomorrow and I'm going to be so tired and I'm going to look exhausted and there's no power and I don't even know what time it is because my clock isn't working and please, please, please let everything be better in the morning.

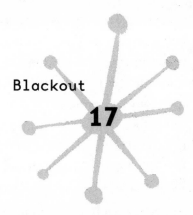

Blackout

17

I'm awakened by Miri's screaming, "No, Tigger, no! Leave Billy alone!" and realize that maybe everything does not always seem better in the morning. I look at my alarm clock, but it's black. Please don't tell me that the power is still out.

And then I remember the goat, so I get out of bed to see how our houseguest is doing. I find Billy on the kitchen table, bleating like crazy, Tigger hissing on a neighboring chair, and Miri failing to manage the ménage.

"What time is it?" I ask, rubbing the sleep from my eyes.

"Eight-thirty," Miri answers.

I groan. "I'm going to be late for school!"

"There is no school," she says, pulling Tigger's chair across the room to the sink. "Power is still out."

She points to the radio next to the sink. I carry it to the kitchen table and turn the volume up. Hmm. Good thing we're out of lithium batteries and not AAAs.

The voice coming from the radio is loud and crisp. "At 2:09 a.m. eastern time, the entire island of Manhattan was hit by an unexplained blackout. Subways stopped midtunnel, streetlights went out, and electricity consumers are still waiting to have service restored. The cause of the blackout is still unknown. All schools are closed today, and most businesses are expected to remain closed until power is restored, hopefully by tomorrow morning. The bell on Wall Street will not be ringing. . . ."

You've got to be kidding. Oh. My. God. "Miri! Are you listening?"

Billy bleats. The cat hisses. I sigh.

Instead of listening, or caring, Miri watches Tigger as he leaps off the chair and onto the countertop, and she scoops him up before he attacks the table. I sink into Tigger's vacated chair and cradle my suddenly pounding head in my arms.

"What do you think *bleat* means?" Miri asks.

"I think it means 'I miss my mother,' " I say.

262

"In other news," the radio announcer continues, "exotic animals have been appearing in unexpected places all across the country. This morning, a dance troupe in Birmingham, Alabama, found a seven-thousand-pound elephant on the stage of the BJCC Arena."

That's it. I've had enough. "Sit down, Miri." I must look serious, because she slithers into a chair, holding Tigger tightly on her lap. "Do you realize what you've done? By trying to save the circus animals, you caused a citywide blackout. Plus you've endangered the animals you tried to save! They just found an elephant in Alabama! There could be an alligator in Maine!"

"An alligator wouldn't have been born in Maine," she says, reddening.

"How do you know? Stranger things have happened! My

point is, you have to realize that all your spells have consequences. You have to think, and I mean *really* think, about each and every action before you end up ruining everything!"

"B-but I thought the animals were b-born in the wild . . . ," she stutters.

"I'm sure some of them were, but you didn't do your research and lots of people—and animals—are going to get hurt."

Her eyes fill with tears. "I just wanted to help."

"I know you did, and that's very honorable. But you're not helping! You're making things worse! What do you think is going to happen to that elephant? They're not going to fit him with tights and ballet slippers and give him the starring role in *The Nutcracker*! He's going to be tranquilized and could be hurt. Is that what you wanted?"

263

"No," she whimpers. Billy bleats.

"Don't you see? Everything comes with a price. The cows had to go *somewhere*, so they went to the school gym. The oranges had to come from somewhere. The Mercedes had to come from somewhere. Nothing comes from nothing. You're not making something appear from nothing, Miri. Your magic just moves things from one place to another."

"Stealing," she says, and starts crying all over again. "You're right. Helping just made everything worse. I'm the worst superhero ever!"

Finally, my message is getting through to her. "And I still haven't figured out what happened to the oil you zapped. I'm hoping it ended up in a gas station or some lucky guy's backyard. But don't you see? You're just like Mom. She's a magicoholic. You're a do-goodoholic."

She nods. "From now on I'll mind my own business. Keep my nose in my own books."

Good. Well, not exactly. "That's not what I meant—"

"Stop trying to make the world a better place," she says sadly. "I'll never help anyone again."

Now she's just going to extremes. "Miri, you don't have to stop helping *anyone*. You have to stop helping *everyone*."

"Huh?"

I walk over to the table and sit on it, facing my sister. "You have to learn that doing a hundred things partially means you're not doing anything a hundred percent. In the past two months, you've tried to feed and clothe the homeless, stop the bushfires in California, fix the ozone layer, and save circus animals, among other things. It's too much. You need to try to make a difference one issue at a time so you can give each issue your all. Every action has costs, even every nonmagical one. What you have to do to make a real, positive difference is plan. Map out your potential actions so you can figure out what the consequences are ahead of time. That way, you'll do good, not damage."

She dries her eyes with the backs of her hands. "That makes sense."

I pat Billy on the head. "I know. I'm very smart."

The phone rings and we both jump. I grab it before it wakes my mom. She needs her rest.

"Rachel? Are you okay?"

"Hi, Will. I'm fine. How are you?"

"Not so good. I just called Penthouse Fifty and the prom is officially canceled."

What now? What else could possibly have gone wrong? Why is this prom so cursed? Why, why, why? "Because of the power?"

"Yup," he says, sighing.

"But we still have the space, right? Can't the band sing without a microphone? We could light up the room with candles. It would be really romantic!"

"We could, but the room we rented is on the fiftieth floor. So everyone would have to walk all the way upstairs."

Oh, right. No elevator. "Don't they have any rooms on the ground floor?"

"They do, but the other problem is that the doors all have key cards that don't work without power." His voice cracks. "I just can't believe this."

"But can't they move the date?" I ask, feeling desperate. "We can have it tomorrow, or next week—"

"Rachel, everyone's booked. The band and the rentals can't make it another day and they won't return the deposits unless it's tonight. So unless the power comes back on, it's over."

Not only have Miri and I caused a major blackout in the metropolitan area, we've ruined the prom. Again.

I hang up with a depressed Will and recount the latest news to Miri, Billy, and Tigger.

"We have to wake up Mom," Miri says.

"No," I say firmly. "She's recuperating. We're not asking for her help. We have to deal with this on our own. Let's try the spell reversal."

"But the animals—"

"The *animals* will be better off. If we reverse the go-home spell and the animals return, maybe this whole chain of events will unravel. Billy wouldn't have run into the subway, you wouldn't have had to save him, and the power wouldn't have gone out. I know it's a long shot, but it's worth a try."

"Okay." Miri sighs, and I follow her into her room. "But I need to recharge the crystal in the salt for an hour. And I can't promise it will work."

"I know. But let's give it a go."

By noon we buy new batteries and transport ourselves back to the convention center. Luckily, the goat is light, and Miri is carrying him in a satchel over her shoulder while I'm on her back wearing the crystal necklace and holding up the umbrella shield.

266

Bright light!

We pop up behind a police car. Good—no one seems to have seen us. Bad—there is a police car. Four officers and a crowd have surrounded the front door to the convention center.

"Damn animal rights groups," someone says.

We head back to the side entranceway. "We're actually going to circle the entire building backward?" I ask in amazement.

"Since the crystal is already enchanted," she says. "Can you do it? I'm a jinx these days."

I would, but I know that I'd be doing more harm than good. She has to learn to pay the consequences. I shake my head, and hand her the crystal necklace, and she passes me the goat satchel with a sigh.

"This had better work," she says. "Billy misses his mommy. Ready?"

"Yup," I say, and begin leading Miri around the million-square-foot block-long building, reflective shield hiding us from prying eyes.

Twenty minutes and six stumbles later, we're back at the side entrance. As she takes the final step, we hear an explosion of roars, bleats, and howls from the animals now inside. A little cranky, are we?

A trainer throws open the side door and yells to a nearby policeman, "The animals are back! It must have been some sort of publicity stunt!"

I remove Billy from the bag and set him free toward the door. "Run, little goat, run! Let's get out of here," I say as a policeman and onlooker approach the door. We sneak back toward the street, hoping to see working traffic lights. To our disappointment, they're still not on. So much for the great spell unraveler.

Miri sighs. "Next plan?"

We find a five-broomer light spell, but before we try it on the city, we test it on the apartment. Our curtains catch on fire.

My mom is now awake in her room, chatting on the phone, oblivious to our role in this catastrophe.

So we listen to the radio, which tells us that they've located the problem. Reportedly, a power blockage around Times Square caused a surge, which made the lights go out on the entire island. Who caused the blockage isn't, of course, on the news. The newscaster also reports that the power is expected to be back up and running by early tomorrow morning. I give Miri a dirty look.

"Great," I say. "One day too late."

"Should I try another spell?" Miri asks.

"No," I say, resigned. "It's too risky. What if it goes wrong? They say they'll have it fixed by tomorrow morning, so we'll have to wait."

"But your prom is tonight."

I shrug. "It's just a prom." I try to smile.

"I feel awful," Miri says. "If only you could have it someplace out of the city."

"Like where? Disneyland?"

"Very funny." Then she jumps up. "I know! I know! Didn't you say the theme was Oscar night?"

"Yes. But I doubt we'll be able to have it in L.A. Unless the entire class is going to climb on your back."

"What about the drive-in? You know, the one we flew over? It's only about forty minutes away. They're not in the city, so they'd have power."

"How would we even get there? We can't fly everyone out there on brooms, and the subways aren't running. It's not like we know anyone who owns a car, never mind a bus."

She sighs. "That's true."

We hear my mom's door open and she comes out in a bathrobe. Her roots are back to normal (dark), her nails are back to normal (ragged), and her breasts are back to normal (small and saggy). But she's smiling. "Morning, girls!"

"You seem happy," Miri says gloomily.

"I slept very well, thank you. And I just had a very nice conversation with Lex. Remember him? He called to see how we three girls are holding up in the blackout. Wasn't that sweet of him?"

Aw! That *was* sweet of him. "Lex is a really nice guy, Mom. You should definitely go out with him." Wait a sec. Lex is a tour guide. And a tour guide definitely has bus access. I start jumping up and down and I'm so excited that I can barely talk. "Call him back! Lex! Bus!"

As comprehension dawns on Miri's face, she starts jumping up and down alongside me.

"We need to get to prom! Upstate! Because of the power failure! Do you think Lex will help us?"

My mom looks confused. "It doesn't hurt to ask. Um, girls, you didn't have anything to do with the power problem, did you?"

The next four hours are a bit of a whirlwind. First we have to explain it all to Mom, which we do, and luckily she doesn't freak out. Instead, she gives Miri a big hug.

"Like mother, like daughter," she says, smoothing Miri's hair back. "We forgot about the importance of moderation, didn't we? And we both paid the consequences."

"If I had powers," I say longingly, "I would so use them carefully and sparingly."

My mom and sister take this as a cue to begin laughing uncontrollably.

When she calms down, Mom warns us that now that

she's *back*, she'll be monitoring our shenanigans far more closely. And that, yes, Miri is still allowed to use magic but not unconditionally. Then Mom helps us *non*magically track down the drive-in (hello, phone book) and then the owners, who live just down the road from the theater. They're a sweet elderly couple who only charge a thousand dollars. Plus they offer to play any movies we want in the background all night. *Pretty in Pink! Grease! Carrie!* Okay, maybe not *Carrie.* I'd be happy to see any movie at all, except *The Sound of Music.* But anyway, Mom calls Lex back, and he agrees to pack his bus with eager prom-goers. He also asks some bus driver pals of his to help us out.

Then I call Will to share the good news.

"You are the best," he says. "I'll get Kat to start calling all the seniors. Bosh, River, and I will head out early to lead the setup committee. Is it okay if I meet you there? Or do you want to bring your stuff and come with me and get ready at the drive-in?"

"I'll get ready here. I need lots of time to beautify." I don't even want to think about my under-eye circles.

"You're beautiful as is."

He's the best boyfriend ever. I mean, really, what else could I ask for?

As I get ready, I can hear Mom and Miri chatting it up in the kitchen. Mom is making homemade veggie egg rolls ("I'll try to cut down on the tofu overload, I promise!") as she helps Miri with her homework.

The phone rings as I'm towel-drying my hair. "It's me!" screams Kat. "I can't believe you saved prom! You are a star.

Honestly. It's too bad you're only a freshman, otherwise you could so run for president next year. Just wanted to say you rock! Have a great time tonight."

And that's when it hits me, and I know what I have to do.

Pretty in Pink . . . Sneakers 18

I pull my hair back into a ponytail, put on one of my new pairs of jeans, and slide my swollen feet into my sneakers.

"You sure?" Miri asks.

"Yup." I hang the garment bag over my left arm and lift the two smaller bags with my right.

She gives me a hug. "Have fun. If you need me, I'll be here not saving the world."

"Good," I say. "You need to relax. Why don't you read?"

"I thought I'd watch *The Sound of Music*."

"Ha-ha."

She laughs and returns to her room.

There's a knock on the door. Who's that? "Hello?" I ask.

"Hi. It's Lex!"

What is he doing here? "I thought I was meeting you at the school."

"He's coming to get us," says my mom, sashaying out of her room in an old pair of jeans and a cotton blouse, looking like her old self. "Miri, come say good-bye and give us a hug!" she hollers.

Huh? "You're coming?"

She blushes. "Lex asked me to keep him company on the trip. If that's all right with you. He thought he'd pick us up first and then we'd stop by the school. If you'd let him in." She eyes my outfit quizzically. "You're planning to get dressed at the drive-in?"

I open the door to find Lex flushed, sweating, and smiling. He's also holding a corsage. "For you," he says to my mom. Aw. "Ready, ladies?" he says, and tips his hat.

"Yup," I say, picking up my bags. "I just need you to make one quick stop before going to school."

He takes the bags from my arms. What a gentleman, I think, thoroughly impressed.

Kat unlocks her front door and throws it wide open. "What are you doing here?"

"I've come to pick you up," I say.

She laughs. "What? Why? I'm not going anywhere."

"Yes, you are." I hand her the garment bag. "This is your prom dress."

"W-what . . . ," she stutters, surprised. "I can't go. I don't have a date."

"Yes, you do."

"Who?"

I smile. "It's a surprise. What size shoe are you?"

"Six."

I toss her the second bag. "It's your lucky day. They're even broken in."

She's holding up both bags, looking at me like she just woke up on a different planet. "I don't understand."

I hear Lex honking outside. "Now, hurry up and get dressed. Your pumpkin awaits."

As we pull into the drive-in, I can already see the rainbow of girls in their prom dresses dancing on the cobblestones with their tuxedo-clad dates. The massive screen is playing an old black-and-white movie I don't recognize, and the band is singing one of those songs that's always on the radio. Under one of the rows of glowing lanterns are the dinner buffet and beautifully set tables. The party is in full swing. Two empty buses, some cars, and a few limos are parked in front of us.

"Are you sure you're okay?" Tammy whispers to me as we join the line to get off the bus. "I don't get what's going on." She peeks at Kat, who's a few people behind us. "Why is she wearing your dress?"

I give Tammy's arm a squeeze and ignore the question. Luckily, she spots Bosh through the window and goes into giggle overdrive, forgetting all about me.

"Look how cute he is in his tux," she gushes, straightening her strapless red dress.

As I climb down the stairs of the bus, I spot Will in *his* tux, and my throat feels dry. My heart pounds faster, louder, until I can feel it in my neck and fingers.

He's talking to the photographer, smiling and nodding at something he's saying. When he looks up and sees me watching him, the smile lights up his eyes.

He doesn't even notice that I'm wearing jeans. Gripping my final bag, I walk down the red carpet toward him. "Hi," I say when he's only a foot away. I remove the crystal necklace from the bag and slip it over my head.

He's going to make some girl very happy, I think as I circle him. Just not me.

"What the . . . Why did you do that?" He blinks repeatedly, not knowing what just hit him. As I take my final backward step, he opens his mouth. He closes it. He opens it again.

Okay, I'll admit it. A fraction of me, my ego, is thinking that he'll still love me. That his feelings for me have grown stronger than any spell.

He blinks again.

Oh well. A girl can dream. But the truth is, while what he felt for me wasn't real, what I felt for him was just as illusory. I was enamored with all he represented, his hotness, his social status, his never-ending supply of licorice. But there was never any *real* magic between us.

I take a deep breath. "Listen, Will, we have to talk. You're a terrific guy, but I don't think we're right together. I didn't want to leave you stranded tonight, so I got you another date." I point to the bus just as Kat is stepping off the last step.

His eyes follow my finger. And light up. Kat looks beautiful. The dress flatters her figure in a way that capris and hoodies never could, and her hair is wavy around her shoulders. She and Will smile shyly at each other.

"Hi," she mouths.

"You look amazing," he mouths back, not losing her gaze for a second.

Kat walks toward us and looks at me quizzically. "We broke up," I tell her. "Would you mind being his date tonight?"

275

Kat's head swivels between the two of us. "Are you sure?" she asks incredulously.

I nod, smiling, and walk away. He takes her hand and they head toward the dance floor.

So.

What to do for the next four hours until I can hitch a ride back to the city? I guess I'll wait in the bus. Or maybe in my tree?

I climb to the spot where Miri and I once watched *Spider-Man* and get comfortable. A slow song begins and echoes through the night. From my perch, I see Will and Kat in each other's arms, moving to the music. Behind them, Lex and Mom are also dancing, totally oblivious to everyone around. Under a lantern, Tammy and Bosh are looking deeply into each other's eyes. All the couples are back where they belong. Just like in the end of *A Midsummer Night's Dream*. If we witches have offended, think but this, and all is mended.

Almost all. I swallow the lump in my throat when I spot Raf and Melissa slow-dancing, her head on his shoulder, his arms around her waist.

My heart races at the sight of him. Even though I've tried to convince myself that I don't care, that old feeling comes back with a punch. Or maybe it never really left me in the first place. All is back to normal, including my feelings for Raf. If only he felt the same way about me.

Suddenly, he lifts his gaze into the tree and our eyes lock. And he smiles at me. Is it possible? Could he feel the same way I do?

And that's when a raindrop lands smack on my forehead. Two drops. Three, four. I look up through the branches to see the sky disappearing behind angry black clouds. Suddenly, the clouds crack open. Within two seconds, the entire senior class is shrieking and searching for nonexistent cover.

Oh, no! Prom will be ruined after all!

I lift my face to the downpour. Good thing I'm not wearing mascara.

I close my eyes, pulling all the energy I can muster from every pore of my body, until I can feel it imploding inside me, and wish with all my heart:

Rain, rain, go away,
Go instead to help L.A.!

I feel a wave of cold and then . . . nothing. I open one eye. And then the other. It stopped raining.

Huh? Did I . . . ?

I watch as the dark clouds swiftly disappear, leaving a gorgeous starry night over the prom once more.

And as I realize what just happened, my body tingles with electricity.

I did that.

I. Did. That.

Omigod.

OMIGOD.

Yes!

The magic continues—at camp!—in
***Spells & Sleeping Bags,* coming in 2007!**